LEGEND OF THE PIRATE QUEEN

Piracy, Mayhem, and Majesty on the Seven Seas

Melissa Saari

Van Rye
PUBLISHING

Cover design by Vila Design

Published by Van Rye Publishing, LLC
Ann Arbor, MI
www.vanryepublishing.com

ISBN: 978-1-957906-00-3 (paperback)
ISBN: 978-1-957906-01-0 (ebook)
Library of Congress Control Number: 2022935810

Warning

LEGEND OF THE PIRATE QUEEN is a fictionalized account of life as a slave and pirate in the 1500s and 1600s. As such, this book necessarily contains language and scenarios related to murder, torture, and abuse (emotional, physical, and sexual) that might be triggering for some audiences. Reader discretion is advised.

Dedication

This book is dedicated to my daughter, Tonya Kish, who has always been a ray of sunshine in my life.

Contents

Chapter 1

1594 BEGAN WITH NO difference from any year before it. But by the end of the year, life would change forever. It would change for a young girl, her mother, and her father. And the entire world would be altered by these simple people.

For now, 1594 was just a maker's mark to Keela, appearing below her signature on the green ribbon that wove through her daughter's hair. The braided hair that ran through the ribbon represented innocence. Keela knew the magic of this image was strong enough that she needed to use it in her painting.

Keela meditated on the image of her daughter, Caitlin, as it worked into the painting before her. Soon, the ribbon, the hair, and her daughter's dress became the focus of the painting, and the hills and valleys in the background were covered by a dancing girl. The grass hid behind the girl, forgotten and covered by the brilliant paint depicting her dancing form.

In County Cork, by the sea, Keela O'Hara painted the luscious landscape of Ireland. Before her stretched the actual landscape: endless sweeping fields, stopped only by the persistent ocean where her husband, Joseph O'Hara, fished nearby every day. Keela didn't expect her solitude to be broken, but Joseph came up behind her unannounced and softly massaged her shoulders, releasing the tension she'd been holding against the paintbrush. She put the paintbrush down on her easel and removed the pin holding her long red hair. Her hair came tumbling down, and Keela moved her easel out of the way so the hair wouldn't get painted like the canvas, green and blue.

With the other fishermen dotting the water in their tiny boats, Keela hadn't noticed Joseph's approach from behind her because she took so much delight in the sight of those fishing vessels that brought the area's main export home from the ocean each day. It was a scene perfect for painting. She always found new sights to inspire her on the ocean's surface and in the sky above it.

As Keela set her easel down, she noticed that Caitlin had joined them too. Keela sighed with satisfaction at seeing her daughter's favorite green satin ribbon tied into her hair. Keela's mother had given it to her years before, and she'd passed it on to Caitlin as soon as her beautiful red hair had begun to grow.

"I got a tuna," Joseph announced, lifting up the catch from the grass. Keela turned to gaze at the massive fish. It was still wet from the ocean and hanging motionless from the rope in Joseph's arms, seeming to lengthen his limbs.

"Wonderful! It'll be perfect for tonight's soup!" Keela replied.

Joseph and Caitlin headed down the hill and back to their thatched-roof cottage in the nearby village. Joseph had strengthened the roof with powerful beams from oak trees he had harvested at the top of Mount Gabriel. The mountain had become the inspiration for many of Keela's pieces of artwork.

Keela returned to her painting, polishing off a few details before picking up the canvas and the easel and heading back to the house to make supper. The house was strong and well-built. Heavy stones stuck through the plaster to provide a stable structure, difficult to destroy. There, inside the strong walls, Keela felt safe as her knife sliced through the dark-pink tuna, tearing it into small pieces so she could find all the bones. Once all the sharp prongs were gone, she dumped the meat into the cauldron over the fire. Then, she cut up the vegetables and tossed them into the soup along with the fish.

That night, Keela enjoyed a good dinner with Joseph and Caitlin. It was a delicious soup, and they all enjoyed it. Something about the soup stayed in Keela's mind—something memorable that she didn't think deeper of until later that night. It was a sense that the tuna was fresher than usual, or the soup was more satisfying, and then just a lingering feeling of contentment.

After dinner, Joseph entertained Keela and Caitlin with songs on his fiddle. Soon, Caitlin was falling asleep, and Keela felt that sense of contentment again. She looked at her daughter fast asleep, and she relished that sense of contentment. They all went to bed early. And they were soon sound asleep, with Joseph's arm draped over Keela's body, making her feel safe and secure.

* * *

The next morning, Keela went over to her neighbor Maggie O'Ryan's house and asked Maggie if Caitlin could stay with her for the day so she and Joseph could go fishing together. Keela's neighbor happily agreed to watch Caitlin. And Joseph and Keela headed off to the coastline.

Keela tremendously enjoyed fishing with Joseph. It gave her time away from the village, and she got to spend time with her husband as he worked. As she reached the boat, she got more excited. The small boat was large enough for both adults to sit comfortably—that is, until fish filled the deck. Riding the waves beneath its single sail, the boat had bright red paint on the hull to keep barnacles away as the boat sliced through the water.

Years before, Joseph had taught Keela how to sail. She untied the sail with a single tug, and it hung loose as she strapped the sail to the mast one hole at a time. She drew the rigging tight, pulled the sail against the wind, dropped the moorings, and let the moorings hang loose in the water with the nets while they sailed out into deep water where the schools of fish waited for Joseph's nets. The breeze was good and stiff behind them, and the boat made good progress through the waves, with the bubbling wake behind them standing on the surface as the swells rolled across the ocean. Keela relaxed, watching their smooth, relentless course away from the coastline, which was falling far behind them.

Once they were away from the shore, Keela pulled the sail in and let the boat coast. She enjoyed the quiet time with her husband as the nets slowly filled with fish. Keela and Joseph kissed passionately, without speaking a word, as the breeze continued to blow across the waters.

After enough time had passed, Joseph and Keela pulled in the nets together because the nets had grown heavy from flopping cod and even a few tuna. But their biggest prize of the day was eight gigantic cat-sharks, which had earned their name from the little black spots on their scales. They were four feet long and, despite looking slender, each catshark would provide two hundred pounds of meat for the village, with plenty of leftovers for the hungry dogs.

The fish and sharks flopped around in the bottom of the boat, gasping in the air and wishing for the water. Keela knocked them in the head to stop their flopping before they bruised their tender flesh all over and lost their good taste and color. She had heard that fish feel no pain whatsoever, but she always wondered if they suffered when they were dragged from the water.

By the time Keela had raised the sail, the breezes had changed, and they now blew toward shore. It was time to return home. She was grateful for the fair winds. It would have taken hours to return to the sandy shore if the wind had been against them. She played the potential of that nightmare scenario through her mind as she sailed easily home, imagining the endless tacks back and forth had she needed to fight the intention of the winds.

The sky was getting darker as Keela and Joseph sailed into their village, pulled up their boat, and waved to the townsfolk. Maggie came running to greet them first, with Caitlin right behind her. Then Tom and Catherine O'Quinlan, from further down the way, came as well.

As more people came out of their houses, Joseph began waving his arms in greeting. They realized he had enough fish to feed everyone, so they gratefully approached the boat, bringing buckets to carry all the fish. Keela smiled at all the happy faces around the boat as the fish were loaded and hauled away. The boat began to rise out of the waves as the load began to lighten, and soon, the boat no longer looked ready to sink into the shallow reaches of the bay.

Keela was so proud of her life in the village that she was fit to burst. She beamed from ear to ear as the community came together and celebrated. On the beach, the men started a fire and began to put some of the fish on stakes for roasting. They expertly sliced the sharp stakes through the soft flesh of the fresh fish, with the stakes missing all the bones and cleanly going through the other side.

The smell of frying fish was intoxicating. It made Keela feel hungry, and the feeling contrasted with her earlier sense of comfort. It was an urgent need and a feeling that she wanted something more. She accepted one of the fillets as villagers carried them away from the fire three at a time and began handing them to other villagers.

While Keela enjoyed her time on the beach by the warm fires, she continued to eat fillet after fillet because they kept being offered as they came away from the fire. The surplus was great enough to feed everyone more than three fish fillets each, and many of her friends were already full by the time she ran out of appetite for the juicy chunks of fish. Keela remained on the beach with the other villagers until after dark, when she finally went home and fell asleep.

* * *

Keela knew it must still be late at night, but she woke up to amber and yellow light outside the windows of her house, shining through the curtains and leaving her home bright enough for her to navigate through. As she rose from bed and started to approach a window, she felt pain in her kidneys as the panic began to rise, for she already knew from the flickering shadows that the orange glow was coming from a fire. When Keela looked out the window, she knew nothing she imagined could have prepared her for the scene in the village. The scene burned into her mind more vividly than all the paintings she had carefully crafted.

A deep well of nausea rose within Keela and threatened to make her sick as she realized with a deep horror that nothing would ever again be the same in her village. She fought back bile and tried to concentrate on the scene before her. As she looked down the street, she counted at least three houses that were already ablaze. Several more had smoke pouring out the windows, while the rest were glowing with fresh lamps in the rooms as people woke up and tried to find out what was going on.

A fear rose up in Keela like she'd never felt before. A fire in the village was a complete disaster—one that would set these simple fishermen back years as they rebuilt their homes. Fear made her want to run and help put out the fire, her heart pounding in panic. Then, she saw a man carrying a torch walk brazenly into one of the houses, and seconds later, it too was ablaze. She realized it wasn't safe to go out and help anyone, and her heart began to pound even faster with fear as she remained rooted to the floor.

The black smoke crawled up above the houses, with the roofs glowing red from flames licking into the air. As the roof beams collapsed into the houses, they fell on beds and curtains, setting them ablaze. As this progressed down the road one house at a time, the screams of astonishment grew louder and louder.

A great number of people were running around in the street, many of them foreigners wearing strange clothing. These people all had three-pointed sailor's hats and white clothing—nothing like the local fishermen and shepherds wore. As people poured out of the smoking houses, they found an even worse situation outside. The sailors began to grab their hands one by one and pull them behind their backs, roping the villagers' hands together faster than they could struggle free.

Although many of Keela's neighbors fought back, the sailors were much stronger, and as the villagers were being tied up, she realized that the men attacking her village were slave merchants. According to rumors she had heard, slavers had been attacking up and down the coast of England but had never raided Ireland before. All the women were being chained together, and all the men were being rounded up for an identical fate. One sailor strode between the groups of his friends, looking from side to side and running a count with his finger of how many slaves he had created so far.

Keela went back to her bed and shook Joseph awake. "Get Caitlin, we've got to hurry," she whispered. "And be quiet; slave traders are everywhere."

Joseph ran across the room to Caitlin's bed, scooping her up in his arms and carrying her to safety. Keela opened the cellar door, and

Joseph went inside first with Caitlin. All three rushed to the back of the cellar, where they tried to maintain their silence. Keela reached out for Caitlin and smothered her in protective hugs. As Caitlin began to whimper in fear, Keela immediately put her finger across her lips.

Keela heard furniture moving around upstairs with loud scrapes and boots stomping everywhere on the wood slats. She also heard the voices of two or three strange men upstairs. She listened intently to every word, trying to glean every detail she could. Her mind was in a full-blown panic and hypersensitive, and every scrape on the boards made her skin crawl and prickle with terror.

"Keep looking. More men have to be here somewhere. I know they're hiding, Ron," said the first voice, wheezy and high.

"The women are just as valuable as the men, James. Deas needs them all alive!" cried a second voice, rough and deep.

"I know they're around here somewhere. Nobody just leaves a fire going." The third man's voice was keen and sharp—two qualities realized as being very dangerous in men.

Keela shook with terror and shame as she realized that in her frozen panic, she had forgotten to extinguish the fireplace. The crashing upstairs became much louder. By the time Keela realized that the cellar door had been broken open, it was too late. The heavy boots thundered through the cellar, and Joseph cried out as two hands grabbed his elbows.

Joseph pushed backward with his elbows, trying to dislodge the attacker. Although he shook one elbow free, the attacker grabbed a club from his belt and swung it down on Joseph's head, leaving him stunned. A second man came up behind Joseph and grabbed his other elbow, and together, the two men were strong enough to subdue Joseph.

The men dragged Joseph away, leaving Keela and Caitlin downstairs. One of the slave traders gave Keela an evil sneer but, realizing that he couldn't bring more than one captive upstairs at once, he turned around after a few seconds to help drag Joseph away. He ignored the elbow strikes to his ribs as Joseph tried desperately to get away.

Keela could tell that Joseph was upstairs now because she heard the unmistakable clang of the latch on the cellar door. She heard more stomping of boots as he was dragged to the kitchen. Then, she heard punches, but she had no idea what was going to happen as she quivered against her will in the cellar. With each punch, she flinched, not knowing if it was Joseph or a slave trader who was getting hit. Deep inside her, something switched as Joseph cried out. Terror turned to rage in one swift second as she stood beneath the floorboards.

Keela was about to go upstairs and risk her life in the process when she heard the cellar door open, and the punches stopped. She had no choice but to keep hiding because she knew the only person capable of stopping these brutal men had to be their ringleader.

"This one's been causing a lot of trouble," came the wheezing voice from before, which was wheezing even louder now. "He busted one of my ribs, the little bastard! We've got to teach him a lesson, John Deas!"

There was a brief pause in the noise upstairs, and Keela realized that the leader was named John Deas. In the quiet that ensued, she heard the cocking of a musket. Her heart froze in her chest.

"Are you the only one here?" asked a man in a deep, threatening voice. Keela had never heard his voice before, so she knew it must be her unseen nemesis, John Deas.

"Yes! I'm alone! Now get out of my house!" Keela would recognize Joseph's voice anywhere, and she was glad he could still speak. It meant he was still alive.

"Kill him, Ron," uttered the dangerous voice again. There was no doubt he was the ringleader Keela had seen surveying the work in the street.

In the calm following the remark, Keela heard the screams and crashing timbers outside in the street. "You can't do this! You'll never get away with this!" a villager shouted. Then, she heard a musket shot ring out, and Joseph screamed.

Keela saw red blood pour across the floorboards above her. Earlier, she had felt like time was slowing down, but it froze solid after the musket shot rang out. Before her husband's body could even hit the floor, she could already see his blood accumulating and coming through the floorboards. Even though time continued to flow, it seemed like the blood hovered above her head, unready to drip. She heard a loud thump as Joseph hit the floor.

Although her child hadn't cried out yet, Keela knew Caitlin would soon figure out what was dripping between the boards. She kept Caitlin close to her and clasped her hand over her young daughter's mouth, praying for her to stay silent and praying that Ron had forgotten about them.

John Deas's deep, cruel voice burst forth upstairs. "You see any other men giving you that kind of trouble, just shoot them dead. They're no good to me at all. They won't make good slaves, and I won't make any money off them. Tear through this place. Make sure there's no one else hiding here!"

"I promise I got everyone," said Ron.

The man with a deep voice said, "The colonel is not going to like this. The colonel said he wants them alive!"

John Deas turned to the sailor. "If you say anything about what you saw here, I'll shoot you dead, too! And I don't trust you, Ron. No man lives on his own. I'm sending another crew in here." Keela heard some boots departing, but as John Deas's voice faded, she heard him say, "If you see any more women in the village, I want you to capture them alive. That's a standing order! Not one more murder, do you hear me? If you kill one more of these slaves, you're a dead man!"

New boot steps approached, and another man entered the house. He cried, "Bring a lantern in here!" Keela began to shake uncontrollably as the footsteps got closer to the cellar door. She pushed herself backward, further back into the cellar, into the darkness.

The banging of boots stopped, and Keela thought she might be safe. But she never heard anyone close the door behind them upstairs, so she stayed alert. The longer the silence carried on, the more confident she became in her safety. She listened even more intently, hoping she could pick up clues in the silence.

Outside, Keela heard repeated shouts down the street as the order Deas had given was relayed. Every banging door and distant scream created further panic in her as she shared the fear her neighbors were going through. As the blood continued to drip through the floor, Keela couldn't hold it in anymore. She began to shake harder and harder until she thought the invaders would be able to hear the repetitive thrumming of her joints. She had the sense of her life becoming a spiral of water that was spinning down and away and draining through the floor, and if it ceased, she would no longer exist. She had her back to the steps, hoping to push an intruder back into the stairs, possibly toppling him against the protruding slats.

Loud boots stomped downstairs, and before Keela knew it, rough hands were wrapping around her. She fought back at once, with all her built-up fury and fear releasing at the same time. She followed her first instinct and buried her teeth into one of the big hands trying to grab her. She clenched down with her jaw, straining her tendons in the process, releasing some of her anger but not nearly all of it.

The man who had grabbed Keela pushed her mouth away with his own, diseased mouth, but she managed to get a chunk of his lips between her teeth as he leaned forward. She felt flesh tearing as he continued to maintain his grasp on her. The slave trader then grabbed Caitlin's legs and began to pull as hard as he could, stretching her legs and bringing an involuntary shriek of pain from the girl. The cry filled Keela's heart with determination and fury.

One of the slavers tugged hard against Keela's arms, and he shouted, "Get out here, you wench! They told me you were down here. Hey, James, give me a hand here! We've got two of them. One of them is a little girl. Hurry! Both of them are feisty!" He had an even deeper voice than the other men.

Keela tried to hold on to Caitlin with all her might. "Let go of her!" Keela screamed. The other slaver, named James, stomped down the steps behind the first slaver, who twisted to the side to let him past, stretching Caitlin even more in the process. The fight never let up between Keela and the man who held her, and she felt something cold wrap around her ankle, but she didn't care.

The slaver continued to wrench Caitlin loose, spitting viciously on the floor as his torn lip dripped blood. Keela had to adjust her grasp to keep Caitlin from slipping away forever. The slavers attacking Keela had managed to bind one of her feet in a manacle during the struggle, and James was using the chains attached to the manacles to try and knock her over. She held her ground against the first slaver while the other slaver continued to pull on her waist, trying to make her submit.

As James grabbed Caitlin's other leg, doubling the pull, Keela realized her daughter would soon be taken away from her. She tried to memorize every detail of their vile faces as they dragged her daughter out of her arms. She cried out to them again, to buy more time for her daughter.

"Please!" Keela screamed for mercy. "Take me instead! Leave her alone! She's only seven years old! She'll be no good as a slave, and she hasn't done anything to deserve this! Leave her alone!"

James spat on the ground, laughing in scorn, and each peal of laughter was a scythe against Keela's ribs. "Never!" he replied. "They make better slaves! They fetch a higher price than adults right now!"

"No!" Keela screamed, panic rushing through her like a whirlwind.

At the sound of panic in her mother's voice, Caitlin began to scream even louder. "Save me, Mommy! Don't let me go! Mommy!"

Keela was desperate to save her daughter's life, but as she grabbed hold again, she realized that the only part of her daughter she held in her hand was the green ribbon. The satin ribbon hung from her hands as her daughter disappeared into the darkness, screaming, "Mommy! Mommy!"

Keela had no time to grieve because two more slavers had already entered the basement and grabbed her by each arm, their great strength overpowering her and stopping her fight. A third man, grabbing her manacled legs, hoisted her up in the air. Keela fought desperately, even while bound and suspended.

No matter how hard Keela struggled, there was no getting away from three of these men at once, and now, she was in complete danger. Anger switched back to mind-numbing terror as her brain began to block out emotions to protect itself from harm, leaving her in a strange lucid state. She was in utter shock but still aware of her surroundings.

The slavers dragged Keela out into the street while another slaver hauled Caitlin up ahead of her. Caitlin was kicking at the slaver with all her might, but the slaver seemed to enjoy it, or at least the sneer on his torn and ragged lips indicated so. Instead of punishing her, he chose to humiliate her, swatting her on her behind every time she kicked him. Keela's head began to spin as her rage soared to new heights.

"These here gave us quite a problem!" said one of the slavers holding Keela.

"We'll have to teach her a lesson then, won't we?" John Deas replied.

"*You're* the one that needs to be taught a lesson!" screamed Keela. She took aim at the nearest hand. One of the slavers had his hand wrapped around her left arm near the shoulder, and she decided to make him pay for his mistake. She quickly bit down on the knuckles as hard as she could. The slaver screamed and backed away momentarily, clutching his hand.

With one slaver out of the way, Keela kneed the other slaver as hard as she could between his legs. Even though the slaver was rather large, for about twenty seconds, he couldn't do anything to her or anyone else. She punched him in the face while he was motionless, and she tried to escape, running for her daughter as fast as possible.

Keela was surprised when the bloody hand of the other slaver came at her out of nowhere in a vicious fist. She was distracted by the blow to her head, and she swerved to the side to miss the next swing. She thought this was a good idea at the time, but she misjudged the situation. To her left stood another attacker, who was able to deal a second impact, this one to her skull, along her upper jaw. The nerve in her jaw sang, and her face seemed to go numb.

Keela ran forward and tripped over something in the road. She felt the interruption through every bone and wondered what had obstructed her. She lifted her head up to look behind her, and she witnessed death. It was a unique sight for her to see a dead person. She had only seen dead fish before. But now, she saw Joseph's body on the ground. She knew the slavers had killed him, but she had not yet seen his corpse.

The blood from Joseph's head covered his body. A deep scream escaped Keela's lungs, but her body was completely paralyzed with pain and fear. She had no way to fight back as the slavers grabbed her. The sight of her dead husband was too much for her. And Keela realized that there was no escape.

"Quite a set of lungs on her, too. Good catch! Tie her to the tree backward!" Deas instructed. "I've got an idea."

Keela was unable to fight back as the slavers hauled her to her feet and dragged her to a tree, her legs unwillingly following behind her. She was thrown against the tree so hard that she lost the rest of the air in her lungs, and her head rested against the tree as she tried not to pass out. The tight rope around her back made it hard to breathe, but she fought for awareness, seeing her daughter on the other side of the tree.

As Keela stood there, trapped, the slavers stood on each side of the captive woman and ripped her clothes away. Keela never took her eyes off Caitlin. As tears ran down Keela's face, Caitlin sobbed. "Don't cry," said Keela. "I promise I'll come and find you."

Keela's captors held the ropes tight. John Deas hovered behind her, but his face was tilted toward her, making sure she could look into his eyes. "I'll make sure you never see your daughter again," he said.

Deas's promise cut Keela's heart deeper than he could ever know, but she filled her words with anger so he would never forget the pain he caused her. "You'll never be able to get away! No matter how far you run, I'll hunt you down!" Keela could do nothing but shout while tied tightly to the tree.

John Deas stared back at her with pure evil in his eyes. "I'm not going anywhere yet."

"Close your eyes, Caitlin! Close your eyes!" Keela begged.

As the people from town began to lower their heads, ashamed to see what Deas was about to do, the slavers smacked them in their faces hard enough to draw blood. One by one, the slavers forced the villagers' heads up by the hair until they had no choice but to look. "You watch, men!" one of the slavers grunted.

One man tried to close his eyes against the madness and the violence. But another slaver reached over to his eyes with fingernails that hadn't been trimmed in weeks. Slowly, he peeled the man's eyelids open, yanking the lids apart and causing drops of blood to hit the ground.

John Deas returned to his position behind Keela, and she felt his hot breath on her neck. It made her gag. He whispered in her ear, "I'm really going to enjoy this." Immediately, with no other pretext, John

Deas pounded himself into her.

Keela screamed in pain as every sense of security was ripped from her. Never in her life had she ever felt so helpless. Her body shook with the force of the rape. Not a tear fell from her eyes, though, and not a grunt or a whisper escaped her while she was violated. This made John Deas even angrier.

Deas grunted, "This is too hard! I'm getting tired. I want you to really feel this." He untied Keela, ripping the rope free and throwing her to the ground. "Hold her down!" he screamed at his men. His pants were still hanging down around his ankles. As Keela lay forced to the ground by the men, he got to his knees and unsteadily crawled toward her, eager to rejoin the assault.

Deas fell on top of Keela, sweating, and he violated her again as she was helpless on the ground. The combination of sweat and violence filled her with revulsion. He pounded her mercilessly. Shockwaves of pain rocked her from her ribcage all the way to her skull.

Just as Keela was sure she would pass out from the pain, a man dressed in full battle armor came over and raised his sword high above his head. "Enough, John Deas!" he cried with enough authority and force to compel Deas to immediately stop, pull himself out, and crawl away unsteadily on his knees as he tried to pull up his pants. Deas turned to look at the colonel, along with everyone else, while still yanking his pants up around his hips.

"Leave it alone!" shouted the colonel. And Keela realized she was in even worse hands now. "It needs to be with the rest of the slaves! If you damage my merchandise, I can't make any money off it!"

"As you say, colonel," Deas reluctantly agreed.

"And put some clothes on it. We're not savages! We're businessmen!"

Keela was quickly dressed in rags, and then her hands were tied behind her back. The colonel said, "That's just in case you get any ideas that you're not a slave now."

Keela's head began to clear. She looked around, frantically scanning for Caitlin. "What did you do with my daughter? Where is she?"

John Deas turned to look at her, casually glancing at her as though he didn't care what he had just done. The look on his face made her blood curdle. "The only reason I didn't kill that little girl is because I can make a lot of money off her," Deas said. "A lot more than the likes of you, that's for sure."

"I'll never stop hunting you down!" Keela screamed. "I'll never rest until you pay for what you did!"

Undaunted, John Deas stared her right in the face and whispered, "That's going to be pretty hard when you're all the way across the ocean in Haiti, and I'll still be here, raiding more towns and getting more slaves."

Keela felt something hard strike her head. Then, as her senses faded, John Deas turned away, and everything went black. When Keela woke up, she was in the hold of a slave ship, chained to hundreds of other slaves.

Chapter 2

A FTER THE COLONEL cried out to John Deas, all commotion had stopped in the street. Caitlin was frozen, but the slavers behind her were not. She was dragged away as the colonel took over matters. Even if Caitlin had been free, she knew that she would have been powerless to move at the sight of the scene around her.

Caitlin finally came alive and tried to fight the traders dragging her away, but they brought her to the shore, where a ship waited for its new slaves. It was a smaller ship. And as Caitlin was dragged onto the ship, cold horror washed over her.

One of the slavers presented Caitlin to a woman. "Take good care of her," said the slaver who passed her off. "John Deas wants this girl for Margaret."

Lily's eyes opened wide, and she reached out and took Caitlin by the shoulder. "There's a girl," she soothed. "Let's go get you cleaned up, right?"

Caitlin refused to have any of the young lady's sweet-talking. She reached down with her head and bit Lily's thumb, holding on for a couple of seconds before releasing the thumb and making a break for the gangplank. Both slavers looked terrified. Though they stood in front of Caitlin and pushed her hands down, refusing to let her leave, they took their orders not to hurt her seriously.

"Whoa, whoa, whoa, there, young lady. Just cool down now," one of the slavers said. "There's nothing you can do about it, so just get used to it. Come on; there's a bed for you and everything."

Lily came up behind Caitlin, and even though Caitlin was still scared, the fact that no one was hurting her for the moment made her relax slightly. "I want my mommy!" she cried out.

"I'm sorry we got off on the wrong foot," Lily said, "but that can't happen today. You've got a new mom to look forward to, though. You've got Margaret as your mother now."

"But I want my *real* mommy!" cried Caitlin.

Lily stayed where she was, still rubbing her hand. Caitlin knew she had every right to be mad. After all, Lily's finger was still bleeding. "This is not the time to have this conversation," Lily said. "It's too cold out here for you to be standing around in the dark. Come into the cabins, where it's nice and warm."

Caitlin had already been feeling cold, but when Lily started up about the warm cabins, Caitlin began to feel a chill settling into her bones. She nodded her head, still sniffling, and walked inside, where Lily made sure that she got cleaned up and into new clothes.

John Deas made little appearance at all during the subsequent voyage, and Caitlin stayed in her cabin amidships most of the time anyway. She was grateful that she didn't have to see that beast of a man.

The voyage to the jungle island was uneventful. But Caitlin missed her mother horribly by the time the ship sailed into the blue-green waters of the quiet harbor on the island. The ship's small dinghy was released, and it carried Caitlin, Lily, two slave traders, and John Deas to the island.

The sandy shore felt excellent to Caitlin beneath her shoes, and she enjoyed the sight of coconut trees and ferns immensely after a week of sailing through the open ocean. In Ireland, she had never been exposed to coconut trees or ferns, and she didn't even know what they were called yet. Despite her lack of knowledge, she had no problem absorbing new experiences.

While Caitlin had never seen parrots before, she had heard of them. She recognized a parrot as soon as it squawked loudly and flashed its brilliant colors as it flew from tree to tree. Just like her mother's paintings were filled with bright colors, so too were the parrots. The magical painted birds brought a whole new level of mystical world to the jungle island.

Suddenly, a parrot spoke, and this new magic amazed Caitlin. "Hola," said the bird.

Caitlin was astonished at the words coming from the bird. Bluebirds never gave voice to any words, only producing songs. She had been sure that this portion of the tales surrounding parrots could not be true. "What did you say?" she asked the parrot, too astonished to avoid talking to it.

"Hello," answered the bird. Caitlin remained astonished and confused.

John Deas walked a bit further up the beach from Caitlin, toward the trees. Then, he turned to Caitlin, and when she looked at his face, she felt uncomfortable. Scars on his face told her of fights he had won. Caitlin wondered how he could even look her in the eyes after what he'd done to her mother, but when he spoke to Caitlin, his voice was soft and reassuring.

"Come here, Caitlin," he said. "Let's take you to meet your new mother. You'll like her."

Caitlin was surprised by the man's kind approach to her after capturing her and dragging her away from her home. "What's your home like?" she asked, still unsure of the situation but following him into the jungle anyway. Being abandoned on the beach was too terrifying a prospect for her to entertain.

"It's not just a home; it's a castle. Here, on this island, I'm King John."

"Would that make me a princess?" Caitlin asked, suddenly thrilled at the idea.

John Deas made a quizzical face, pulling his neck up straight and looking less evil. "Yes, I believe that would make you Princess Caitlin. Lady Margaret wanted a child for so long. I'm so glad you finally came along. You should always refer to my Lady Margaret as Mother."

"But she's *not* my mother." The comment seemed innocent enough, but the way Deas stopped walking when Caitlin said it told her how angry it made him.

John Deas spoke in a calm voice, even though he was upset. "Lady Margaret is your mother now," he answered.

Lily had been quiet during the long walk through the jungle, but now she spoke up. "That would make you my sister, wouldn't it, Caitlin?" It was impossible for Caitlin to miss the connection. If she were Lily's sister now, it would be even harder to ignore her.

Lily was friendly toward her new sibling. If Caitlin was really being kidnapped, Lily had already gotten under her skin, and she didn't want her new sister to be upset or scared.

Caitlin continued following Deas but knew in her heart that she wasn't there willingly. She was still young, but she was old enough to know that her life on a tropical island was not going to be a pleasant one. Two of John Deas's strongest slave traders walked behind them, and behind the traders strode the rest of the salt-covered sailors who had taken care of the boat during its uncountably distant voyage. For all Caitlin knew, this could have been the distant fairy kingdom Tir na Nog so often spoken of back in Ireland before she was taken away.

The castle took Caitlin's breath away, and she nearly forgot that she would become a servant here. The high walls were reinforced with copper spikes to prevent invaders, and the ground floor was protected behind a massive wall, with only ramparts above it. Only one window peeked out of the ground floor of the castle. From that window, the steam from a fresh pie was pouring out, and the smell of the berries took Caitlin the rest of the distance to the door. Once she smelled the fresh food after weeks of dry biscuits that the slavers called tack, she couldn't resist going into the castle, even though it would become her prison.

Inside the castle, Caitlin discovered a kitchen, a dining room, and a large hall. The woman baking the pie entered from the kitchen, and the blueberries had stained her apron blue, leaving the aroma of blueberries all over her. "Who is this young urchin?" the lady asked.

John Deas cleared his throat. "Lady— Um, *Queen* Margaret, may I present Caitlin to you?"

"What a wonderful child," she said. "I've always wanted to have one!"

"I thought you might like it," said John Deas. "That's why she's all yours."

"*All mine?*" Margaret spluttered, trying too hard not to giggle loudly.

"Yes," John Deas confirmed.

Caitlin had nothing to say during the exchange. Her mind simply wandered off.

"Young Caitlin, would you like some blueberry pie?" Margaret asked.

She seemed sweet enough on the outside, and Caitlin couldn't resist the temptation of hot blueberry pie after days of hard tack and the occasional jerky. "I'd love some blueberry pie!"

"You didn't say that quite right," Margaret responded. She blinked her eyes and squatted down before Caitlin. "John says that I'm your mother now. So, what do we say, daughter?"

Lily stood next to Caitlin, but her presence did nothing to reassure her. It only left her in a more vulnerable position because she didn't want to disappoint her new sister, no matter how much she didn't trust her friendship. "I'd love some blueberry pie . . . Mother," Caitlin said, although the last word was expelled from her after a pause. Caitlin couldn't understand exactly how this worked because Keela said that she'd always be her mother as if it was a point of fact. But now, this woman was saying that she was her mother instead.

"Well, if you want some pie, then I hope you don't mind cleaning this apron for me," said Margaret. "It's become hopelessly soiled, but the nuts on the island provide us with soap. It's better than anything your father can provide from afar. It won't take too long to clean, and then the pie will be cool enough to eat."

Caitlin didn't mind doing chores at first because she was already prepared for that treatment. John Deas had warned her about it. And she felt that the position of these people as her parents left her defenseless to say no to them. She knew that she was too young to stand up to these new people that had hauled her away. She dutifully put the apron in the water and started trying to clean it with soap, but even with her good effort, it took her a good ten minutes to get the blue stains out of the plain linen apron.

"That looks much better, daughter. What did your father say your name was again?"

"Caitlin," she answered, only moments later uttering, "Mother" in an apologetic rush.

"You're going to love it here, Caitlin," Margaret assured her.

Try as she might, Caitlin still struggled with the idea of Margaret Deas being her mother. But the blueberry pie was fantastic. After Caitlin was done eating, Margaret took her by the hand and led her outside. "I want to show you your new bedroom," Margaret said.

"Where is it?" Caitlin asked, growing more concerned as they drew away from the castle. Lily followed Margaret and Caitlin out of the lovely castle. And Caitlin's dreams of living in a castle vanished as surely as the castle itself receded the further they walked away from it.

"Right over her," said Margaret. Caitlin looked where she pointed. A number of servants' huts, small and humble, filled the far side of the lawn, by the looming coconut trees. "This is your new home. You can stay in the castle during the daytime, but at night, your home is here. You might be my daughter, but you're still living by the rules. You help out with the chores, or you won't be welcome anymore."

"Yes, Mother," answered Caitlin quietly. But the more promises that got broken, the harder it became for Caitlin to trust her new mother.

As they reached the huts, Margaret ushered Caitlin inside one of them, and Caitlin couldn't distinguish it from the others. She knew she had to leave something identifying her hut so that she wouldn't get confused. But she suddenly realized that she hadn't held onto anything when she was torn away from her mother. Even her favorite green ribbon was missing.

Inside the hut, Caitlin noticed a bed, a fireplace, and some clothes that looked to be about Lily's size. She quickly realized that Lily lived here too. And the idea of someone she didn't know very well living in the same hut as herself didn't feel very comforting. As she surveyed her new home, she began to sniffle.

"Don't you dare cry, you ungrateful twerp!" Margaret chided her. "Be grateful your mother is putting a roof over your head! I took Lily in years ago, and she's never cried or talked back to me. I expect to see you at the castle by sunup for your chores!"

Caitlin had stopped sniffling by the time Margaret finished her tirade. "It's okay," said Lily. "I'll show you how everything works around the castle."

Margaret scoffed at Lily and spun around. She marched out the flimsy door of the hut, swinging it shut behind her. Caitlin remained inside the small house that had now become her home with Lily, and as she sat down on the bed, Lily asked her, "Are you all right?"

Caitlin looked at Lily with sadness in her eyes. "I'll be fine. I just need to get some sleep. I just know my mommy will come and find me someday."

"Of course, she will, little Caitlin. Don't lose hope. May you have pleasant dreams tonight," Lily comforted.

Although Caitlin still had her worries, she rested against her pillow and was soon fast asleep.

Chapter 3

K EELA WOKE UP SLOWLY, with shackles connecting her hands and feet in cold metal loops. Her body was wracked in pain from head to toe. Her wrists stung from the shackles, and her legs hurt as well. She looked down and saw dark red blood on the rag that had been thrown over her body. She knew she was sitting up, but she was unclear how she survived the attack and her kidnapping. She thought she was bleeding to death and tried harder to regain her senses.

As she awakened further, Keela discovered that hundreds of other people were chained together with her, side by side. They were so close together that they couldn't even lay down; they had to stay sitting up. She realized that one of the women sitting beside her was from her village. It was Maggie O'Ryan. The chains ran between the two of them, and Keela realized she was chained to a dying friend. The grim reality pushed her into a higher level of awareness and pulled the clouds of sleep from her mind.

Keela had never been on a slave ship, but the reality of her new life was not unheard of. She had been horrified by the stories of abuse and other mistreatment, but she thought they were the same dangerous lies as dragons and fairies and other such myths that suddenly didn't seem so impossible. Though dulled by the blows to her head and the deep shroud of unconsciousness that had followed, as Keela's hearing became sharper, the sounds of distant moans emerged, and some close by as well. She looked beside her and noticed that the blood on the rag wasn't coming from her body but from a deep cut on Maggie's exposed torso, dangerously close to her kidney.

As Keela sat there in the darkness beside her neighbor, Maggie began to speak in a lilting, trance-like voice that filled Keela with horror. She knew that voice all too well. Every time someone she had known was dying, they would start talking very strange just before they went. Keela thought of this strange quality as a death lilt. To her, it meant that they were running out of air and would soon leave life behind.

"Remember those times we used to make blueberry pies—every Saturday?" Keela whispered to her friend. "Those were good times." Maggie's lips were turning blue, so Keela knew she was already done for. Keela tried to keep her face calm as she looked at her friend drawing her last breaths. Although Keela was filled with dread and sorrow, she forced herself to remain calm on the surface, and she tried to keep herself from trembling. She wanted to stay strong for Maggie's sake.

"Hold on, Maggie. Hold on. We're going to make it. You're going to be all right. Lean against me," Keela said.

As tears poured down Maggie's cheeks, she rested her head against Keela's shoulder unsteadily. Her breathing grew more and more labored. "I see Tir na Nog," Maggie whispered in her delirium. Finally, Maggie stopped breathing, and Keela paused once more, still chained to her dead friend, unable to move a muscle but also completely unwilling to move.

Keela stared at her friend, who used to make pies with her and play with Caitlin, until she could no longer bear the sight of her dead body. She turned her gaze forward to the slave chained in front of her, trying to ignore the weight of Maggie's lifeless body leaning against hers. She had no idea how many hours later it was when the slavers finally came down to inspect their cargo. Two of the slavers came over to Maggie, and they looked at each other with silent gazes before they started to unshackle poor Maggie's body.

The men unshackled the dead woman from the slaves around her and dragged her away by the arms and legs as if she were a sack of grain. They never even looked down at the body as they left the hold, instead speaking calmly to each other as they walked like the body wasn't even there. They never even looked at Keela or bothered to acknowledge that she was alive. "This one's going to be food for the sharks," said one of the men as they left.

Keela had no idea how two people could be so completely heartless. She began to feel uncontrollable shaking overwhelm her, but as she tried to wrap her arms around herself, she discovered that the chains were too short to even afford her that luxury. As she continued to shiver, she began to listen to other voices around her to try and calm her mind.

The moans and cries of the other slaves did nothing to calm Keela, but they did distract her from her own physical distress. As she waited in the darkness, many hours passed, punctuated by a feeding, which was nothing but hard tack and fresh water since they were only a day out from port. Keela knew the provisions would soon begin to rot and stagnate. She had been on fishing boats long enough to know that food carried in boats would be eaten by maggots, water would turn sour, and the only liquid would be wine, which would be a cold comfort indeed to starving slaves.

Keela shuddered at how easily her mind could accept her new position in the world. But deep in her subconscious, the keys of rebellion were hatching and were pushing to the surface as a screaming desire to no longer be in that position of slavery. She wanted to be free again. For now, she eagerly consumed the hard tack, realizing she had to conserve her energy if she was to survive the entire voyage.

Hours later, one of the slaves decided to hang his own neck from the chains by wrapping them around a post and slumping forward. Not all of the slaves on the ship were Irish. Some of them were criminals from Spain, some had been collected from Africa weeks before, and others were dark-skinned but not African. One of the slaves insisted he was going back to his homeland. In retaliation, the slavers used a sword to rip his head from his body in front of the other slaves. The slaver who wielded the sword said, "Well, his head's not going back to his homeland. His head is going right to the bottom of the sea." After that, none of the slaves spoke for several days.

Even though no one broke the silence, inside, Keela was screaming. As the silence lingered and grew thicker, she was forced to accept its presence. But inside, she was fighting back with every ounce of her will. She refused to ever fall into silent depression and falter on her path. She knew exactly what her path needed to be, and that path led to her daughter, no matter how much pain and terror she had to endure to get there. It was important for her to keep working to find her daughter and take her back from the man who took so much from her. It kept her motivated to survive.

Every day, Keela was dragged out on deck and forced to eat food with the rest of the slaves. She knew that many of the slaves were dying from various causes because she saw fewer slaves on the deck each day during the daily feeding. As they sailed through the hot sun, day after day, the food became worse and worse. After a while, the hard tack became inedible because it had been ruined, but the slavers made sure that fresh fish was always brought on board.

The fish was much better than the hard tack. And even though there was nothing to cook the fish over, it was better than starvation, and nothing on the fish went to waste except for the thin ribs. As for the water, the hotter the sun became, the worse the water tasted until three of the barrels of water were poured overboard because they had gone green.

When a rainstorm swept through, and rain poured through the grates that only existed in the ceiling so that the slaves could have oxygen, everyone on the entire ship was grateful. The ship's crew saved so much rainwater in buckets that the slaves were even able to bilge out the slave decks. The layers of body fluid and grime were slowly removed from the floor, but only with a lot of scrubbing and bilging. Slowly, the filth was removed, and the floor was made clean.

After that, fewer deaths occurred for a while, though one of the slaves, a man in Keela's section, asked to be strangled because he couldn't take the pain in his legs any longer. An older man reached out with his shackles and wordlessly held onto the other man's neck until the man's jaw stopped twitching and his horrible convulsions stopped scraping his legs against the floor. After his death, a silence hung over the slaves in Keela's section for many days.

Weeks later, Keela heard the screaming of seagulls and realized

26

immediately that the ship was close to its destination. She was hauled to her feet with the rest of the slaves and dragged on deck, reduced to following physical commands. She heard one of the slave traders say, "We're in Haiti. Time to leave," and a sense of disorientation hit her. All she had heard about the island of Haiti is that Christopher Columbus from Spain had lived there and that the island was in the New World, on the other side of the globe from her home.

The Nightingale sailed into La Isabela, Haiti, in 1595. The slaves aboard did not enjoy their arrival, despite the warm sun and the green hills rising in the distance. Haiti tempted them with warm sandy beaches, lush palm trees, and black rocks that stood on the shore as if they had been planted there hundreds of years ago. The slaves knew they would not be afforded the pleasures the island held as they squinted at their new island home.

As Keela emerged into the blinding sunlight, it took a while for her eyes to adjust from the dark hold of the ship. As her brain throbbed, she covered her eyes with her hand for shade. She noticed that the other Irish people that survived the journey had nearly bone-white skin. It shone in the tropical sunlight. She realized that her skin was paler, too, after a month away from sunlight.

As Keela regained her vision, she could see the ship clearly. All the other slaves, no matter their color, were on deck together. She realized that they had been stored on different levels. Her realization that they were being treated like cargo instead of people made her willpower even stronger.

Keela was near the edge of the group and could see all the slavers surrounding them. Many of the men had their mouths covered with bandanas to block the smell of the slaves on deck. On the main deck, she saw a placard identifying the ship simply as *The Nightingale.* Keela had no idea how many weeks she had been trapped below deck, but she found some comfort in the fact that she was no longer trapped inside the stinking belly of *The Nightingale.*

The warm Caribbean Sea beckoned visitors to Haiti. The warm waters encouraged sailors and traders to establish colonies long ago. Keela could see the young Spanish boys in the water, pointing at the ship and jumping up and down as it sailed into the harbor.

One by one, the slaves were led into the hands of their masters. Two of the slavers stood before Keela. One of them spoke: "You lot— the ones who made it here—have been purchased by Jonathon Omari. Follow me."

The slave trader carefully undid the shackles on each end of the slaves he had addressed and isolated the slaves that Omari had bought. Then, he started pushing them one by one, urging them to move off the ship. "Go on!" he cried. "Get down there to your new master!"

The other slave men and women followed the instructions without giving the slave traders any trouble. But Keela was not like the other people on the ship. She wasn't about to be cowardly, even though she was destined for seven long years of work at the hands of Mr. Omari, the plantation owner who had purchased her.

Haiti was extremely warm—too hot, really. And Keela was already sweating by the time the slave traders got to her among the row of slaves. The traders started shoving her rudely on her back with their palms and then their fists. In retaliation, she swung her elbows back as hard as she could muster after weeks trapped sitting up, angry that they would dare touch her like that.

In response, Keela felt a punch to her kidney from one slaver and a kick from the other, who was much heavier and stronger. She grunted in pain and dropped to her knees as she heard a strong male voice call out from somewhere. "Don't you lay another finger on my property, or I'll take those fingers off your hands! I was promised that none of the people would come to me injured, and it looks to me like you're injur- ing her."

The two slavers immediately stopped touching Keela and took a couple of steps back from her. Both slave traders kept staring at Mr. Omari as they backed away from Keela. "Our apologies, Mr. Omari!" cried the smaller thug. "She's just very stubborn, as you can see!"

Left alone, Keela rose to her feet again and opened her eyes to see a tall, handsome plantation owner riding on horseback toward the boat. He continued berating one of the slavers as he dismounted to approach the boat. "Why do you think I bought her, you sea crab? That's what I *want* in a worker!" Mr. Omari strode up the gangplank, stomping his boots on the rickety ladder. "You'd better give me those keys, too," he said angrily.

A sailor handed the whole large brass ring full of keys to Mr. Omari. "You'd better tell me which one's hers," Omari said, tapping his boot and making the now-emptied *Nightingale* boom with echoes.

The sailor grabbed the keys and nervously dug through them, snatching up a key with a red thread wrapped around it and holding it up. "This one."

Mr. Omari quickly undid Keela's shackles from around her hands and her ankles. He looked directly into her big green eyes and said, "You're my number one servant as of today. You're tough enough to keep the other servants in line. Nobody else I bought today has an ounce of courage."

Keela had not been expecting a compassionate slave owner. Her new owner allowed her to ride on horseback until he got back to his carriage. He tied the horse to the carriage and allowed Keela to sit inside with him. The other slaves walked behind the carriage, escorted by a guard. They went back to his plantation, which rested miles away from La Isabela, in the green hill country. Keela had never heard of Jonathon Omari before, or his plantation, but she knew this was going to be her new home.

Chapter 4

M R. OMARI'S PLANTATION HOUSE was fantastic. It was a structure towering above the sugarcane plantation where other slaves already struggled. They wore only shoes and small pants, going shirtless to cope with the heat and the hard work.

Keela tried to take in the details as they approached the house, but she lost track of the details when she saw parrots flying through the trees. The colors were so brilliant that she knew she had to paint them as soon as she could. The idea of such a colorful bird astonished her, but its existence was as undeniable as the peacocks roaming the grounds. They preferred to walk with their beautiful tails stretched out above them, but when they flew, the tail became fluted and hidden. The profound colors on these flying creatures gave Keela countless ideas for paintings. She wondered when she would have the freedom to paint, if ever.

All the new servants were led to the bathhouse, which was a separate enclosure where the largest pool Keela had ever seen was waiting for them. The roof was simple thatch, and the walls were simple as well. But the beautiful pool of clear water outshined the humble surroundings.

Three women approached with clean towels, but only one of them spoke up. "Hi! You all can call me Miss Ellie. I'm the first servant of the house, and that means everyone else answers to me. Welcome to the Nina—the first and largest plantation started by the Omari clan. We're here to get you cleaned up."

Keela remained silent. Miss Ellie came over to her first, making her feel singled out and vulnerable. Miss Ellie's sympathetic frown did little to reassure Keela. "We'll start with you because those cuts on your back are still bleeding," Miss Ellie announced. "You need to get cleaned up right away."

The other maids went off to care for the other new slaves while Miss Ellie stayed by Keela's side. Miss Ellie drew closer. Keela's hair was so matted and tangled and caked with grime that the bright red hair was hidden. "Oh-wee, it smells like you really need a bath!" Miss Ellie exclaimed. "And we're going to get you some new clothes. I don't think anyone can get this dress clean. How did you survive with all those cuts?"

"A lot of us *didn't* survive," Keela answered. "Many of us have already died."

The maid had been straightening out the deep tangles in Keela's hair, but she stopped and rested her hands on Keela's shoulders. The gentle touch told Keela how much the loss was a personal one to Miss Ellie. The people that didn't survive would have been working alongside her and the other maids.

"I've heard that Jonathon is very upset about that. He paid for sixty slaves, but he didn't get even forty."

As Miss Ellie began to peel the long dress away from Keela's legs, Keela remained silent. Sweat and blood had glued the dress to her body. And she struggled as she remembered the ribbon in her pocket, fumbling to grab it as her dress was being removed. The green ribbon fell to the floor.

Miss Ellie noticed the ribbon. She stopped peeling the dress, and Keela breathed a sigh of relief, which Miss Ellie caught. It immediately brought a blush to Keela's cheeks, which she hoped had not been seen.

"Oh, what a wonderful ribbon!" Miss Ellie remarked. "I'll keep it safe for you here in my dress. You're not supposed to have anything, but I know how important it is to have keepsakes. Now, I'm not going to lie to you, this is going to hurt very bad, but I'm going to bring some shears in to make it easier. I'll have to cut this dress away from you. And it's going to hurt."

So much blood had leaked into the dress that Keela's skin had sealed itself together with the fabric along the deepest whip cuts. Keela refrained from moaning or crying out even as the pain tore through her body. As each strip of fabric was slowly peeled away from her, it felt like her thighs were being torn apart, and she had to grasp the arms of the chair in front of her until her knuckles turned bone white.

"It's okay," said Miss Ellie. "You can cry if you need to. No one deserves to be treated like this. Mr. Omari is not as cruel as some of the other slave owners. He insisted that we take good care of you all."

As the dress was clipped away and peeled inch by inch, the rest of Keela's back was exposed. She could tell just by the horrified moan from Miss Ellie that her back was severely injured. But Keela remained silent. As the dress was peeled past her bruised and aching shoulders, she collapsed to her knees one at a time. But still, she didn't cry out. The pain radiated across her entire back, and she struggled to breathe for a minute, appreciating the silence.

When Miss Ellie had recovered her own voice, she spoke. "I'm very sorry they did this to you. Those cuts are red and tortured. You need lots of ointment, and I don't think you'll be able to start working today. You should take the rest of the day off. Mr. Omari will be very angry when he finds out what they did to the woman he paid good money for."

"Why does he care so much about us?" asked Keela. "What makes him different?"

Ellie was quiet for a while before she answered. Each clip of the shears brought more of the dress away and punctuated the time. "I don't really know the answer to that. But I know that he has a soft heart, and he doesn't want other people to suffer. We work for him because we have to, but he doesn't allow us to be hurt like this. The only time the whip comes out is when betrayal takes place." Keela noticed the clipping of the shears had stopped. "Time to go into the pool," said the maid.

As Miss Ellie helped her into the pool, Keela became immersed slowly, soaking in every second of the experience. The first sensation upon entering the warm, healing water of the pool was the gentle hands of the woman cleaning her face and shoulders. Just the simple act of someone taking care of her was alien after weeks of torture on the ship. Keela began to tremble at the tenderness. She flashed back to Joseph and her bathing together in the old days, in the deep eddies of the ice-cold river. It was one of her favorite pastimes. They would spend hours in the water, laughing.

As Keela entered the water of the pool, the effect on her skin was instantaneous, even though she was still covered in grime and blood. The clean water quickly ate through the grime, and her skin thrilled at the clean water. To avoid the pain as her body was being cleansed, Keela flashed back to another good memory, where she was painting her daughter one day. It had been a bright spring day in Ireland, and the air was full of the aroma from small white flowers in the fields.

Another sharp pain from Miss Ellie cleaning an open wound shocked Keela back to reality. She felt the water surrounding her with fresh sensitivity. Miss Ellie carefully cleaned her back and other places she couldn't get to. Even bending over was impossible for Keela. But suddenly, she started to feel better.

Another memory returned to Keela as she saw Caitlin jumping into the river with her parents. As Caitlin swam with her and Joseph, she had been so happy that she couldn't stop laughing. Keela reveled in the memory, but soon, the hot rage returned as she remembered that her family was gone. Keela felt like she was boiling deep inside, and she wondered how she could hide that anger—tuck it away until she saw John Deas face to face again.

Keela's anger at John Deas pushed the happy memories away, and soon, her mind was no longer a place to escape the pain but rather a grim reminder of the scars he had left. Pain still burned throughout her body from his vicious attack, and the punishment left wounds that had yet to be cleaned. The deepest injuries, the ones on her soul, had yet to be examined or prodded. But the knowledge that she was no longer free had become a pounding demand to escape.

As Miss Ellie cleaned Keela's hair, the grime disappeared, leaving the bright red hair shining in the water. It was so tangled that Ellie had to scrub the brush underwater to untangle the knotted strands of curling, red hair from the bristles. "I've known how to take care of people's hair for many years," she said. "It is a joy to take care of your beautiful hair." Keela had begun to warm up to Ellie's soft, friendly nature, and she allowed Ellie a grateful smile.

All the new servants were properly cleaned in the wonderful pool of water. Keela felt almost baptized in the clean water, with the layers of black tar residue and grime from the hold of *The Nightingale* washing off her body. The reflections from the light bounced off the water and shimmered across the stately columns surrounding it. Keela had not expected such a beautiful place in the tropics.

Keela's rags had been replaced with a clean white linen dress. It was the expected clothing for each house servant. She sat in a chair, remaining patient while Ellie trimmed her curling red locks. Even before she could start trimming back the weeks of growth from the long hair, Ellie had to spend minutes brushing away the dense tangles that persisted in the hair.

A polished mirror gave Keela a better perspective of herself. Now, she could see her face had suffered little damage, and the appearance of the few cuts she had was not as bad as the pain they still caused her. She watched the clippings of hair fall to the floor by her side. Although she had always loved her hair, seeing it fall to the floor felt like a blessing of sorts—a falling away of an old situation to be replaced by a new experience in her life.

After Miss Ellie finished trimming Keela's hair, she tied the green ribbon through the back of the hair, organizing the web of hair into a magnificent braid. She was very proud of her work and stepped back to admire it. Keela noticed the ribbon the moment Miss Ellie began weaving it in, and she was so satisfied by its appearance as it traced through her hair that she was at a loss for words.

"Now your hair looks wonderful!" Miss Ellie proclaimed. "Mr. Omari has a doctor here at the plantation. You'll find that this place is much better than many of the other plantations."

Although she was clean, Keela was taken to the infirmary. It was a small place by the slave quarters. It only had four small mattresses covered in rough ticking, but it was enough to serve as a place for healing.

The doctor was an old Haitian man who immediately wrinkled his nose at the smell of Keela's wounds. "You've got diseased wounds, young lady. I can smell it from here." The doctor looked at her back for several minutes before doing anything. Keela could hardly imagine what took so long to examine, and she assumed it was bad news before he announced it. "These five cuts all have to be cleaned out. The color of the blood here is not good at all. It's turning yellow from disease. You need to drink some sarsaparilla tea at once." The doctor had herbal pastes at the ready. "Please be calm," he said. "This will hurt much less when I am done."

As the minty, herbal paste was applied to each wound, Keela felt the stitching of her skin as if the skin was literally being pulled back together. After she was dressed, Mr. Omari stepped in and said, "I heard that one of the women was injured. What happened?"

"This woman was badly whipped and beaten," the doctor answered. "Her wounds were infected. I've been working to heal them for the last hour, sir." The doctor looked very nervous.

"Stay right here," Mr. Omari said. "I've got some business to take care of, but I'll be back."

Chapter 5

MR. OMARI WASTED NO TIME in heading down to the local tavern. His horse sped down the road, spurred on by a furious rider. Even though he owned slaves, Jonathon Omari was not a cruel man. He only got violent when people were hurt. Surrounded by other plantations, where beating slaves was a way of life, Jonathon had no shortage of enemies among his neighbors, who were men equally as offended by his humanity and compassion.

The tavern was noisy and smelly. Jonathon immediately spotted the cruel lead slave trader from *The Nightingale* drinking heavily by the bar. His face was bright red from the alcohol, and a massive scar ran just below his left eye, by his nose. His black hair was greasy from weeks at sea without a shower. Jonathon stared at him in pure contempt, and then, because the man was too drunk to notice him, he called him out by name.

"Jackson!" Jonathon roared, loud enough for the whole tavern to hear him. The slaver lifted his head toward him, but it was too late. Jonathon was already on top of him. He slammed the slaver's head to the bar.

Jackson was stunned for a few seconds, but he lifted his head up far enough to spit on the bar. Blood and two cavity-riddled teeth landed on the ancient bar. As Jonathon leaned over the slave trader, the trader's breath reeked of rum, and Jonathon realized he was completely drunk.

Jonathon grabbed Jackson by the back of his shirt, yanking him away from the bar. Firmly holding on to his head and shirt, he pushed the slaver outside. Once they were a good distance from the tavern, he dropped the vicious slave trader to the ground and stood directly over him. Even though the slaver lifted his head to stare in impudence at Jonathon, he was too afraid to move another muscle as Jonathon towered above him.

"I want my money back for that one slave you sold me—the one that's been whipped!"

The trader laughed and spat mud from his mouth. "Why do you care?"

"She's damaged. She's got infected cuts, you monster!"

The slaver laughed out loud. His insolence was more than Jonathon could stand. "What are you talking about? I sold her. Now, she's yours!"

Jonathon slapped him across the face but resisted the urge to do worse to him. "You sold me damaged goods, you sard!"

The slaver spat again, and this time, blood came from his mouth. "Why do you care?"

Jonathon resisted the urge to get more violent. "If you hurt her, then you owe me my money back! You swore those slaves were unharmed. You promised! You took innocent people, and then you hurt them. Now, I have to wait for days while their wounds heal before they can even work for me."

"Why do you care so much? I already spent the money on rum! Besides, it's not up to me; it's up to John Deas!"

Jonathon Omari could never tolerate people blaming someone else for their problems. It was a disposition that allowed him to keep things running properly on his plantation. "John Deas is just a no-account, slave-dealing, piece of scum that's not worth the bowels of his ship," Jonathon retorted. "And you can tell him I said that, too! You let over fifty of them die on the way over. In fact, you can tell John Deas that he's going to get what's coming to him one of these days! Tell John Deas to watch his back! And tell him I want my money back!"

"Piss off, you oaf!" the slaver replied. "I'm not seeing hide or hair of John Deas until I get back over there. And when I get there, I don't think he'll be very happy about that little stunt you just pulled!"

Jonathon stared the evil slave trader right in the face for several seconds, trying to make up his mind. "Give John Deas my regards!" Using all his anger, he unloaded a huge punch to the slaver's square forehead. Then, he shook his wrist vigorously, reducing the pain. "That felt pretty good. I've always wanted to do that."

Jonathon looked down at the cobblestones. Jackson was bleeding heavily from his nose, and he was completely unconscious. Between the bubbles foaming from his nose, he was sleeping deeply.

"Didn't see *that* coming, did you?" Jonathon muttered as he headed back to his horse to return to the plantation.

Chapter 6

THE NEXT MORNING, Keela's wounds had begun to heal significantly. Miss Ellie was standing by her side when the doctor pronounced her recovered. "You're ready to work now," said the old doctor.

"You make that sound like a good thing," Keela said. "Now, I have to be a servant."

"Better a servant than a field hand," the doctor replied. "The field hands get the club or the whip every time they don't work fast enough."

"Doesn't Mr. Omari run the whole plantation?"

"Just the house, Keela. The fields are run by Pablo."

"Where am *I* working?" asked Keela.

"You'll be in the house," said Miss Ellie. "No one will be whipping you there. Pablo might think he's the boss, but Jonathon has more power than he does. If Pablo gives you any trouble, just talk to Jonathon, and he'll make sure it doesn't happen again."

Keela needed no guidance to the plantation house since it was the largest structure on the property, but Ellie led the way anyway. Keela noticed that Ellie kept her eyes on the road and didn't turn to look back at Keela even once. She knew that Miss Ellie was hiding something from her, but Ellie had seemed so honest that she couldn't figure out what it was.

As Keela pondered these mysteries, Miss Ellie walked her the rest of the way over to the plantation house, where a nasty little man stood in front of her in the living room. The little man disturbed her greatly the first time she set eyes on him. With a sense powerful enough that she gave credit to her Irish ancestors' spirit skills, Keela sensed a dark vacuum all around him and was immediately on her guard as her skin prickled with goosebumps.

Miss Ellie introduced them. "Miss Keela, this is Pablo, Jonathon Omari's brother."

Pablo's eyes glinted with a dark evil, and he was skinny and shrunken compared to his older brother. His awful sneer reminded Keela she was just a servant. His vicious glare also made Keela even more determined to escape this life of slavery.

As he stood there, Pablo gave all the new servants and the existing workers a long glare. "You're tasked with keeping the house clean. That shouldn't be too difficult, should it?" he sneered. "Go on, time to start cleaning."

Keela headed forward to start cleaning because it was clear from the other servants' movements that these orders were to be followed at once. "Not you," said Ellie, with a careful touch on Keela's arm. Keela froze at once, frightened. Ellie leaned close and kept her voice low, but some of the servants had clearly heard her because they gave surprised glances. "You're the personal servant for Jonathon and Pablo, so you've got different duties. Sometimes, you'll be cleaning, but mostly, it's about the needs of the masters."

Keela felt the obedience to her masters as an automatic response, just like a frightened dog cowers as it approaches its owner. Were it not for the stronger pull of fear, she could have easily begun attacking Pablo with her bare hands.

"Keela, your job in this house is simple. You serve us tea after dinner and help with breakfast and lunch, too," Pablo instructed her. "The tea is very special to us here. Dinner is up to the chef, but I'm sure you know all about setting tables." Keela kept silent, nodding as she needed to so that he knew he was being understood. "Tea is boiled in the teakettle from our private supply of Indian tea leaves, which is Jonathon's favorite tea," Pablo informed her. "Have you made tea before, Keela?"

Keela *felt* like a teapot already boiling over, and she didn't realize she was going to make a snap comment until it happened. "Irish women know how to make tea."

"Well, if you listen properly, you'll learn how to make tea the way Jonathon likes it! He might be my brother, but we have different tastes. He likes cinnamon and cardamon and all that happy stuff, but I don't, all right? When you're serving *my* tea, it's nothing but the tea leaves and milk. I want lots of milk in my tea. Now, on the other hand, my brother refuses the milk, so it's better if you just make our tea on different trays."

Keela nodded again.

"Good. I'm glad you're ready to work. The snack supplies are quite low out here. I think the first thing is for you to head back to the kitchen and learn about the snack containers. And don't nibble on the peanuts. You have your own food, and that's all you're going to eat."

Keela knew she was too skinny, but she kept her head down and refused to admit any weaknesses because she knew that slave owners always kept a watchful eye on the workers. Although she learned how to make tea the way Jonathon liked it, which was far spicier than Irish tea, she never lost her indignant spirit. She already knew how to work hard from when she was fishing and raising a family, and painting had its own discipline. But none of those things had prepared her for the hot weather and the way it beat down the workers—not just the workers in the fields, but the people inside the house as well.

* * *

Over the next few difficult weeks, Keela noticed that the servants in the house were treated better than the slaves in the fields, but not much better. A large house in the humid jungle of Haiti took far more work to keep clean every day than her small house in Ireland. Eighteen other women, all nervous and young, helped her with cleaning the great house from top to bottom so she could keep up with the food services. The others were already used to their roles in the house.

Pablo watched the maids carefully, and Keela noticed the discomfort in the other women's faces. One of the other maids was also named

Maggie. Her name reminded Keela of her fallen friend. But unlike the woman who had perished on the boat, Maggie the servant was British. She said, "I think he likes you, Keela." Keela had taken a liking to Maggie instantly, and not just because she shared a name with her fallen neighbor but because she was genuinely happy despite being trapped as a servant.

Shayna spoke up against the other maid. "He likes *all of us*, Maggie. He thinks that thing in his pants is a cattle prod and that we're just a bunch of cows."

Maggie stood up in her own defense. "Hey, we all know that. But when he looks at one of us the way he's looking at Keela, he wants something more."

When Jonathon walked in the room, Maggie looked up in surprise and held her tongue at once. Jonathon's gaze was fixed on Keela. "I'd like a tea in my study, please," he informed her.

"Right away, Mr. Omari," Keela answered.

"Thank you," he said, opening the study door just long enough to enter.

The other maids winked at Keela and giggled as quietly as they could. She looked down at the tea service and assembled the tea, adding the perfect proportion of spices. Then, she entered the study with the feeling of eyes following her. Undaunted, she closed the door behind her, balancing the tray on her hip so she wouldn't spill any of the tea.

When she came over, Jonathon gave Keela a sympathetic gaze, and it was something she hadn't expected. "I appreciate this so much," he said. "I don't like drinking tea outside. I don't want to run into Pablo." Keela poured the tea for Jonathon, who watched each movement she made. "You have the hands of a painter," he said. Keela looked at him without answering. "It's nothing personal. I'd just like to know a little more about you. You should have a cup of tea as well," Jonathon suggested, pouring the other cup for her.

Keela stood by the table and shook her head. "It's not my place," she protested.

"No, I'm being serious," Jonathon assured her. "Sit down at the table," he insisted. Keela sat down at the table and gratefully sipped the tea. "So, did you use to paint?"

"I did. How did you know that?"

Her surprise did not go unnoticed. "I didn't mean to surprise you, but I pride myself on being observant. You have a special touch with the housework. Only those with well-trained hands are that good at cleaning the house."

"Well, thank you for the compliment. And yes, I have been a painter for a long time. My mother started teaching me when I was very young."

"Wonderful! I've always appreciated the arts. Would you paint for me sometime? I would buy you all the things you need."

Keela nodded. Then, she excused herself and left.

That night, Keela went back to her quarters with confidence to add to her resolve. The servants' quarters were quite shabby, with very thin walls. While Keela was resting in bed at night, she could hear the other women talking in the rooms. She had trouble sleeping some nights because the conversations would turn heated and wake her up. Other times, it was lovemaking that interrupted her sleep. But each night, she grew better at ignoring it. She knew that she needed her sleep, and she avoided the distractions that kept the other women more tired than her, placing her at an advantage over the other servants.

Chapter 7

WHENEVER THE SERVANTS GOT to eat, the meals were corn mash with sugarcane syrup, as well as small pieces of salted fish, if they were lucky. Keela longed for the food of Ireland and would sometimes dream of it while eating her corn mash. Having the same foods day after day became a boring routine, and without potatoes, she felt herself getting weaker. She longed for other foods.

Sometimes, Keela was found down by the slave quarters, helping the slaves out instead of doing her duties at the house. They would have to wash down the corn mash with lots of tea, which spiked their energy and gave them strength to work through the hot afternoon. Cleaning the plantation house was an amazing chore, with many obstacles in Keela's way. When the hot rain poured outside, the wind blew it through the cracks in the walls. And on hot sunny days, the dust would filter in, leaving layers of dust on all the china. Every day, the servants had to clean off every surface at least twice. And during the rainy nights, they had to be extra sure to keep everything dry. In the jungle, anything left unattended would quickly mold and decay.

The unending heat of the jungle left little change in the atmosphere. Haiti was as much a prisoner's world as Keela had ever seen. She didn't see anything good in slavery. It was just another way to make people feel worthless while money was made off the sugarcane. Keela had known nothing like this in Ireland. Only cooperation and friendship kept her sane during her long years of servitude.

1599 was not an interesting year for Keela, but 1600 was a good year for her. She had made many friends during her time on the plantation. And in the year 1600, Jonathon declared that five of the field hands had earned their freedom from the labor they had done on the farm. It was a pivotal year for Keela because she didn't realize there was a legitimate way to escape a life of slavery. She had a kernel of hope ignite inside her, and it burned hotter than the jungle air around her.

Keela's friendship with Jonathon grew stronger with every passing year. No slaves under Pablo's control ever went free, but they did under Jonathon. Jonathon retained control of the villa house and provided Keela with paintbrushes and canvas after canvas while Pablo continued to watch the fields. Jonathon bought large cans of paint from overseas and never bothered to tell her the prices.

Keela hoped to buy her freedom through the paintings, but she didn't understand why Jonathon wouldn't set her free. It wasn't until the year 1600 that she found a bill for the paint cans and realized just how much he was spending on it. The artwork wasn't buying her freedom; it was only adding to her "indebtedness" to him. He'd been keeping a journal of Keela's art supplies and another list with two paintings he had sold for cash without her knowing about it. She was surprised to discover that he had snuck two away without paying her.

And so, 1600 was also the year that Keela came to understand that she was just a checkmark in a book of numbers to Jonathon Omari. She felt bad about the betrayal and the mistreatment, and she didn't realize how deep into her soul it would cut. From that point on, she noticed that Jonathon was selling more paintings, but after the first two, he was honest with her about it.

Keela knew that Jonathon was keeping most of the money from her paintings, but he let her have a guinea or two—sometimes, even four. It was never enough to buy her freedom, though. Her money was just more scratch marks in a book of numbers on Jonathon's desk. One of the scratch marks between the numbers spelled out the word "indebtedness," and Keela only understood the "debt" part. She understood that the paintings could give her freedom in the distant future if Jonathon held honest to the books he kept on his slaves and business transactions.

Every time Jonathon left Keela in his study by herself, she made sure to examine his belongings, so it was easy for her to notice other subtle treasures lying around. But none of them compared to that evil book she found. It showed her that business was slavery's best friend and that she was tied to these people for so long as they wanted her to stay there. It had nothing to do with freedom, and the benefits of painting she thought she was enjoying were just lame attempts to make her feel consoled with the removal of her freedom.

Keela never lost her feelings for Jonathon, but she never could trust a person who treats a human like another number in a book of numbers, and she'd heard enough from preachers to know that books of numbers are the sign of Satan's grasp on a human soul. If the abolishment of her freedom was tied to owing money to become free again, then slavery was truly evil because she could never make enough money from painting to cover the cost of the materials. It was an endless spiral, and Jonathon was keeping her trapped inside of it. Keela began to hope for a different way out.

* * *

When 1601 arrived, Pablo started to attack a servant named Opal in her shack from time to time. Keela knew about it from the first attack because she lived right next door, and that was close enough for her and Opal to become close friends. She knew Opal quite well by then. Opal had a scar above her nose that she was sensitive about. Simply mentioning the scar would result in her glaring at the offender, and the other servants quickly learned not to even bring it up.

One night, Keela heard Pablo enter Opal's room, next to hers. Keela tensed in alarm. The young slave girl gave some frightened gasps, but soon, a hand was clapped over her mouth as Pablo forced her onto her bed. Keela could hear the bed thump quite hard against the wall. Then, she began to hear regular thumping sounds, and the hand was off Opal's mouth because Keela heard one cry of pain after another, rising in intensity as Pablo took Opal forcefully.

Keela didn't know which disgusted her more: that Pablo couldn't keep his hands off the servants or that he didn't care who knew about it. The next day, when they were all working, Keela couldn't help but notice how much Opal was limping. Pablo walked by, interfering with Keela's chance to help the poor girl, and he gave Opal a nasty smile, leaving the poor maid shaking all over and clinging to the table for support. Keela knew that something had traumatized her, and she knew she had to comfort her.

After Pablo was gone, Keela went over and spoke with the servant. "What's wrong, Opal?"

"He took me last night. And this morning, I keep heading to the outhouse with blood between my legs. I don't know what to do."

Keela continued to comfort her, looking around carefully to make sure Pablo wasn't coming back. "I'll take care of this for you, Opal," said Keela. "Pablo's not going to hurt you again. Put away your duster and get to the infirmary. You're not going to get better on your own."

More fully aware of the danger, Opal got to her feet carefully and set her duster down on a table before slowly walking out the door. Keela watched her cautiously from the window to ensure that she made it to the infirmary without being accosted by Pablo. Then, she walked around the large plantation house until she found Jonathon.

Jonathon noticed Keela and beckoned her over. She got comfortable on the sofa beside him. It was almost time for lunch, and she'd been working hard all morning. Getting to sit down on something padded and soft was a wonderful change from kneeling, scrubbing, and dusting.

"I've noticed that some of the servants appear to be in a lot of pain," Jonathon said.

"I thought you should know, but I don't want to make any trouble." Keela looked at Jonathon uncertainly, but he shook his head, dispelling her insecurity.

"It's okay, Keela. You can tell me what's going on. As long as you're not the one making the trouble, you're not going to be in trouble. In fact, I welcome a good conversation. The other women are too scared of me to tell me the truth. What's happening?"

Feeling more secure, Keela decided to tell him exactly what Pablo was doing. "It's about Opal. Pablo has been sleeping with her, but she doesn't want it to happen, and I don't like it. It looks like he really hurt her this time."

"That's true. I noticed her limping quite a bit. Thank you for letting me know what's going on. I'll take care of Pablo myself. He does not have the right to do that to anybody."

Chapter 8

KEELA WAS ENJOYING A sound sleep when, suddenly, a noise woke her up. She recognized the sound as a man clearing his throat and spitting on the ground. Only women lived on this side of the servants' quarters. The men lived on the other side. So, Keela knew something was up right away.

Terrified, Keela lay back down in case the man came into her shack. She didn't want anyone to know she was awake. She would have the element of surprise. Her pulse slowed as she forced herself to stay calm. Then, she noticed the shadow of a man in her doorway. She froze because the man was extremely still. Her pulse got faster, but she stayed prone on the bed.

The longer the man remained, unmoving, in Keela's doorway, the more nervous she got. By the time he started moving toward the bed, she'd already worked herself into a fever of apprehension. She knew it was Pablo because there was enough moonlight to see his face. But knowing who was preying on her only made her more nervous.

Keela kept her eyes open, but only as small slits. Pablo seemed convinced that she was asleep because he shook her shoulder back and forth. She wanted to open her eyes quickly, but she drew it out to look like she was just waking up.

"I heard what you told my brother," Pablo whispered menacingly.

Keela knew the little man was afraid, and that made it easier for her to find some courage. "I don't know what you're talking about. I haven't even talked to Jonathon lately." Keela spoke louder than Pablo,

49

and even though she noticed her voice quivering, she had no qualms about making him feel a little guilty. She slid out of bed to the floor, and she stood on the far side of the bed from Pablo. It gave her a little distance.

Pablo was enraged, and Keela knew he was no longer concerned about anyone overhearing him. In fact, she knew he was waking up all the servants as he started to shout. She hoped that it would also wake Jonathon. "Don't you lie to me, you little spitfire!" he yelled. "I heard you talking to Jonathon about Opal! You just need to mind your own business. Do you hear me?"

Keela stood her ground, refusing to move away from the bed. If he was going to attack her, she was going to make him work for it. He lunged forward to attack her, and the sound of his boots slamming against the hard floor was loud. He stopped once he got to the end of the bed, and Keela knew he was thinking twice about making a lot of noise. He continued moving toward her with quieter steps, but an attack was still an attack. She made quick steps around him as he struggled to grab her in the corner, and she was clear on the other side of the bed before he turned around and advanced toward her again.

"Come back here, you little sard!" Pablo demanded. "Don't you walk away when I'm talking to you!"

"You don't care who knows about it, do you?" Keela asked him.

"I don't care what anybody thinks!" he growled out. "I'm going to have my fun with these women, and there's nothing you or anybody else can do to stop me."

"There's plenty I can to do stop you!" answered Keela.

"And there's plenty I can do to stop *you*, too!" Pablo shouted. Pushing Keela's shoulders hard, he shoved her against the wall of the small room.

Keela had avoided attacking Pablo because the punishment for attacking a master was always death, but now that he was attacking her, her gut instincts kicked in. Pablo wrapped his hands around her throat, and though his arms were thin and sinewy, his hands pushed against her throat with the force of an animal. Keela struggled to break free, wrapping her hands around his wrists and trying to pry them loose. She struggled to break free as his fingers were locked in a death grip, and she couldn't keep a good grip on his thumbs. The sneaky man kept popping his thumbs loose and returning to the task, but Keela was able to grab enough air to stay alive during the short breaks she was gaining.

Pablo continued to choke Keela, making her heart pound with a demand for air and the dread of dying, when suddenly, Jonathon broke into the room out of nowhere. "I heard your stomps! I see your hands around her throat! If you don't get out of here right now, you're done!" he threatened.

Pablo released the pressure immediately but refused to leave Keela's quarters. Jonathon smacked Pablo in the nose with the butt of a whip curled up in his hand. "Do you like that, brother? Get out of here!" Pablo hesitated for another moment, earning him another blow from Jonathon, this time on the ear. "Didn't you hear me? Get out of here!"

Pablo stumbled backward. "That varmint!" he shouted, pointing at Keela. Turning his eyes to her, he made his own threat: "You're going to get it one of these days, you hear me?"

* * *

The next morning, Pablo did not appear until lunchtime. He avoided Jonathon and stayed quiet most of the day. When the next day passed without incident, Keela decided that it would be safe to let her guard down a bit.

Weeks later, Keela was astonished, not by the continuing calm but by a package that Jonathon made sure to open in front of her. It was the latest paintbrushes, canvases, and paint that he had ordered for her. She had trouble capturing it all in her mind. The horsehair on the brushes was pristine, and the brushes had never been used before. The different thicknesses caught her attention at once. And the pots of oil, each one sealed and brilliant, captivated her.

"Don't worry," said Jonathon. "After your chores are done, you can do all the painting you want."

Keela had trouble grasping the magnitude of the gift. When Jonathon opened it the first time, she was amazed, but when she opened it herself later on, she knew she had many tasks to complete. She set up her easel and mixed the different colors together. It wasn't long before she assembled a canvas, and the drafty room she was in was now her studio. Even the process of inspiration was accelerated because no sooner had she set up her canvas on the wooden frame than a bright red parrot flew past the window.

Keela spent a few seconds looking at the parrot as it flew past. She noted flecks of green dotting its wings. Then, she saw a rainbow parakeet fly past the window, and then an Amazon green. She knew what she was going to paint with her bold new colors.

In the unexpected lulls between tea orders and deliveries and other random chores she got assigned, Keela painted picture after picture of the world around her. In the first ones, she always chose a piece of scenery, like the big villa or the servants' quarters. She only painted the servants' area one time because the other servants were not too happy about it. So, she focused on other things instead.

Once, Keela painted a self-portrait, and she noticed that a parrot appeared in the background. She didn't remember painting it, but then she noticed that every picture she had painted had a colorful parrot in it. After she noticed that, there was more of a purpose to her work and also more of an urgent energy. In every parrot, she noticed a green streak through the wing. With the later parrots, she made sure that the streak was in a braided curlicue instead of a simple arch because it reminded her of the green ribbon, which was all she had of Caitlin. If she could capture that in each picture, she could keep hoping to rescue her daughter someday.

To keep people's spirits up, Keela would take time out from her chores to paint the portraits of different workers. The workers enjoyed the breaks since they had no need to work during that time. It was also a chance for the servants to see themselves the way Keela saw them: as hard-working people who didn't deserve to get treated the way they did. These were people who could still smile despite the scars on their arms and legs, and Keela was able to capture the beauty of each person. A parrot always flew through the trees in the background of each of these paintings. One servant kept trying out different poses until Keela almost went crazy, begging the servant girl to stop moving around so much. But they had a good laugh about it.

Jonathon, with his awareness of Keela's painting talents, continued to resupply her with the tools of her craft because canisters of paint always run dry sooner or later. As each ship came from Europe, bearing more slaves and more goods, he would be down by the dock, collecting the goods and bringing them back to the plantation. Each time he came back, more brilliant hues of reds and greens and yellows would be beckoning from the boxes. Keela took them with gratitude, but it was more than thankfulness. Love grew between Jonathon and Keela as more and more days lingered on without any trouble or drama.

The servants were happy because no new slaves arrived. And Jonathon was happy because the pictures Keela painted were quite stunning for him to witness. The work she did was not without reward, either; she saw her paintings gracing the walls of the villa. And somehow, each servant found a way to make the paintings in Keela's shack peek through the doorways of their own humble shacks.

One day, Keela saw Pablo behind the plantation house, chuckling to himself and bending over something. She crept behind him, making sure to catch him in the act. She didn't expect to see her paintbrushes— the most valuable of the possessions she'd earned. But when she got close enough, she counted every single paintbrush Jonathon had given her. Somehow, Pablo had enough intelligence to know what part of the craft she couldn't do without, and he had broken several of her paintbrushes over his knee, with a twisted smirk crossing his face with every breaking paintbrush.

Keela sank to the grass, dropping to her knees as a weight formed inside her stomach and crushed her to the ground. All those paintbrushes had taken months to arrive from overseas, and Jonathon had bought them with his own money. She knew they were valuable because only one or two paintbrushes arrived with each shipment, and the collection had taken months to accumulate.

Painting had been a passion all Keela's life, and to see the tools of her craft destroyed so callously in front of her broke her inside. Like a musician losing an instrument, the loss of her tools was devastating. It meant the end of good times with the other servants and no more release from her servitude as her craft vanished before her eyes.

Even in her despair, Keela refused to cry, stubbornly breathing until she gained the strength to arise. Later, she told Jonathon about it. Jonathon was quite angry but could do nothing to help except to send for more paintbrushes from Sweden.

Chapter 9

KEELA HAD A DIFFICULT TIME waiting for the new paintbrushes to arrive. While she waited, a new crisis hit the plantation and many others as well. The smallpox epidemic started in the city
of La Isabela, brought there by one unlucky sailor. His captain was too
lazy and too stubborn to enforce a quarantine, and so he left the bowels
of his ship and brought a horrible virus to the island with him. As soon
as the infected sailor started coughing, couriers and porters from across
the island encountered him and began spreading the dreaded illness
before the boils even began to disrupt the skin on their arms.

The men in the fields were contracting smallpox one by one. As the
boils began to break out on their skin, they would cough and moan.
Within a few hours, all the men were laying down in the fields, sick as
dogs. Their handlers led them to their quarters, where they rested, and
no work got done in the fields as the sugarcane ripened.

Everyone knew they had to get healthy before the crops were harvested, but survival was difficult in the brutal heat of the jungle. Although the sick men fought bravely, Keela watched one of the older
slaves draw his last breath as he lay on his cot. His eyes were wide and
staring at the ceiling, his last sight the fragile slats of the roof.

The slave quarters were far away from the plantation house, and the
closer Keela got to the quarters, the smell reminded her of why the
shacks were so far away. The shacks smelled all year round in the
endless heat, and they were hard to keep clean. Keela had avoided
falling ill, making sure to drink lots of the Haitian doctor's remedies,

and she worked hard, scrubbing the floors and changing the linens on the sick men's beds so they would at least have clean ones to sleep on.

The old servant was not the only one they lost. Two of the field workers had become exhausted from their daily labors and succumbed to the vile disease. Although they passed at different times, their powerful frames had both been destroyed in the same way. It sent Keela a potent message that not all of the doctor's patients would survive.

Back in Ireland, Keela had discovered that if she changed the sheets, her Caitlin would recover from colds much faster. She also remembered that citrus would bring a fever down. She began stealing lemons from the plantation house's kitchen and bringing them to the slaves to stop their fevers. The fevered slaves would suck desperately on the fresh lemons, staring at Keela in mute gratitude for her generosity.

Soon, the slaves were beginning to recover and were very grateful to Keela for the help. Within days, they were moving around and even helping her clean up the quarters. But all of that came to a stop when Pablo caught Keela at the slave quarters.

"What are you doing?" Pablo barked. "You can't be out here! I've been looking for you everywhere! I want my tea, and so does Jonathon, and it's been days."

Keela was exhausted from her hard work, and her anger was righteous. "Have you noticed the smallpox that's been going around?"

"That's the slaves that are getting sick," he shot back. "*You're* the personal servant! You've got no excuse to be down here with these sick creatures! You could get ill yourself." Pablo dragged Keela by the arm to the barn by the slave quarters. He grabbed a horsewhip from the wall, spilling oats on the ground in the process. Once he had the whip in his grasp, he marched her up the hill to the villa as he coughed from the dust in the air. "I really need my tea," said Pablo. "I should whip you right now."

As Pablo lifted the whip over his head, Jonathon stepped onto the lawn. The timing was too excellent to be a coincidence. Keela knew he had to have been watching the whole time. "Get away from her, you boar!" Jonathon ordered. "She's just trying to keep the slaves alive! What if she had been taking care of your children? Did you ever think about that?"

Pablo's face sunk in horror, realizing that Jonathon was right. "She should still be punished!" he asserted. "She was shirking her duties! You'd do well to remember that, brother!"

Pablo let go of Keela's wrist, and she massaged her hand until the awful tingling in her fingers stopped. Pablo stormed off into the dark, but she knew that he would be a thorn in her side for quite some time to come. Jonathon, on the other hand, was very kind to Keela, and he even complimented her for her hard work. "Thank you so much for caring for my servants. You brought them through this horrible sickness. Without you, they would have died."

"I just have a lot of knowledge about healing people," Keela said, trying to downplay her actions.

"Unlike my brother, I actually value human life," Jonathon informed her. "One of these days, I might even set you free."

Chapter 10

A FEW DAYS LATER, Keela found herself facing the hatred of Pablo again, but this time, he had a legitimate reason to be upset. She knew full well that the twelfth-century ceramic serving trays in the kitchen held tremendous value to the Spaniards that ruled Haiti. Somehow, one of the valuable serving trays had broken. Keela had been carrying it when it broke, but she had never dropped it; it just broke. So, an escape from punishment was unlikely, and Keela wasn't happy about the situation at all.

Pablo already had a green switch in his hand, and he was impatiently tapping it against his other hand, eager to strike Keela's wrists hard enough to sting for minutes. Keela was embarrassed about dropping the plate of pork, though it wasn't her fault. With Pablo backing her into a corner and preparing to whip her, she found herself running short of patience and quite prepared to fight back. Other servants would have been asking, "Please, Master Pablo, forgive me." But Keela wasted no breath on such platitudes, knowing it was beneath her.

Pablo always got angrier when Keela kept her silence because he knew he could get her in more trouble if she started to talk. He switched her hands five times with all his might, but still, she remained silent. The pain was excruciating, but she worked through it just like the pain from hours of cleaning, with no tears escaping on either occasion. The backs of Keela's wrists began to smear with red blood leaking from her skin, but she refused to even flinch. She took every single stinging lash with silence.

"Aren't you going to say, 'I'm sorry, sir'?" Pablo hissed.

Keela held her tongue, but her cheeks were turning red, and she could feel them burning. She kept staring at him with defiance in her eyes as the switch sliced the back of one of her wrists three more times. She looked at her mangled hand that once painted brilliant pictures and wondered how long it would be until she could hold a paintbrush again. She imagined months, if not longer, and the anger she felt within her went from a roaring inferno to a white-hot explosion. She sneered at Pablo in defiance, and spittle flew from her mouth against her will from the deep gasps of air she was pulling through her clenched teeth. She wanted some way to apologize to Pablo, but she knew she had to keep her silence no matter what he did to her.

"You're still not going to apologize? You'd have to work for years to replace the value of the noble family's tray! *You're* not even worth as much as that tray you broke!" Pablo raised his hand in the air, shaking with gleeful anticipation of the next swing.

Just then, Jonathon, who had been waiting expectantly for another serving of tea, happened to walk in on them. His eyes flared with fury as he saw the two of them, and he thundered across the room, much to Pablo's surprise. Pablo still had his arm raised over his head, but Jonathon ripped the switch out of his hand. Pablo stumbled backward and struggled for composure.

"Enough, brother!" Jonathon thundered. "I told you to stop treating my servants this way! How is she supposed to work with her hands all cut up like that? What were you thinking? Get out of my sight! You make me sick!"

"This isn't over, brother," Pablo whined as he crept away.

Jonathon carried Keela to the servants' quarters, where he lay her down on her bed. The doctor arrived, and soon, he was wiping the blood off her wrists. Without warning, he began pouring strong alcohol on her wrists, cleaning the wounds. The alcohol burned like hot fire on Keela's cuts, and her mind was overwhelmed with different sensations: tingling, burning, and sizzling. Even though her mind was saturated in pain, she stubbornly kept her eyes wide open, gritting her teeth, refusing to let any tears fall.

"You're very strong, young lady, to endure pain like this without crying out," the doctor said. "Who taught you such fortitude? This is not normal. You have to let your grief out sometimes."

Keela looked at the aging doctor with kindness in her eyes. She forced herself to speak with calm, despite the pain she felt. "My mother told me, long ago, that it never hurts half as bad if you just remember that it goes away. Pain always goes away. Hope is what stays forever. That's what she always told me. She was very wise." Keela continued to stare into the distance, refusing to hold eye contact with the doctor any longer. Her thoughts drifted to the green ribbon her mother had given her.

"It's okay; you can let it out. You don't have to be brave. It will make you feel better if you scream."

Keela continued to stop herself from screaming until the alcohol had run its course and the doctor was rinsing her hands with cool water. She embraced the heat that replaced the stinging as the alcohol healed the cuts. "Take a good swig of that rum, miss," the doctor urged. "It will help with the pain when I sew your skin together."

Keela looked at the bottle and took a long swig of the sharp liquor. After catching her breath, she nodded to the doctor, already feeling lightheaded. The doctor smiled back at her, wordless. Then, he began the delicate task of sewing her skin back together. As the needle pushed through her wounded skin and poked through the other side, Keela couldn't even feel it. The liquor wormed through her brain until she couldn't feel pain at all anymore.

When the doctor was done, it was already dark outside. Keela felt comfortable in her bed, except for her hands, which hurt so bad that she couldn't really feel connected to them, even though they were still attached. She lay on the bed without covers, but she didn't want them anyway because her muscles burned with an inner heat. She could feel the heat escaping her skin in waves, like when skin hits the cool water of a deep pool.

Keela was conscious of the anger she felt. She knew the anger was part of her, but the strength of her anger made it a separate power—a distinct entity. The anger had a superior strength and power that she herself did not possess. She wondered if some great Celtic warrior lived through her blood and yearned to fight through her arms. She knew the anger was not her own. It would have already consumed her and left her in ashes if she had taken hold of it. Forcing one deep breath to follow the next, Keela lay in the bed, relaxing like a lioness, waiting for her opportunity to strike.

Chapter 11

THE NEXT MORNING, Jonathon declared that he needed to see how things were going at the other plantation he owned. "It should take about two weeks to finish everything there, and I'll miss you terribly, Miss Ellie," he said as he departed. "Would you keep an eye on Keela for me? Keep her safe."

"I promise, Mr. Omari," Ellie assured him.

Jonathon rode off on his horse, and Keela convinced herself she would be all right. She went back inside to dust. Inside the house, so many things still needed to be dusted, and her tasks were far from complete. She buried herself in her work until lunchtime, when she ate a hearty meal. Then, she got right back to dusting.

While Keela was dusting underneath a table, Pablo snuck up behind her. He tried to pull her dress up her legs while she was kneeling and bent over. "Thought you could avoid me forever, carrot?"

Keela was shocked, not just by his rudeness but also his audacity at trying to take her in front of the other servants. It humiliated her. She struggled to get away from him, but she was pinned between the table and Pablo.

"You think you're too good for me? You think you're better than me? I'm going to put you in your place, carrot!" Pablo continued.

Keela knew she was in a bad position, but she still had some capabilities. She grabbed Pablo's neck with her feet. She was disgusted by his attempts to lick her heels, but she continued to hold him back. "I'd rather die than let you touch me, you little prick!"

Pablo was undeterred by her threats. "Oh, I have worse for you!" With a vicious yank, he finally extricated Keela from under the table and pulled her up beside him. His fingers dug into her wrist, where the cuts from his last attack were still healing.

"What do you mean, worse?" Keela was still indignant, and the pain drove her to hate him even more.

"I'm sending you to work in the fields!"

None of the other servants spoke up in Keela's defense, terrified of reprisal. She was getting ready to fight for her life but was relieved when Miss Ellie walked over and put her hands on Pablo's arm, trying to pull his arm away with both hands. "Mr. Pablo, I don't think that's a good idea."

Pablo smacked Miss Ellie hard on her face, knocking her back against the wall and knocking her own arm back into her face. She stumbled away from the wall while holding her hand against her bleeding nose and staring at Pablo in terror. "Anybody else want some?" Pablo asked, looking around at the silent servants.

All the servants evacuated except for Ellie, who hunched back against the wall. As the servants left, Pablo was distracted, and Keela took the opportunity to push him over. Pablo fell onto the sofa, and while he was trying to get back up, Ellie was able to get above him. "You're under orders to leave her alone, Mr. Pablo. You're going to get far worse from your brother if you don't stop."

Pablo stood up and walked away, and the two women shared a temporary victory.

* * *

The next morning, Keela encountered Pablo again, without Ellie nearby to defend her. Pablo took Keela by the wrist and dragged her to the field. "Start working!" he ordered.

"There's been a misunderstanding," Keela told the slave handlers in the field. "Jonathon said I was supposed to stay in the house."

The slave handlers were not sympathetic. "You heard Pablo. Get to work!" one of them shouted.

Another burly handler joined his cries. "Jonathon's not here now, is he? You can complain to Jonathon when he gets back. Until then, you work!"

Pablo stayed in the field with Keela as she started cutting down the sugarcane. She was able to cut the first sugarcane stalk down after three whacks, but that was two blows too many for Pablo. "You're supposed to have those things down in one swoop!" he scolded her. "Try it again!" Out of nowhere, a green lash swooped across Keela's hand. She was astonished to see Pablo's fist wrapped around the switch. She didn't think he'd go that far again.

"How am I supposed to work when you're hitting me?" Keela asked. She swung the scythe with great strength, but her pained hand made it tougher. The sugarcane remained upright but dented. Another whack to her fingers from Pablo's switch pushed her to swing again, unleashing her anger on the sugarcane. The sugarcane fell to the ground.

"Good enough, carrot. Keep going!"

Keela knew how dangerous it was to talk back, but she needed to make her point. "Keep going? I'm *hurting*!"

"Keep . . . going!" Pablo hit her again, twice. Keela swung the scythe with more anger this time, and the sugarcane fell to the ground in front of her. "Good! I'll teach you what your place is. Don't give up now!"

Stalk after stalk fell before Keela's blade as she struggled across the field and the sun crawled across the sky. The blade's handle became slippery as her hands oozed blood, and the red stains worked their way into the wood grain. As Keela waded through sugarcane, the heat overcame her, and she collapsed to the ground, passing out.

Keela didn't revive until the sting of alcohol on her back made her wake up. She didn't know where she was at first. Then, as she looked around, she realized she was in the doctor's hut, and she heard Miss Ellie's comforting voice coming from above her. "Please roll over," Ellie requested.

Keela rolled over without arguing, and Miss Ellie noticed two infected whip marks. She covered them with gauze at once, and the pain made Keela aware of her injuries. "I shouldn't have abandoned you," Miss Ellie said. "I'm so sorry."

"I understand. It's okay. You have every right to be afraid of that monster. But I'm not going to let him ruin my life," Keela asserted.

When Keela had recovered enough, she went back to the plantation house. Pablo showed up out of nowhere as soon as she got inside. "What's it going to take to break you?" he asked. "You're no good for field work now, so I guess it's back to women's work. Get down and shine my boots."

As Keela bent over and spat on his shoes, shining them, the cuts on her wrists stung, but she endured the pain. She even endured Pablo laughing at her. But she never uttered a word, only silently fuming.

Pablo looked at his boots. "I can see myself in them now. I look pretty good. Good work, carrot." He walked away, leaving Keela to head off to the kitchen. But he turned around just before walking out the door and said, "Oh, carrot, I'm saving the best for last."

After Pablo left, Keela felt safe enough to whisper, "Not if I kill you first." She finished her trip to the kitchen, where she gathered supplies and medicine for her wounds. After escaping back to her quarters, she waited for Jonathon to return, keeping a horsewhip close by her in case Pablo showed up at her door before Jonathon did.

The sun was already down by the time Jonathon got back, and Keela was still in her quarters. Her hands were covered in many small cuts from the switch, the rough handle of the scythe, and the heavy work. She pushed the horsewhip aside, and Jonathon only had to look at her once before his face started turning red. He began to shout. "Look what he did to your hands, Keela! That's why I asked Miss Ellie to look out for you! It's a good thing she told me what was going on. She did fight back, didn't she?"

Keela felt compelled to speak up on behalf of her friend. "She did, Mr. Omari! She used her strength to stand in the way, but he overpowered her, too. Nobody else dared to stand."

"I'm getting you away from Pablo, and I'm getting Ellie away, too," Jonathon decided. "My other plantation, the Santa Maria Ranch, needs more hands anyway."

Chapter 12

THE SANTA MARIA RANCH WAS more beautiful than the one Jonathon had taken Keela to originally. Unlike the first plantation, with its ancestral villas overlooking the fields, this property was almost a vacation lodge. It was grand and imposing but surrounded by pools of water for swimming. Here, she was treated respectfully because no one like Pablo worked there. Here, all the workers found respect, and they were given time to swim in the water. They worked even harder than the workers at the first plantation because the cool water kept them refreshed.

Keela was still a maid, but life was much easier. She felt free to live a normal life. The pools of water and the rushing river helped her escape the heat of the day, and so did her new bedroom. It was not a shack like at the old plantation but an actual room of the villa, with her own private bathing area that she didn't have to share with anyone.

Jonathon purchased paintbrushes for Keela. But when they arrived, she was surprised because he'd kept it a secret. She didn't know about the paint either, until he escorted her to her new studio. A canvas there sat elegant and blank, and Jonathon had expertly hung the canvas on a frame for painting. A newer easel gave Keela much more room to mix pigments.

Keela was astonished that Jonathon had learned how to prepare a canvas. She gasped in shock. His look told her that he knew why she gasped, and he laughed knowingly. "Would you make a portrait of me?" he asked.

"Absolutely!" Keela replied. Although he tried to sit still, Jonathon could not help rearranging his legs. Keela tried to cope with it, but it became impossible to make a rendering of his legs. "You're moving too much," she said.

"My legs are going numb," he countered, laughing.

That got Keela to laugh as well. Jonathon put his legs back in roughly the same position. "Close enough," Keela said.

As Keela kept painting, Jonathon tried not to chuckle, but he failed. After several minutes of painting, he interrupted her again. "Are you done with my legs yet, Keela?" he asked. "I've been sitting still for ten minutes now."

She nodded, chuckling. "It's not the most complicated part of the painting." As she kept working, Jonathon stretched out his legs and relaxed. "Are you sure you want to be smiling? People might not take you seriously."

Jonathon tried to stop smiling, but every time he pulled his lips down, they came back up. "How am I supposed to not smile when I'm looking at you?" he asked. "Even if I look over your shoulder, I can still see your beauty."

Keela blushed. "Just try it for a little while," she said. "Think about something that makes you angry. Think about Pablo." She didn't want Jonathon to get upset, but the thought of his brother did stop him from smiling for several minutes. It was long enough for her to capture the face of her master in a way that would earn other people's respect. "I still have to finish your hair and things," she said. "And the chair, of course."

When Keela was done, Jonathon couldn't believe his eyes. "Wow!" he said. "I can't believe how well you painted me. It's a perfect likeness! I need you to visit me in my quarters tonight. It's the only way I can repay you."

Keela went to Jonathon's bedroom that night without hesitation. He had asked for her presence, after all. "Can I show you how much I appreciate this portrait?" he asked when she got there.

"Yes," Keela answered. Jonathon began to kiss her at once. The kiss was passionate, and by the end of the kiss, she was already working on undoing the buttons of his shirt. He reacted quickly, running his hand down her back, then tracing it up the same skin. The fabric of her shirt brought more sensations sliding up her back and made the experience more intense.

Although they still kissed, Jonathon moved to Keela's back and embraced the scars that still lingered there. She got more excited and started to gasp. Her heart pounded loud in her ears, but she knew it wasn't fear. As he eased her down on her back, she began to grow more excited, and as he touched her skin, she remembered how it felt to be loved.

As Jonathon's hands traced across her thighs, Keela couldn't believe the sensations. He teased her legs to the side, lowered his head, and vision became meaningless as she faded into bliss. Wave after wave of thrills shot through her. She felt strong walls melting around her heart, and she reached out to hug Jonathon in her arms as he drew close.

Lost in this intimacy that she'd been denied for months, Keela felt bliss overwhelm her senses, and she felt elevated to some paradise far above, separated from her pain. During her bliss, not one shiver of pain ran through her body, and she wanted the experience to go on forever. But time ran its inexorable course, and when she had to return to herself, she stretched out on the bed and, surrounded by Jonathon's embrace, rued the pain that she had to feel again. The pain poked through the surging numbness and reminded her of her human condition.

After the great bliss departed, Jonathon slowly traced the lines of Keela's scars. She couldn't tell what he was doing, but without uttering a complaint, she let him touch the scars that John Deas had left behind.

Chapter 13

ELLIE REMAINED AT THE Santa Maria Ranch, helping Jonathon keep the plantation organized. She settled in quickly there, but she was still uneasy about what was going on at the other plantation. By now, Pablo could be making things far worse for the servants. But she also knew that he needed some time to calm down, so she waited several more days before returning to check on the servants.

When Miss Ellie went back to the plantation now ruled by Pablo, she noticed that the pigs had broken loose and destroyed the side of the creek running through the plantation, crushing the fragile, sandy bank with their big hoofs. Although the water was cloudy with mud from the ruined edges, no one had been tasked with its repair until that day. She saw a few slaves walking over with hoes to start repairs, but the water had already washed so much dirt away that a small pond had begun to eddy along the side.

Ellie stepped in with the rest of the group. But even with all five of them working to repair the side of the creek, it was not enough hands. The large pool grew, separated by a natural sand barrier, and the swirling currents dragged the new sand away as they were depositing it. Progress was slow.

When Pablo came over, Ellie stood up and tried to act natural. He headed straight for her in spite of the nonchalance she carried. "Where did that hardheaded Keela take off to?" he asked Miss Ellie.

"I couldn't say, Mr. Pablo."

"No, you just don't *want* to say! Don't worry, I'll find her."

Pablo marched off, never looking back at Miss Ellie. She realized that he hadn't even noticed her absence, so she went back to work as if nothing was wrong. She was about to slip away when something hard hit the back of her neck. When she woke up, she was chained up inside a small shack.

"Can't have you ruining all my fun, can I?" Pablo whispered in Ellie's ear. Then, as she tried to fight against the chains, he walked away and closed the door. After several minutes, no one had come to her rescue despite her screams. She knew that with Jonathon gone and Pablo in charge, no one else on the plantation would come and save her.

Ellie attempted to break the wooden timbers of the shack she was chained to free, but the boards held steady. Nothing she could do would break her out. As the day wore on, the heat became more unbearable. At first, she grew dizzy, and then she started to fall asleep. It was only when the other servants pounded on the iron door that she realized she had passed out.

"Please help!" Ellie called out.

"We're trying, Miss Ellie," was the answer she received from outside the door.

As the men kept pounding, Ellie noticed the top of a metal bar shoved through the edge of the door. Once the bar made its appearance, the banging stopped. Ellie wondered what was going on now that they had partially broken through the door. She waited in the darkness and realized night had begun to fall while she had been asleep.

With a coordinated series of grunts, the slaves worked on prying the door open as a team. With a great screech, the door came loose. Their work was far from done, though, because they still had to break the shackles around Ellie's hands. Without the key, all they could do was heat the iron shackles with a red-hot stake from a fire until the chains melted away from the shackles. The hand clasps remained around Ellie's wrists, but she was free of the shackles.

"Why did you get put in there?" asked one of the slaves. "What did you do?"

"Nothing," Ellie answered. "He just needed to stop me long enough so that he could hurt Keela."

"Well, where is she? I want to help," said one of the servants.

"She's at the Santa Maria," answered Ellie.

Chapter 14

O N THAT SAME DAY, at the Santa Maria Ranch, Keela was
painting outside while Jonathon was away. Pablo approached her
from the river's edge, leaving her blocked in between the river and the
thick trees behind her. She stood up from her canvas and rushed to the
left, hoping to make it to the house. She was good at running, so she
made it to the door before Pablo. The door led to the basement, and
once she was there, she could get the door locked.

Keela raced down the stairs, but Pablo was fast enough to catch up
to her. He grabbed her shoulder hard enough to stop her and slammed
her against the wall at the base of the stairs before she could reach the
sanctuary. Pablo was quick this time. He disrobed so quickly that Keela
didn't know how to react. She only knew the horrible pain of being
entered from behind without any way to stop it or even see her attacker.
As Pablo took her in the worst way, every part of her body began to
heave with revulsion and pain.

After Pablo was done, he pushed Keela out of the way and left her
on the floor of the basement, walking away before she could recover.
Getting off the floor, Keela was horrified to discover blood all over her
legs, but she couldn't find cuts anywhere on her thighs. She realized she
was bleeding from the inside, and that could only mean one thing.

Keela crawled from the basement and told another servant to call
for a doctor. She didn't realize how difficult it was to stand up until she
actually tried. The first time, she fell over. But the second time, the
servant was there at her side, ready to lend her shoulder so Keela could

use her arms to get to her feet. Keela relied on the support to make her way up the staircase and across the lawn.

The doctor, another Haitian, wasted no time in examining Keela and forcing her to drink more sarsaparilla tea, along with dandelion tea and other curatives, to bring her out of shock. "You had a baby inside you, but the poor little thing is no more," said the doctor.

Keela felt numb for a moment, but the grief pushed through the short calm, and she could not stop her tears. She bid the doctor goodbye and spent the rest of the afternoon dazed, resting in her room, unable to get out of bed. When Jonathon returned, she was still in bed, staring up at the ceiling.

"You look like you're on death's door," Jonathon declared.

"It was just an accident," she lied. The lie tickled her throat and made her cough violently.

"What happened? Did my brother do this to you?"

"I fell in the kitchen," Keela lied. The lie clung to her throat and added to the first, almost making her choke. Although Keela knew how to lie to save her own skin without any problem, she hated lying to the man she loved.

Jonathon leaned over, directly in front of Keela's eyes, forcing her to look at him. "You've never had an accident before, but you've never been dishonest with me either. Tell me the truth, woman! Did my brother do this?"

When Jonathon got down to her level and stared right into her eyes, Keela knew she had no choice but to tell him the truth. She nodded. "Yes, Pablo did this to me."

"What else did he do to you? What aren't you telling me?" Jonathon was starting to pace back and forth, and Keela knew that he was starting to feel violent. Any second now, and he might decide to use that violence on her. She knew she had to act fast, and she knew she had to tell him the complete truth.

"While you were gone, the doctor came, and he told me that I lost your baby," Keela informed him. Jonathon pounded his fist on the table, leaning over in agony. "You didn't know I had a baby? Oh no, I . . ."

As Jonathon absorbed the double impact of the news, she could see his anger spike. She realized he had been pushed over the edge. "You were carrying my child? Now you're not? This is what my brother does to me?"

Keela felt terror grasp her in its icy grip as she realized what would happen. "Jonathon! No! Don't do it!" Pain shot through her as she sat up.

"Keela, you have several broken ribs. You can't move until they get set. Stay right there. I'm going to take care of this once and for all!"

Jonathon was on his way to his horse before Keela could call out behind him. She knew he was out of earshot, and she began to rethink her idea of speaking up anyway, remembering what Pablo did to her. Resting her aching, cracked ribs back against the bed, she knew at once that she had to stay in bed until she healed. Although she wanted to witness Pablo's beating, she knew that she had to stay in bed.

While she stayed planted on her back, Keela's hand curled up into a fist, which she relaxed and opened back up before forming another curled fist. In her mind, she imagined the bruises on Pablo's face and the pain he would be suffering. Despite these pleasing thoughts, Keela found herself unable to fall asleep, and instead, she waited for Jonathon to return home.

Chapter 15

JONATHON OMARI POUNDED THE front doors of the villa wide open and stormed into Pablo's room. He dragged Pablo out to the front of the house in his pajamas. Then, Jonathon dragged him to a field where the sugarcane had already been harvested. "You evil bastard! You're not my brother anymore!"

"What?!" cried Pablo. "How dare you!"

"You know what you did, you bastard! She was carrying my baby, and you hurt her so bad that the baby is dead now. You actually managed to kill a baby. I hope that you're proud of yourself. You've always caused problems for me, little brother."

"*You're* the bastard!" yelled Pablo. "You just admitted that you had sex with a servant! What compelled you to do *that*?"

Jonathon hadn't expected that response. It disgusted him that Pablo would stoop so low, but it gave him an excuse to dig even deeper. He remembered the attacks on Opal and realized that Pablo enjoyed taking advantage of women. "You're a coward! You took her against her will, and you can't even own up to what you did."

"Fraternizing with the slaves? I mean, really, Jonathon. What would our father have said?"

"*You're* the evil one, you vicious coward! Our father would beat you black and blue for talking like that. I'm going to knock the evil out of you. Don't you dare back away from this one!"

Pablo laughed out loud, unfazed by the verbal attacks. "How did you get that blood on your hands, Jonathon?"

This last dig was one too many for Jonathon. He knew Pablo was aware of the damage that he'd caused Keela, and that meant that Pablo was specifically trying to hurt him, not Keela. Everything Pablo had been doing was to make Jonathon's life more miserable. This last revelation was too much for Jonathon to take, and it pushed him over the edge. "Because she's bleeding, you evil bastard. And now, I'm going to make *you* bleed!"

Jonathon grabbed Pablo's head with both hands and made sure he had a good grip on his ears before he slammed his knee into Pablo's mouth. He knew he only had one good shot before Pablo could fight back, and he wanted to make it count. Pablo's head hit the dirt right before the rest of his body. Jonathon rolled him over, and Pablo's eyes were open and glinting. Jonathon had failed to knock him out, but he was stunned. He straddled Pablo to pin him down and punched him in the face, one blow after another until Pablo's blood covered Jonathon's knuckles.

"Coward!" Jonathon screamed as he pounded Pablo's head. "Coward!" Each time Pablo's head bounced off the dirt, it brought dust into the air, and Jonathon started to cough. By then, two of Pablo's friends had woken up and were starting to pull at Jonathon's arms, trying to save their friend. "Stay away from me! Go to hell!" he yelled, knocking them back with his large arms. One of the men began to bleed from the nose, and the other man was cradling his jaw. Neither one of them wanted to continue the fight.

Pablo seized the chance to scurry away to safety, rising to his feet and sinking his head like a wounded animal. "Your friends aren't going to be able to save you next time," Jonathon roared after him. The three grown men backing away from him didn't look that dangerous anyway.

"That baby . . ." Jonathon started before another coughing fit stopped him from shouting. He was able to speak again soon enough. "*My* baby. His blood is on Pablo's hands!" Even though the nearby men were grievously injured, Jonathon stepped forward as they retreated. "You remember that, men! You're working for a murderer!"

Pablo shot back one last insult as he retreated. His friends had already vanished from sight, and he was alone. "Keela and Ellie and the rest of them are *slaves*," he wheezed. "Why do you care so much about them? They're scum! They're tools, to be used at our whim and disposed of!"

"You unholy bastard!" Jonathon screamed. "They're still human!" He urged his horse into a dead run toward Pablo, only turning aside at the last moment as Pablo dove out of the way. Then, Jonathon rode back to the Santa Maria Ranch, with blood still dripping from his clenched knuckles.

Chapter 16

WHILE PABLO LAY IN the dirt, he noticed how wet his pants were. He discovered that his hip flask had shattered during the fight, and all his whiskey was gone. Once he was able to get to his feet, he decided to drown his sorrows in tankards of ale. He left the plantation behind and headed down to the local tavern, nine miles away. Every night, the tavern was full of people getting drunk. Unlike at the plantation, alcohol was always in good supply at the tavern.

When Pablo got to the noisy tavern, it was busier than usual, but he had no problem getting someone to serve him a bottle of rum. He noticed blood dripping onto the bar from his nose, and he leaned back to prevent the blood from getting into his rum. He started pouring the liquor into a glass himself. The bartender was too terrified to even get near him. Even when he finally worked up the courage to wipe off the blood drops, he still refused to say a word to Pablo.

All this fear around him made Pablo feel stronger and more confident. He could strike fear into people. He could get his way when he wanted to. He projected his dangerous attitude with a gloomy silence, knowing that no one would have the courage to challenge him.

Pablo was staring at the half-empty glass of rum in front of him when his friends started to show up at the tavern and get drunk too. Although they laughed and joked, Pablo remained gloomy. After a few minutes of laughter, Pablo's friends wanted to know what was going on. "Why are you coming down here with that bad attitude?" Joseph asked him. "Wouldn't you feel better if you were whipping some of those slaves?"

All of Joseph's friends laughed at that one because they all shared Pablo's line of work. They all managed slaves at one plantation or another, and they all had plenty of time to visit the bar and get soused. "The servant girl won't spread her legs anymore?" inquired Samuel. Another gale of chuckles followed, but Pablo stayed quiet, sipping on the rum.

Pablo finished his glass of rum before answering, and he poured a new drink before the bartender even had a chance. "I don't want to talk about it. Just some trouble with the field slaves, that's all." He took a long drink, not caring that he was already beyond tipsy.

"What about your old man? Can't he do anything about it?" Joseph asked.

"What's wrong with your memory, Joseph?" Pablo replied. "My father has been gone for a year now, and you were there at the cemetery, so you should know that! He left almost everything to Jonathon and only a few of the house slaves for me!" He drank some more rum, even though he couldn't feel his cuts anymore.

"Well, you still have power!" Samuel shot back. "Why don't you just sell the bad slaves? Go behind your brother's back. What's he ever done for you anyway? There's a slave boat leaving in the morning, but you have to hurry. Captain McGill can buy your slaves, and then they won't be your problem anymore."

Pablo finished the rum in his second glass. This allowed him to pour a fresh glass for the walk. He jammed the half-empty bottle of rum into his shirt pocket. "Take me to him right away," he said, standing up from the bar.

"Whoa, Pablo, are you sure you can walk?" Samuel asked. "It looks like you angered one of those horses."

"I'm fine," Pablo answered, even though he wasn't.

Samuel shook his head but led Pablo out of the bar. Pablo wasn't about to admit any weakness, but the bruises on his face had resulted in a severe headache, and the rum was only making it worse. Stubborn and furious, he kept taking drink after drink as he ambled along behind Samuel.

The walk through the streets was muddy and dangerous, but Pablo pushed forward, bullied along by the pain in his head. He finished a final glass of rum and threw the glass into the puddle-filled roadway, where it sank into the mud at once. As they continued walking, Pablo started to complain while now drinking directly from the bottle of rum. "How long is this walk going to be? Didn't you have a horse yourself?"

"I did, but short Jimmy had a poker game last night, and now, it's the little man's horse."

"You're kidding, right?" asked Pablo, taking another swig from the bottle. "How did he beat you at poker?"

Samuel used a hip flask, too, and Pablo wanted to take the flask away from him to replace his broken one. He didn't make a move right away, but he knew he would steal it at some point. When they arrived at the inn where Captain McGill was staying, Pablo recognized it as one of the most dismal of establishments, but he didn't really care where he was. As long as the walk through the mud was over, it was an improvement.

Samuel knocked at the front door of the inn but stayed outside in the shadows, out of sight. "I need to talk to the captain," Pablo said to the inn keeper who answered. The man ushered him in.

Captain McGill was a cold-hearted man, but he openly offered Pablo a glass of rum when he entered the room. "I would like to sell some slaves," Pablo announced after he had a hearty drink of the rum.

"Perfect!" said Captain McGill. "I'm in the market for twelve slaves. Well, maybe thirteen if a few of them are skinny enough. I have one cage left, and it would be nice to leave with a full stock."

"What if I told you I know exactly which twelve slaves I want to sell you?"

"That would make it easier. For a sharp man like you, I'd take them for a hundred. No, I'm feeling generous, for . . . a hundred and twenty pounds!"

"That's a very splendid offer. Let's do nine pounds a head, and all thirteen are lightweight. I'll accept that offer." Pablo's head was swimming, and the throbbing in his skull would not abate for anything. But he was so excited about the news that he started to take deeper breaths.

Captain McGill handed him a sheet of paper. "Why don't you help me by writing down the names of the thirteen slaves you want to get rid of the most?"

Pablo wasted no time in writing "Keela" at the top of the list, followed by other servants that had been giving him trouble over the previous few weeks. Pablo completed the list very quickly, and he proudly handed it back to Captain McGill.

Captain McGill signed the paperwork. Then, he took out a large pile of one-pound coins, counted out Pablo's payment, and closed the coin purse tightly. He then rolled up the agreement, poured hot wax from a sealer down against the paper, and pounded his very own special seal against the wax. The imprint of the whale shone on the seal. "There! Now it's official!" he announced.

Once Pablo shook hands with the captain, he knew the deal was done. He wanted to celebrate the moment, but something inside him left his stomach irritated and his throat burning. He wanted to enjoy the moment, but some deep guilt nagged at him. Taking another long drink of the rum, he felt steadier, and even though he needed the arm of the chair to help him rise to his feet, he insisted on walking out the door unaided.

Samuel returned to Pablo's side once he was back in the mud. "So, how did that go?" he asked.

"He's actually a pretty great guy," said Pablo.

"Are you kidding me?" asked Samuel. "One time, he dropped a whole chain load of slaves over the edge of his ship, just because one of them started a fight."

Pablo took a moment to savor the image in his mind. "That doesn't bother me," he answered. "I'd drop those nasty slaves into the ocean myself if I had half a chance. But now, they're sold. And tomorrow, they're on their way to Amsterdam."

The hip flask clinked against the rum bottle as Pablo and Samuel toasted each other. Somewhere along the long walk back to the tavern, Pablo removed the hip flask from Samuel without his friend even noticing.

Chapter 17

THE NEXT MORNING, A loud knock woke Jonathon. As he opened his front door, he saw Captain McGill standing at attention. "I want your slaves," McGill said. "I've got order papers for them right here!" Pablo stood next to him, grinning at his brother as he held up the form.

"What's going on here, Pablo? Explain yourself!" Jonathon demanded.

"Read it and weep, dear brother! Twelve . . . no, thirteen slaves are on their way to Holland. We need to get them to Holland as soon as possible. Don't slow us down. This man is very impatient."

"But you're taking all my slaves!" shouted Jonathon. He got up close to his brother, about to strike him.

"I'm sure you can buy some new ones, brother. Here, ten pounds should help." Pablo pushed the heavy coins into Jonathon's hand, closing his fingers around the hand so Jonathon couldn't refuse the gift.

As another servant was being dragged away, Jonathon told her, "Don't worry, I'll find a way to bring you back."

"Good luck with that," said Pablo as he walked away to a carriage. "I've got to get these slaves to the harbor as fast as possible. I don't have time to talk to you now."

Jonathon held his hand up. "You're not going anywhere. Captain McGill, how much do you want for the slaves?"

"Not a half a penny less than three hundred," answered the captain squarely.

"That's a fortune! That's more than I have. Isn't one hundred and fifty pounds fair enough? I want my servants back!"

Pablo turned around and laughed at that comment. "What are you buying for those servants, brother? Fancy clothes or something?"

Jonathon glowered at his brother, but he couldn't have a good response because the captain standing before him was an obstacle. "Three hundred, or they're legally mine," Captain McGill insisted. "Do I have to escort you out of here, or are you going to get out of my face on your own?"

Jonathon knew he was stronger than the captain, but the captain was being assisted by several slave traders, and most of Jonathon's servants were already on their way to the ships. As Keela was being dragged downstairs, Jonathon saw what was going on and started to lose his temper. "What are you doing?!" he shouted at the slave traders. "That one's not even for sale!"

"Don't let them take me, Jonathon!" Keela cried. "I can't be on that slave ship again!"

"I'll come and find you!" Jonathon cried. "I won't stop until I get you back!" Jonathon was getting angrier by the moment, but Captain McGill had already departed down the road for the harbor, leaving Jonathon alone with Pablo and two of the slave traders. "What have you done, Pablo?"

"What I had to do, brother. That whore was no good for you."

Jonathon punched his brother in the face. "That's it! You're going down!" He readied himself for another punch, but Pablo was quicker, drawing a musket from his pocket, aiming it straight and Jonathon's head, and taking a pot shot at him. The small musket misfired, pushing the short barrel to the side, and the ball missed Jonathon by feet.

Once his brother had fired the weapon, Jonathon couldn't take any more. He didn't mind the broad shot, but he minded that his brother could be callous enough to even try and shoot him. He changed his tactics and kicked Pablo's skinny leg as hard as he could. He heard a sharp cracking as Pablo's kneecap shattered, and Pablo fell to the ground, crying.

Pablo didn't have time to get off the dirt before Jonathon came over to him. He got his leg on top of Pablo's back so he couldn't move, and he quickly undid Pablo's belt and yanked it from his pants. He tore Pablo's shirt off his back, and he reveled at the high screech as the fine silk clothing ripped. He took the belt in his hands and whacked Pablo as hard as he could. "That's how it feels when you do it to the slaves!" Blood sprayed from Pablo's back as the buckle of the belt hit his skin. Jonathon noticed a horsewhip within arm's reach and grabbed it without taking the pressure off Pablo's hips. "You want some more?"

"Stop! Stop!" Pablo begged. But the whip cracked down on his back, lacing it with hot red lines. As Jonathon struck Pablo's back again and again, the blood began to spray off the tentacles of the whip.

The two slave traders with Pablo pulled Jonathon away. "Stop, Mr. Omari! You don't know what you're doing!" one of them shouted. "It's a legal contract! They'd throw you into the dungeons for trying to stop it!"

Jonathon stopped trying to fight back against the slavers, choosing instead to glare at Captain McGill's carriage as McGill completed the process of claiming his new possessions, including Keela. When the slave traders had all gone, Jonathon had no more slaves on the Santa Maria plantation.

Chapter 18

AS JONATHON'S SERVANTS WERE being taken, they were pushed and shoved and even punched for trying to protest. The women were moaning as they were loaded into the back of horse-drawn wagons. Keela clicked her tongue at them in a scolding manner, and the other women turned their heads toward her and changed their moans to whimpers. They looked at her with just as much fear as they stared at their masters with. Keela knew how terrified they were, and she knew they would give up if she didn't encourage them.

"No more of this out of you," Keela insisted. "They treat us like animals, but we don't have to act like mindless cattle. Be strong, be smart, and we'll get through this. Hold your heads up high. Don't let them win." The weeping stopped, and the wagons rolled to a stop.

The women and Keela were herded onto the slave ship that would take them to Holland. It was a three-mast man-of-war that would have been glorious if it wasn't a slave ship. The women moved forward as commanded, but Keela was proud to notice that many of them kept their heads high, silent, and proud, even as they were being pushed down into the belly of the ship.

Keela wondered what it would feel like to sail a ship of her own again, and the dawn of a plan began to hatch in her mind. She was still a slave, but that didn't mean they could take her mind away. If she could just get out of her cage, she could take over the entire ship with the skills she'd learned. So many men had tortured her that, by now, it seemed commonsense to rip throats open and leave legs sliced and quickly bleeding out. *It would be so easy to take over this vessel*, Keela thought.

Keela paid close attention to the details of the ship as she was being hauled aboard. She counted two layers of fifteen portholes each above the water. As the other slaves continued to walk slowly, she had plenty of time to study the ship and count the number of slave traders as they came in and out of the hold. She counted seventeen slave traders on board the ship and three more on shore, plus Captain McGill. She noticed that the slaves easily outnumbered them.

It was obvious to Keela that there were not enough slave traders to handle the slaves if there was an escape. As she walked across the deck, she carefully noted the locations of tools tucked into the ropes running along the sides of the ship. Most of the tools were sharp picks and spears. And even though the spears were meant to be used to wedge the wheels when the sailors turned them, they could also be used as dangerous weapons.

The slaves were shoved into cages with nothing but raw hay on the floor. It made Keela feel like an animal. Once they were packed into the large steel cages, there was no room at all to move around, but at least they were free of their chains.

Keela spied a slaver drop one of his many keys as the man was struggling to get her into the cage. She prayed that he would not notice his mistake as she feigned pain in her leg to try to distract him. He shook his head at her apparent distress as he began to shove other women into the cage after her. He was too busy laughing at her limping to notice that the key was missing. The slaver moved on to the next cage, beginning to fill it up. Once all the cages were full, the slave handler returned to the deck, leaving all the slaves with no guard at all.

Every ten minutes or so, a guard would come downstairs to check on the servants. But there was plenty of time between visits for them to do whatever they chose with their time. Keela's slender wrist snaked through the bars of the cage just in time to whisk the key away before the guard returned. By the time his head turned toward her, she was hidden inside the huddled mass of bodies.

The next time the guard finished his rounds, Keela started to talk to the other slaves. "I have a plan," she whispered. "We have to wait until we're out at sea, but I have a plan, and I have a key to open our cages."

As the darkness closed in on them, Keela looked around as best she could. The remaining daylight leaked through the small portholes, but it was still dark inside the hold of the ship. She waited until they were on the ocean and the sun went completely down so they could use the darkness to their advantage. She kept waiting until she knew the slave traders were getting exhausted. The regular footsteps on the deck had begun to dwindle to once every few minutes. The guards were starting to get slack as they got sleepy. She continued to wait.

It was midnight, with no light at all except for faint beams of moonlight poking through the small portholes. No more footsteps echoed on deck. The men were either asleep or too drunk to walk around. Slowly, Keela slipped the key through the bars and toward the latch. She had a few seconds as she quietly nudged the key into the latch. She struggled to sink the key into the lock, and her hand began to ache from the strain. Still, she kept trying until finally, the key slipped inside. Her hand screamed with pain at the torturous angle, but she knew it was her life if she didn't break free.

The huge padlock slipped free and fell to the boards with a clang, and Keela quietly escaped her cage. Her eyes hunted through the darkness, trying to find a tool to free the prisoners in another cage. The rest of the people from her cage began to hunt around in the gloom as well.

As Keela hunted around in the darkness, she came across a sharp file. She triumphantly picked it up and tiptoed back to the cages. "I'm getting you out of here," she whispered to the cage's occupants. "Be quiet."

"What? There's nowhere to go?" one of the occupants said.

"Yes, there is! We're smarter than they give us credit for. I can steer a ship this size. I've been on sailing boats my whole life. This is not a problem."

"What about the other women?"

"You men are stronger. You'll come with me first. One of you can stay back to file the other padlock and free the remaining women." Keela kept rubbing the file against the bar of the padlock. The file shirred back and forth in the darkness. She could not keep track of the time, but the guard did not return while she worked. Once the top of a bar was loosed, she moved to the bottom of the bar, hurrying until the bar was fully separated. Two cages full of people were now emptied out.

"You're all warriors now," Keela told the freed men. "It's time to go kill the slave traders, and the captain, too. But leave the sailors alive for now. Get any weapons you can find down here, but there are lots of picks and spears along the side of the ship as well. Be quiet when you approach the slavers, and make sure to get them into the water. That should take the fight out of them pretty fast."

Keela found a chisel and gripped it in her hand. Then, forty-five former slaves crouched and tiptoed through the darkness, led by Keela. They all moved toward the solitary guard by the hatch. Everybody tried to stay as silent as possible, but the soft footsteps were audible in the quiet hold, and Keela was convinced that they would be found out. When she got closer to the guard, she could smell the rum from dozens of feet away and realized they could have made much better time. He was too drunk to hear them.

When Keela got close enough to the guard, she didn't want to waste any time. Raising her arm above her head, she drove the chisel into his neck with crushing speed. The massive pain and rage boiling inside her flooded out like a huge wave, and she used every ounce of that energy to drive the chisel through his neck to the other side. The rusty chisel severed his spine and left him gurgling on his own blood as he slowly choked to death on his own fluids.

The dying guard was unable to move a muscle below his neck. He was only able to move his eyes back and forth as he gurgled away. Keela left his body where it lay. There was no need to send him over the edge of the ship.

Keela felt liberated and powerful, and as her power returned to her, she realized that vengeance was a sweet and beautiful thing. She knew right then that she would taste vengeance until John Deas was lowered into the cold hard earth. She celebrated her new freedom by yanking the chisel out of the dead guard's neck and relishing the small thump his body made in the silent hold.

The other slaves swarmed around Keela, and they all went silently onto the ship's deck. Shadows in the night, the silent warriors took out every slave trader with whatever knives or weapons they found. Captain McGill was on the poop deck, manning the wheel, and was too busy surveying the ocean to notice the two large men approaching him. When he finally noticed them, he drew his sword. But he failed to see a third slave who came up from behind him and ran a knife against the captain's neck. "Make one move, and you're dead," whispered the slave.

Captain McGill dropped his sword and raised his hands in the air. "What do you think you're doing?" he sneered. "You'll never be able to control a ship this big!"

Keela's pale, sweating skin reflected moonlight that also danced on the wet deck as she walked up the stairs. The captain stared at her like she was a ghost, with utter terror in his eyes. "Don't worry, Captain. I know how to handle this ship," she said. "We don't need you anymore."

The slave that had Captain McGill by the throat spoke up. "Keela, can we just cut his throat like the rest of them?"

"No, that's too good for the captain," she answered. "Throw him overboard. I'm sure the sharks won't mind rotten food!"

As four strong men hauled Captain McGill from the deck, he began to scream. "No! No! No! No, no, no, no, no, no!" Captain McGill sailed over the side of the ship and dove into the cold black water below, vanishing without a trace.

Rather than watch the ocean, Keela immediately turned back to the slaves. "Listen to me! If you all follow me, I will avenge every single one of you. I won't rest until I've avenged every one of the injustices."

The freed slaves roared in unison. Only then did Keela turn around to the ocean, curious about the captain's fate. In the dark water, she could see his head bobbing up and down and his eyes blinking. Underneath the moonlight, his bald head shone like a beacon until the sharks arrived. When Keela saw him disappear beneath the water and the blood shimmer on the surface of the waves, she knew the sharks had taken him.

Chapter 19

"**N**OW, YOU ARE ALL PIRATES," Keela told the freed men and women aboard her new ship. She was getting used to her new role leading others, and she had no problem with it. Anything was worth the prize of getting her daughter back. A great cheer rose up. "We need to find more fighters, and we need to focus on freeing more slaves to accomplish that."

Keela didn't expect any answers right away, but soon, a voice arose from the crowd. "I know where they are kept," came a voice from the deck as Captain McGill was being digested in the waters below them.

"Come forward," Keela directed. A large man stepped forward. His muscles bulged from his arms, and Keela wondered how he ever got captured. "What is your name?" she asked the man.

"Akua," he answered. He looked sincere enough, though Keela still found it hard to trust anyone.

"Have you seen anything that will help us?" Keela asked.

"There are many islands where they keep the slaves between boat rides. It prevents them from starving to death, but it's not much better than a hold. I was held on one of the islands for a while, then taken to a different one. And there was one that reeked of death and despair more than all the slave pens I've been through." Akua fell silent, too troubled by the memories to relive them.

"Name the worst island," Keela said. "Go on."

"Aruba." The name made him shiver, and some of the other slaves flinched as well.

"A terrible name for a terrible place. How many slaves?" Keela asked.

"Hundreds," answered Akua. "No, thousands."

Keela's eyes opened wide. "With those kinds of numbers, we'd be an army! This is a wonderful opportunity! How many handlers did you see?"

"No more than twenty. They are on a small island in the ocean, so they could never escape on their own. There is no need for lots of guards when there's nowhere to go." Akua looked around the deck and found thirty faces staring back at him with fists clenched. "We would have them outnumbered with ease."

"Do they have any weapons?"

"No, there's no need for weapons there. No one dares to rise against them. They just use horsewhips when they want to torture the slaves or keep them in line. It's easier to grab than a sword or a bow." Akua twisted his neck as he tried to rid himself of the bad memories.

"I'm all too familiar with horsewhips," Keela responded. "That makes me want to go there even more."

"We need more than moonlight before I can show you the way," said Akua.

"We should get some sleep, then," Keela suggested. "I'm sure you could all use some rest."

After another cheer, the pirates found their new sleeping quarters. No one rested near the cages.

* * *

Early the next morning, the pirates assembled on deck as the sun rose above the endless water. There was no need for Keela to call for an assembly because she could see that all the pirates were committed to her cause.

After Keela obtained blank papers from the captain's quarters at the stern, Akua drew her a map as best he could. He drew out many small details, including a path between three islands that would lead them to their destination without getting lost. Keela had learned navigation from

Joseph, and looking at the map, she figured they were only a couple hundred miles out from Aruba.

Keela addressed the crowd of pirates, stepping away from the map and perching on the railing that separated her from the main deck. "Here's the plan, everyone! Some of you are white, and some of you are dark. Those with whiter skin, like the slave merchants, will carry weapons and dress like slave merchants. The rest of you will pretend you're still slaves being brought there to be traded. That's when we'll take them out—when we're on the inside and can do the most damage. Who can look like a captain?"

A man named Daniel spoke up. "I can dress like the captain."

Keela looked him up and down carefully. "You're about Captain McGill's size. You'll do quite nicely." Daniel smiled, happy to be of help. "Didn't I see you back at the Santa Maria?" Keela asked him.

"Yes, but I kept stealing the sugarcane, and Pablo got tired of it and put me on this boat." Daniel looked embarrassed, but he got a few whoops and cheers from the other freed people on deck who had also been sold by Pablo.

"Yes, it would work well with you as captain," Keela confirmed. "I'll just pretend to be one of the sailors. I'll go find some clothes, and then we'll be on our way."

Keela returned to the captain's quarters and searched for something they could wear as disguises. She found two leather straps in a trunk and strapped her chisel around her leg, under her dress. She grabbed more straps for the others and stowed a large knife underneath a leather strap on her other leg.

Going through another trunk, Keela found women's clothing. She found some red dresses with strong lines that she studied in the mirror as she wore the outfits. And she found some wonderful hats that made her look like a sailor. She wondered which woman Captain McGill had been stowing these clothes for, but she quickly turned her head to other thoughts, reminding herself that the entire crew was sinking in the water behind them, and these clothes were now spoils of war.

The most magnificent of the dresses Keela found did not fit her well. It was made for a taller woman. Keela had to cut the bottom away, and it worked well enough. She found a pair of long boots, and she quickly put them on as well, knowing it would make her look more intimidating.

Then, Keela found some functional pants in another truck, and she quickly realized that opponents could ensnare her if she wore a dress. She cut far more cloth off the dress, leaving an attractive red bodice, and then she added the trousers to her attire. She also discovered a small jacket at the bottom of the trunk, and she wrapped it around her to fight off the cold salt spray from the ocean. Then, finding a thick shirt, she chose to wear it within the jacket. The shirt had several dozen strips of thin metal inside, which she figured would help shield her from sword blows without alerting the enemy to their presence.

Finally, Keela found a large red bandana and used it to tie up her beautiful red hair so that no one could grab it in their hands. Then, she went out on deck. "Daniel, it's your turn. You get to look like a captain now." Daniel went into the captain's quarters. When he reemerged all dressed up, Keela laughed. "You actually look like a captain."

"Well, I feel like one, too," said Daniel. "Doesn't every ship deserve to have a captain?"

"Yes," Keela answered. "We'd look pretty strange sailing around out here without one. Everyone had better start getting used to their new roles," she said. "We'll reach the first island by tomorrow, and I want you all to be ready. We need to look as much like sailors as we can to get by these people. They're going to have ships in the water, sailing past us to make sure everything's okay."

Keela looked through the captain's quarters a third time and discovered the shipping manifests. She looked in horror as page after page of names turned in front of her. Every page had hundreds of names, and at the top was the location where each group was sold. The records also mentioned the number of slaves who died on each voyage. The pages referred to the dead slaves as "losses of merchandise."

Keela discovered her friends' names on the list going to Aruba. Her best friend, Millie O'Reilly, and Joseph's friend Thomas from down the road were both taken to Aruba as well, and they were then sold forward. As she continued looking at the names, Keela discovered another list that gave her more information. She read that Pablo sold all the slaves for only a hundred and twenty pounds, not the three hundred Captain McGill had been loudly demanding at the Santa Maria. She pounded on the table.

"Jonathon could have bought us back! Pablo didn't even try to let him!" She pounded her fist on the table again, snatched up the Aruba manifests, and then left the captain's quarters with her eyes dark with vengeance. She knew that the papers from Aruba would be an excellent way to fool the guards there.

Back on deck, Keela addressed the crew again. "Does anyone besides me know how to steer a ship?" No one spoke up. "Well, I'll be at the helm, and I'll teach you how to man the sails. It won't take long for you to learn. Any of you that know how to cook, start raiding the mess hall and the kitchen. I'm starving."

About an hour later, the women cooking the food came out of the mess hall and announced that it was time to eat. Not a single soul was left on the deck. As they all crowded into the mess hall, they tried to cheer and celebrate while eating and drinking at the same time. It was a joyous, raucous celebration that all of them were involved in, and Keela relished the celebrations. As everybody began to relax, she felt a warm glow in her chest and realized that this new life she had made for herself was going to be fine indeed.

Chapter 20

THE NEXT MORNING, Keela stared up at the admiral's Dutch pennant and realized that someone should head up the mainmast and remove the pennant from it. "You ladies know how to sew a table-cloth, right? Well, lowering a sail should be easy, and getting up there to remove that flag should be even easier. This is your moment, people! Get up there and take down that awful Dutch flag! This is *your* ship now!"

As the women and men ran up the rigging, taking over the jobs the sailors had done, Keela pulled a large green ribbon out of her pocket. She stared at Caitlin's ribbon as the women who had removed the blue Dutch flag came back down. Keela put the ribbon in a sailor's hands. There was no mistaking its purpose.

The women scurried back up the mast and hoisted the new, green flag high above the sail. Then, the rest of the women dropped the mainsails. Four of the men got to work attaching the mainsail to the boom. Once everything was in place, the wind caught the huge sail and sent the ship moving forward.

Keela headed to find the ship's aging doctor, whom they had spared, and demanded that he go to the mess hall where the other women were resting to take care of their injuries. "Why should I take care of your servants?" he responded. "You mutinied and took over the ship! Why should I listen to you?"

Keela thought that tying the doctor up below deck in a cage would have changed his attitude, but she could see she was wrong. "I can see that I haven't punished you enough yet." She pointed her sword right at his face, between his eyes. He stared cross-eyed down the sharp blade and gulped mightily. With his hands tied behind his back, Keela knew he was defenseless, so she was free to speak her mind.

"*You?* I don't care at all about *you*, doctor! I don't care if you live or if you die! The only people I care about are these servants, and they are my closest friends. They are suffering and poorly fed, and you are going in there to take care of them, do you hear me?"

The doctor had stopped panting and glaring, and his eyes were now sullen and downcast. "Yes, I hear you."

"Good, because if you don't start taking care of these women, you will be eaten by sharks, and I will personally make sure that you're wide awake as it happens." She unlocked the cage and set the doctor free to help the injured servants. She had only spared his life because he was a doctor. Everyone else had forfeited their lives the moment they took her prisoner, but she knew better than to leave her ship without a physician. The doctor went to the galley while Keela returned to the deck.

* * *

By the next sunrise, most of the women and men had recovered. Keela watched as the first island came into view. It was magnificent, with palm trees that grew higher than anything she'd ever seen in Haiti. She steered clear of it, and none of the ships near the island took any interest in her or even diverted their courses as she sailed past untroubled. She knew that in sailor's code, a green flag meant neutrality. The ribbon was not a flag, but it was close enough to convince people that she meant no harm.

Keela reflected on this neutral position as she sailed past ship after ship, all bearing slave traders and captured slaves. They were on their way to Aruba, and she wondered what they would think if they knew what her army of soldiers was capable of. She also wondered if they might encounter these same slavers once she got to Aruba. By then, she could see a tavern on the shore of the island, and the noise coming from that location was sufficient to carry all the way out to sea. It was still midmorning, and she knew from what she was hearing that the captains would be too drunk to pilot their own legs for the next few days. She sailed past the island.

The next day, Keela saw another island come and go, with another place serving liquor and creating a scene on the beach. This time, hearing the raucous celebrations made Keela angry. Then, when a third island came into view the day after that, she knew they were getting close to Aruba.

Aruba was a beautiful desert island. But the slave-trading fortress looming several miles from the shore was an eyesore and an abomination to Keela. It infuriated her that a horrible slave-trading operation would be done here, in such a breathtaking place.

Another ship was already sitting at anchor in the harbor, so Keela did likewise with her ship, drawing anchor a few leagues away. As her crew walked through the desert, she began to dislike the desert environment that had seemed so welcoming from the boat. She found it too dry and dusty—far different from the oasis promised by the green aloe bushes. The green cacti also stood proud above the desert scrub grass. The cacti were prickly but provided water if cut open. The crew paused in the hot sun and drank the cactus water before moving on.

The slave-traders' dungeon was surrounded by tall stone barricades arranged in a perfect and intimidating square that was four stories tall. Keela could sense the evil emanating from the building, and even though her crew waited a mile away, the stench of death—unique and disturbing—wafted through the air from the fortress. The smell made Keela feel sick.

"Why does the smell travel so far?" Keela raised her bandana over her nose as she asked Akua.

Akua already had a bandana over his face. He lowered it carefully and spoke in one breath. "Before they throw the bodies out to sea, they let the corpses rot inside the pens so the others can see what death does to them." Then, he pulled his bandana back into position.

As the crew drew closer to the evil dungeon, Keela noticed a young girl by the side of the road. She was a simple native girl of Aruba, traveling to her desert village. Not too long afterward, two native people carrying a load of hay between them emerged from the mirages that swirled across the landscape. Suddenly, Keela realized that people could see them walking through the desert and pointed that fact out to Daniel.

Daniel stared across the landscape with an eyeglass that he'd taken from the ship. It made him look even more like a captain. Then, he put the eyeglass down and immediately assumed his role, shouting loud enough that any nearby travelers could hear him. "Hey! Kenneth! Make those slaves stay in line!"

Keela turned to her "slaves" and started saying things that were distasteful to her. The comments preserved the image of them leading a group of slaves to their obvious destination, which was growing ever closer. She used a deep voice to sound more masculine. "Keep moving, slaves!"

Keela—or Kenneth—reminded herself to use the horsewhip. She snapped it in the air but made sure to stay well away from any human targets. The whip was convincing as it snapped wickedly in the air, but she made sure it stayed feet away from her pirates. She didn't want any of them getting injured before the upcoming battle.

The "slaves" hunched and flinched quite convincingly. Keela and Daniel made a convincing team. As more villagers passed them, they paid no mind to the group of slaves, as it was an everyday occurrence in Aruba. Keela was horrified that slavery could become so commonplace.

The closer they got to the complex, the more nervous Keela felt. The two guards in front of the complex looked surprised at the convoy, though it was something they saw every day. They began to question Daniel and Keela. "What? What are these, *slaves*? We didn't have any slave transfers scheduled for today!"

Daniel spoke up first, acting every inch a captain. "These slaves are coming here, and if you don't like it, you can take it up with John Deas when he comes here next month. Kenneth has his order for the slaves to be brought here."

Keela held up the transfer orders. The guard squinted at the paperwork for a moment, then nodded and waved his hand once he saw the notice. The other guard withdrew and slowly opened the gate. The first guard growled at Daniel, "I don't like John Deas any more than you do, but I'm not going to be the one to make him lose his temper. Head in there before the merchandise gets too hot."

Keela felt no need to back away from her role as she started yelling at the people in chains, making sure to keep her voice deep. The hot desert air had left her thoroughly parched, helping to make her voice rough and dark and quite convincing. She really sounded like Kenneth, not an Irish lass who had been a slave the previous year instead of a pirate. She was now a man of the sea, complete with a thick Spanish accent she had deciphered with the help of her captors. She was grateful to them for that one gift—an accent that wouldn't draw attention. For everything else they did to her, she reserved her mercy. Until the time was right, she would keep acting the part, even though the slavers made her sick.

"You heard the man. Move it, worms! All of you are worms! Get in there now!" Keela had trouble faking the intentions, but she had no problem faking the low-toned, dominant voices the slave traders used.

Keela and Daniel started leading their "slaves" into the dungeon, with the guards close behind. The slaves were about to enter the cages when Keela screamed, "Now!"

The jailors had no time to react. They were instantly surrounded because they had never expected the slaves to be carrying weapons. Their surrender was immediate. "You'll never kill all of us!" shouted the slave traders' leader.

"We don't have to," answered Keela.

"What are you going to do, then? Didn't you think this through?"

Keela already knew what she was going to say. "Open those cages and let the slaves out."

"What? Why would we do that?" The trader's panic was palpable.

"So that we have somewhere to put you idiots! Start opening those cages! Now!" Keela's voice was so dark and intimidating that the men had no choice but to comply.

As a guard started unlocking the cages one by one, the lead slave trader continued to protest. "This is ridiculous! You're interfering with our trade!"

Keela looked at the trader with disdain. "Your trade is unholy! Your trade is inhumane! It doesn't even deserve to be called a trade! I want you to capture these monsters, not kill them," she directed her crew. "They're coming with us. You hear me?" Then, turning back to the slave traders, she said, "Every single one of you is going to be sold, just the way you sold us. It's time that you learn your lessons."

The traders tried the whips on the slaves in a last-ditch effort to keep them inside the open cages, but there were too many of them, and they were all well-steeped in rage from weeks and months and years of bondage. As the cells emptied of slaves, they began to grab the slavers, overwhelming the slavers and wrapping their arms in ropes. The entire thing was over in seconds.

As the slave traders fell to the ground, they cried and whimpered in fear, reduced from their high posts as slavers to sniveling mongrels on the ground before Keela's feet. As their fortunes changed, Keela felt herself rising taller and taller inside her armor. She looked down at the captured slave handlers and noticed how fast they had absorbed their new positions. The cowering looks and shaking bodies only made Keela happier because she had stripped away their power and they were suffering more than she had. She didn't feel one bit of remorse, only satisfaction at the power shift.

Before long, hundreds of former slaves were roaming freely around the dungeons. Keela continued to walk through the mass of free people, searching for her Irish neighbors that she knew were on the island. She also hoped to see her daughter. As she searched, she saw the occasional handler dragged away in chains.

"These people told us what to do," one of the slaves said to Keela. "Now, we need *you* to tell us what to do."

"Take whatever you can salvage," she responded. "Their food, their wine, their clothing; everything they said you could never have, it's all yours. You've earned your freedom. Fight with me, and we'll stop the slave trade forever!"

The reaction was more than Keela could have hoped for. The freed people roared in unison, and their hands went up in the air in throngs of celebration and support. "Whatever you feel like eating," she continued, "go ahead. But there will be lots of food left over. When you're full, start carrying the supplies out to the ship. We're not going to go hungry on this journey."

With little effort, Keela got used to the idea that she was commanding a legion of warriors. But she knew that any army needs food to survive. She relaxed and refused to rush anyone as they tore into the sweetmeats and cured salami, which were delicacies after weeks of biscuits and near starvation.

As Keela continued to search, she recognized Mr. and Mrs. O'Reilly in one of the cells that had just been opened. She was full of joy at seeing her long-lost friends but horrified at their skeletal condition. Their appearance left her shocked for a moment, but she shook it off and moved toward them after confirming they were still alive. Their torture had clearly been worse than others' because the meat on their bones was almost gone.

Keela sat down in front of her friends and presented them with a rolled ham. The meat was wrapped inside a white linen cloth that they could not unwrap fast enough. As the O'Reillys began to devour the succulent meat, Keela motioned to some other women, keeping her voice dark. "Take care of these two. They're very important to me." Then, she turned back to her friends and asked them, "Do you know where they took my daughter?"

Millie O'Reilly stared at her with sadness. "We saw the big man that runs everything leaving with her, but he was on another ship. We don't know where they went."

"I'm sure I'll learn everything I need to know. Are you all right?"

Millie kept eating, and her husband swallowed three times before saying, "I'm still quite hungry."

"Come to the ship with the other people who are free now," Keela said. "I trust you more than anyone alive, and I can't lose you again. You can have all the food you want on board the ship."

Akua brought two men over to the cage that Keela and the O'Reillys were in. She expected Akua to bring people over, but she didn't want to be sitting by her friends when it happened. So, she went outside the cage and met them there. "What's going on?" she asked. "Who are these men?"

"These men know where John Deas is hiding."

Keela's back straightened at once. "*Where?*"

"He was here two weeks ago," one of the men Akua had brought over informed her. "He said he was going to the Canary Islands."

Keela turned to her friend for confirmation. "Akua? The Canary Islands. Do you know them?"

The big man nodded. "Our informant says that's John Deas's home base."

Keela paused to take it all in. After seven years, she finally knew where her daughter was. A plan started to form in her mind, but she didn't reveal it right away. Once she had taken a moment to recover from her shock, she answered. "We need many more forces before we take him out," she explained. "I think it's time we sent a message to the Dutch government. I want good money for our new prisoners. We'll ransom them and use the money to build an army. Put those two slavers in a cage and follow me."

Keela went outside to where the free people were gathering and celebrating. Her presence grabbed their attention at once, and they gathered around her, with their faces raw with emotions. She stood before them and spoke. "The slave traders came out of the blue!" she started. And with each subsequent point she made, a rush of sound came from the crowd, making her feel more powerful and influential. "Burned our houses!"

Louder shouts this time.

"Killed our loved ones! Stole us and stole from us!"

The intense emotion of the crowd rose feverishly. Keela realized how fast her message was being absorbed and decided to build up more fire for her cause. "Chained us!"

Screams.

"Whipped us!"

Wails of understanding.

"Starved us!" As she spoke, Keela could feel her ears growing deafened from the roar of the free people, but she left her ears uncovered and continued. "Forced us into hard labor! They said this is the way that it has to be!" She paused for breath, then continued. "But if you fight by my side, we'll free as many slaves as we can so that no one else has to be a slave again! You should *not* be slaves! And now, you are free! Free! *Free!*"

A rousing chant of "Free!" arose around Keela, coming from every mouth. She felt her hearing subside even more, but she didn't mind because her heart was pounding faster and faster with each cheer, and she knew that her excitement was making the blood churn through her head. The power surged around her from the roaring crowd, and she suddenly started to understand how much power she had. It was intoxicating to her—a powerful elixir to taste after being a slave for seven years.

When Keela left the fortress, she made sure that everyone had been removed so they could leave the jail abandoned. She didn't know who would take over the building once she left, and she didn't care. She had no interest in owning a prison, but she did envision owning more ships. She had big prospects for her future, just no intention of owning any prisons.

As the traders were dragged away, the freed people spat on them. Keela had never suggested that particular punishment, but she approved of it. By the time the traders reached the ship, they were already completely miserable. Keela's face was hurting from her extended smile. Even the pain she still felt could not make her feel miserable or stop her from grinning.

Chapter 21

B ACK AT THE SHIP, the slave traders were locked in the same cages the slaves had once been confined to. From time to time, the former slaves would move the traders around from cage to cage—sometimes to isolate one person or other times to put two people together in an attempt to make them both angrier. But the attempts to destabilize the hardened slave traders were not as effective as the crew had hoped.

"Your father would help get us out of this mess," muttered one of the traders to another.

"Shh!" countered a young man near Keela, shackled like the rest of them.

"Oh, I heard that!" Keela said, with her attention now focused on the young man. Her frustration melted away as she realized the stress had finally made someone crack. "Your father is important, is he? That's great news!" she said, mocking the young man. He flinched as Keela got closer. This amused her, so she used slow movements to touch his chin with a gentle stroke. "Who's your father?"

The man suddenly seemed less emboldened. "Someone you wouldn't ever run into," he said.

"Oh, he's too good for me, is that it? Do you even know my story? Is this father of yours some big, strong man who's going to come and rescue you? Or is he just a whiny little old man who's too afraid to defend his own children?" With each insult, the young man drew inward, almost crouching in submission, but his friend was getting more agitated with each snub, grinding his teeth and popping his head side to side. He was only hurting himself, though, so Keela ignored it until he uttered his own words.

"Hey! Don't talk about the governor that way!"

"You shut up!" shouted the young man.

"Too late," said Keela. "What's going on here? Did the Governor of Holland really send his own son to be a slave jailor?"

"You need to learn to keep your mouth shut," snapped the young man to his friend.

"He did nothing wrong. In fact, he gave me a great idea," Keela continued to mock. "Thanks to your friend, you are worth something to me alive. Consider this your lucky day." Keela now had the young man's full attention. "Let's have a chat about your father."

"I'm not telling you a thing," the young man hissed. But his shaking legs revealed his terror.

"You're going to tell me exactly who your father is, or you're not getting out of here alive, and that wouldn't be good for anyone, would it?" Keela moved around the room until she found a wooden chair with no arms. As she formulated a plan, she started ordering her people into action. "Now, I've given you a chance to answer nicely, but you've given me no choice. Tie him to this chair!"

Two of the biggest men on Keela's crew came over to tie the young man down to the chair. After they were done tying him down, they looked at Keela silently, awaiting further instruction. "I can handle this myself," she said. "Stay outside. And bring the other man with you."

The men nodded and walked away, closing the door behind them. Keela felt a sense of great power as the men bowed to her command. And it made the young man extremely confused and agitated. He looked at the woman before him in sheer terror, with his eyes pristine and sparkling.

As Keela came closer to the man, she gave him a reassuring wink. "Don't worry! I'm not going to hurt you." He stopped struggling as she reached down and began to push her hands across his chest seductively, enjoying the way he flinched and shuddered as the strokes reached his brain. "I bet it's a long time since you've had sex, isn't it? Why don't we have a little fun?"

Keela backed away from the man long enough to unbutton her shirt, revealing two perfect white breasts. As she touched her nipples, she began to shudder and moan. The young man continued to stare at her, with his horror replaced by lust. She looked him up and down just to pique his interest, and then she slowly reached down to his pants with one smooth gesture.

As Keela began to rub the young man's crotch with her hand, he began to reach out in new ways, pushing his hips as far as he could up into her hand while moaning. Frustrated by his restraints and unable to do more than fidget, he began to make strange noises under his breath. Keela moaned again and brought her face close to his pants. "What have we got here?" she asked.

Keela pulled his pants open and, after admiring him for a second, said, "Isn't that something! Let me kiss your musket!" She reached down with her jaws and grabbed a piece of skin between her teeth. Then, she stepped backward and yanked as hard as she could. From the side of the man's member, a stream of blood was pulsing from a ragged tear in his foreskin. Keela spat the flap of skin out of her mouth, and it flopped to the floor.

The young man shrieked in pain and rocked back and forth in his chair. "Men?!" Keela called out. Her men came back into the room. They looked shocked at the scene but stayed silent. The ropes holding the young man down had been weathered for decades in the salt spray of the ocean, so the ropes never once frayed or stretched. As hard as the man tried to break the ropes or the chair, he couldn't escape.

"You'd better start talking, or you'll bleed to death," Keela warned him. She spat more blood out of her mouth, and she knew how frightening it must have looked to everyone around her.

"All right, I'll tell you everything. My father's name is Jan Ducal. I'm Jacob Ducal."

"I'm not interested in *your* name. Tell me more about Jan Ducal."

The young man shivered. "My father has lots and lots of money. He's the Governor of Amsterdam. He'll pay handsomely for my freedom. Every Sunday morning, my mother insists on going down to the market for fresh flowers, so we can meet them there."

Keela wrapped a rag around Jacob's ragged member, which was still pumping blood from the torn skin. The skin hung loose on each side, flapping back and forth as the spurts of blood continued. Keela squeezed the rag as tight as she could around his prick, which made the pumping stop. Jacob screamed in agony. It was a high-pitched scream that made Keela smile with glee. "Can't have you dying on me, now, can I? Send in the doctors," she directed her men.

The doctors—there were two of them now—were more than happy to enter the room. And the room was becoming crowded. "That cut on his prick looks really bad. I think it might get infected. You definitely need to seal the skin after you close the artery," one doctor said to another.

"The artery?" the other doctor responded.

"Yes, the artery," Keela interrupted. "He would have bled to death if I hadn't saved him. Thank you for helping him."

"Right away," said the doctor. "Bring the alcohol over here, please." After carefully sterilizing the instruments, he left a poker over a fire so he could cauterize the wound. Then, he ordered his assistant to remove the rag. As the torn penis was exposed, the artery began to pump blood again. The doctor motioned with his hand, and the assistant returned the pressure.

"Alcohol, immediately!" the doctor demanded. Jacob was visibly relieved when he saw the rum, and he reached his head forward, desperately trying to claim some. "No, it's not for that!" scolded the doctor. "It's for the infection." He began to pour the strong rum onto Jacob's injury. Jacob screamed even louder this time. It was such a high-pitched scream that the doctor had to cover his ears.

"Now, give me those needles," the doctor further instructed his assistant. "I need to close the artery as fast as possible." As the sharp needle sutured the artery shut, Jacob couldn't take the pain anymore, and he fainted in the chair. After the doctor finished stitching the artery, he held out his hand and said, "Poker." The assistant brought the poker, which was yellow-hot after being on the fire for minutes.

When the poker cauterized the skin, the pain was so great that Jacob regained consciousness and screamed out loud. "Are you trying to kill me?!" he shouted.

"Don't be ridiculous," said the doctor as Jacob gasped for air. "We're trying to save your life. You're a very valuable hostage. You're worthless if you're dead."

Terror swelled in Jacob's eyes as he realized he was on his own. The doctor and the assistant gathered the tools of their trade and left quickly. "I hope this teaches you a lesson," Keela said. "No woman will ever want you now."

Jacob Ducal stared at his now useless prick in silence as Keela walked away and left him alone. She roamed the dungeon, finding one former slave who stood out from the rest. "What's your name?" she asked.

"I lost my name while serving in Governor Ducal's mansion. Now, I am Michael. They sold me off, but I used to serve them."

Keela had to pause before answering. "You *lost* your *name*?"

The man nodded. "I was born as Anthony."

"Then, you are Anthony again. Anthony, how do you think we might get a message to Governor Ducal?"

Anthony thought about it for a minute, then answered. "I know exactly when we can slip a letter to him. Every Sunday morning, the governor's wife insists on getting fresh flowers at the marketplace. That's when we might have a chance to slip a note into her basket with the flowers. We'll just wink at her, and she'll think nothing's wrong. She'll find the note when she gets home, and then she'll show it to the governor."

Keela pondered the situation. "Yes, I'm sure she'll read the message. And then, she'll show it to her husband, who will be forced to act!"

"What do you want the message to say?" asked Anthony.

"I'll just write it down real fast," Keela said. "Find me a piece of paper."

Anthony shook his head. "We need to go upstairs. The guards kept all the paper away from the slaves, hidden in the slavers' quarters. But they're gone now, so all the paper is yours."

Keela smiled broadly. "Let's get upstairs, then. It's time to write my first ransom note!"

After finishing the note, Keela needed someone who would deliver it, but the slave traders were still lashing out in the cages, and she was forced to wait. Three days later, she decided to negotiate with a slave trader who was beginning to get very weak. After being deprived of food and water, he was on the edge of collapse. She knew it would be easy to get his cooperation now. Daniel joined her in the negotiation because he was part of her plan.

"If you don't help us, I'll hunt your wife down, I'll hunt your children down, and your whole family will die," Keela threatened. "You've already seen what I can do, right? Or you can help us and be rewarded handsomely. I'll even give you freedom. So, what do you say?"

"My name is Malcolm. I'd be happy to leave this cage. I'm willing to help deliver the note."

"Why bring this wild brute with me?" asked Daniel.

"He'll make a suitable slave," Keela answered. "You need a good cover. Dress him properly, and no one will think he was ever a free man. We'll need somewhere for the pirates to stay until we attack, though. It won't be a permanent base, but we need somewhere to wait until the governor answers the letter."

Malcolm kept pressing his case. "I'll help you with that, too. There's an island called the Big Red, or the Gran Roque, or the Big Croquet—take your pick. It's a tiny island in the middle of the ocean. No one would ever find you there. Meanwhile, I'll sail back to Holland and pass the message to the governor's wife."

Keela wrote down the instructions. They read:

I'm sure you've heard of me by now. I am Keela the Pirate. And I have your son Jacob Ducal. I want fifty marks for your son, twenty-five for each of the other six of your men who survived, and I want all your slaves released and free. If you do this, I will set your gorgeous son free, unharmed. The slaves are nonnegotiable. You must free your slaves. Slavery is an abomination on this land. If you don't do what I ask, I'll come to your home and burn it and every

109

slave trader's home to the ground. Drop your answer in the bin of yellow gardenias in front of the old flower vendor with the parrot. We have eyes everywhere. Go there alone. You will be watched.

Keela released Malcolm the trader and sent him with his large guardian, Daniel, upon the waves. She watched as their small boat sailed away into the ocean. Then, she rounded up the rest of her people and sailed off in the direction of the island.

La Gran Roque was larger than the trader had suggested but still small enough to be invisible if one was not sailing smack dab into it. Small patches of jungle broken up by volcanic outcroppings provided many variations of cover and of darkness, light, and shadow. As hundreds of new pirates crowded onto the tiny island, the island was soon filled with cheers and whoops as they explored their new paradise.

Chapter 22

CAITLIN SCRUBBED DISHES IN the cold water of the washbasin. She hoped for hot water every time she scrubbed the dishes, but Margaret insisted the cold water was better for her constitution. So, Caitlin had to use cold water, which made her hands as red as the skirt she was wearing.

Beside Caitlin sat a toy that John Deas had bought for her at one of the markets. It had been for her twelfth birthday, and it was a bright red dress top. But it didn't make up for taking her away from her mother and father. "Take it away!" she said when he gave it to her. "You're not my real father! Why should you celebrate my birthday?"

John Deas threw the top against her dresser, and it then fell to the floor. "Pick that up. Don't leave a mess!" Caitlin did as she was told. She folded the top so she could gain his approval. "You're going to wear this skirt," he continued. "You're also going to learn how to be more grateful."

Deas had left the top with her. And now, she stared at the bright red top in fury, with the anger fueling her as she scrubbed the dishes in the icy water. She planned to bury the foul thing after her chores were done.

Caitlin hated scrubbing the grease-covered plates as her hands slowly froze in the cold water. By the time she was done rinsing them off in the clean water basin, her hands were icy cold and tingling on the skin. But the redness was temporary, and her skin was now bloodless and pale. A deep ache from her frozen finger bones left Caitlin even angrier. She rubbed her hands together vigorously, her teeth chattering as she rubbed. She blew warmth on her hands, and for a second, it helped.

Lady Margaret and John Deas confused Caitlin. On the one hand, they were nice to her, giving her food and shelter and calling her princess. But on the other hand, she had to clean dishes, clean clothes and bed sheets, and do everything else a slave was expected to do.

Lady Margaret entered the room, but even with her dangerous presence, Caitlin couldn't stop rubbing her hands together to warm them up. "Don't you think about getting sentimental on me, daughter."

"Never, Mother," Caitlin answered, still rubbing her hands.

"Are you going to cry?" Margaret asked. "You know I hate it when you cry!" Caitlin held her tears inside, focusing on happy memories with her mother to drive away the sorrow. "Your mother would have surely fought harder to save you if she really loved you!" shouted Margaret. "You should be grateful I took you in. What kind of mother leaves her own child behind?"

Lily stepped up behind Margaret and distracted her, to Caitlin's relief. "Lady Margaret?" she asked.

Lady Margaret turned around. "Yes, Lily?"

"Your bath is ready, my lady."

Margaret smiled and nodded her head. "Thank you very much, Lily. Caitlin, you should pay attention to Lily. She'll show you how to truly make me happy."

"And how is that?" asked Caitlin.

"Ask her yourself," Margaret said while walking out of the room.

Caitlin stared at Lily desperately. Lily grinned and told her, "She really loves her baths. That's her big secret. Next time, I'll let you heat up the water and surprise her." Caitlin thought this was an excellent idea. She was still rubbing her tingling hands but was feeling better. "You know how you described your mother, Caitlin? Well, someone matching her description escaped, and now she's a pirate. Everybody at the market keeps talking about this pirate with long red hair and a green pennant."

"That *is* my mother! That's my mother! I know it for sure. It's my green ribbon."

Caitlin ran outside, only stopping long enough to grab a small trowel by the shed. She hurried out to the back of the yard, far from any prying eyes, and hid behind a coconut tree. Twilight was falling, but Caitlin didn't care. She started whacking the tall grass away with her trowel, then started to pound the earth with the small tool, pressing the wooden handle hard against her palm and leaving splinters. Tears poured down her face as she stabbed the earth again and again, breaking through the sod and finally bringing up clumps of earth with the small trowel.

The trowel was just a simple instrument, frail from years of service. And under Caitlin's fury and pain, the handle cracked wide in her hand, and the rocks in the dirt broke the metal spade. The whole trowel disintegrated at once. But this was not enough to deter Caitlin. She reached her hands into the small hole in the ground and started digging with her fingers, pulling up the loose dirt first but finding the soil beneath full of rocks and thick clay that sucked back and resisted her efforts.

Determined and furious, Caitlin kept burrowing her hands into the dirt, breaking her nails apart on the hard rocks and scratching her hands with the sharp edges in the ground. Her hands were cut and bleeding in the dirt. But she still wasn't deep enough to bury the red top. Furious, Caitlin kept digging with her fingers, even though her skin shrieked in pain and her wrists began to ache and pop from the exertion. Once she got deep enough to bury the top, she rudely shoved the red gift inside the hole and started covering it up right away. As she began to disguise the hole with fresh soil, Lily came running over with a lantern.

"Child, how can you even see in this gloom? Look, you've cut yourself, Caitlin! You need to come inside at once so I can get you cleaned up before you get sick. You don't want to lose your hands, do you? Then, you'd be useless to John and Margaret." She ushered Caitlin away from the jungle as she spoke, leading her into the darkened lawns around the servants' huts. There, Caitlin started to cry, feeling alone and helpless.

"Oh, Caitlin, I didn't mean it like that!" Lily soothed. "You're my friend, and I don't want to see you get hurt. Ever! And now, you're out here hurting yourself. I told you, I'm not going to let anyone else hurt you, so I can't let you hurt yourself either. Come on, Caitlin. Let's get on back to our little home."

As twilight faded, the deep horror of outer space loomed. And hanging within that immeasurable darkness, the bright basket of Venus twinkled above Caitlin and Lily, yellow and warm amid the cold, distant stars. Caitlin stood where she was. She stared at the stars and prayed to the sky. "Please let my mother come and find me. Please!"

Lily turned around, looking almost like a shadow in the gloom, and shouted to Caitlin. "Caitlin, come on! Hurry up, or you'll get lost in the dark! Come on!"

Guided by her companion, Caitlin returned to her hut.

Chapter 23

THE GOVERNOR'S WIFE, Annaleis Ducal, was no stranger to fancy treasures. She had several magnificent treasures strung around her neck. She didn't like the pale face staring back at her from the mirror, but powders were all the rage in Amsterdam, and she had to fit in with her neighbors.

Annaleis enjoyed the view from the governor's mansion, not just because it was designed for all-encompassing views but also because she felt she had earned it. What she had done to earn it had taken place long ago, and she had almost forgotten how she ended up married to the now-richest man in Holland. Now, she was too satisfied with her position to admit that she had ever been anything other than rich and successful. Her dressing stand was filled with exotic makeup and perfumes, porcelain hair clips, and many other treasures.

Annaleis still needed one finishing touch to her makeup, and she called for her maid, Bridget. "Child, fetch me that Russian hair clip, would you?" she called, though Bridget was no longer a child.

The maid reached for the hair clip, which was adorned in bright-colored gems and worked in fragile copper. Bridget always got rushed along, so she worked as fast as she could. In her haste, trying to arrange the hair and pin the clip in place, she dropped the hair clip, and it clattered to the floor. A rainbow of colors scattered across the carpet.

"Stupid Bridget! Do you know how much that cost me?" Annaleis scolded her. She slapped the maid as hard as she could, and Bridget fell to the floor, whimpering. "Koen!" Annaleis shouted so loud that the rafters echoed.

The strong servant master, Koen, entered the room. "Yes?"

"Have this lady whipped, and bring me someone that knows how to take care of expensive things!"

As Annaleis continued to fuss over her makeup, trying to get just the right shade of rouge, Koen pulled Bridget from the room. The sounds of a whip cracking down the hall and the cries from Bridget didn't bother Annaleis one bit. Her hand didn't even flinch as she applied the makeup until she was completely satisfied with her appearance. She had caught a few cracks in the powder beneath her eyes, and each of these flaws was important to cover.

When the new servant entered, Annaleis said, "I've got one thing left to do, dear. I need to get my hair clip in. You can do that, can't you?" The new servant nodded, and Annaleis's hawk-like eyes saw the curt nod from the mirror. She waited silently while the new woman installed a new hair clip perfectly. Once she was done, Annaleis couldn't see a single hair hanging loose. "Good work, girl," she said to the speechless servant. "Keep it up, and I won't have you whipped."

The new servant visibly flinched as Annaleis passed by her terrified frame, brushing the servant's buttocks with her nails and enjoying the involuntary cringe the poor girl made. Annaleis knew the woman was terrified, but she didn't see any reason to feel pity. She left the room and closed the door. The new servant exhaled deeply, quickly organized a few things, and left the room, heading down the hallway in the other direction to make sure she did not cross paths with Annaleis.

Before leaving for the market, Annaleis Ducal had to speak to her husband. She loathed having to ask the governor for permission, but as with everything else about her marriage, it was a "needed sacrifice"—as Jan himself phrased it. Jan's overbearing nature irritated her too, but she tolerated it for the power and prestige it gave her. She also enjoyed her extravagant dresses and wore them whenever she could.

"I'm going to the market for flowers," Annaleis said.

"You can't go down there, dear," her husband responded. "It's too dangerous with the rebellions going on. Just stay home for once."

"Darling, I've been doing this my whole life. You're not going to begrudge me my favorite pleasure, are you?"

Jan Ducal was angry, but he relented, hanging his head in a short bow and trying to hide his embarrassment at her winning again. "As you wish, Annaleis. But don't stay too long."

Mrs. Ducal smiled and turned away, her massive collar replacing her face as she departed. Jan Ducal stood in place as she left, staring at her massive collar as she retreated. Time after time, he had warned her, and time after time, she had come back safe. But still, he worried.

Annaleis left the governor's mansion and strolled down the road leading to the market. The main road ran straight to the market at the end of town, where the river bent and arched around the back of the city. Amsterdam was protected by water. The water had granted all of Holland's occupants shipping skills, and waterways were almost as common as roads in the great city.

As Annaleis turned to look behind her in spite, she saw the governor in the archway, engulfed by his great mansion. Three stories tall, it towered above the other red brick houses in the city. In the middle, a grand courtyard allowed everyone in town to gather if they so wished. But all Annaleis wanted to do was visit the market and the nice people there and get away from her massive home, which felt so lonely when no parties were happening.

When Annaleis passed the lush parks filled with happy people, her spirit was more at ease. And as she passed the grand displays of tulips and trees, the landscape opened up to reveal the wide river, where a canal spread between her and the market to allow easy access to the market by water. That way, the vendors could resupply their stalls by canoe or paddleboat instead of having to haul armloads of cheese through the busy streets of the marketplace.

When she entered the marketplace, Annaleis knew where she was headed. The massive wheels of cheese and aromatic salami did not interest her. Instead, she was on the lookout for the most beautiful flowers. She often walked through the entire flower market before making her choice. She passed a stand selling blue crocuses and snapped at its thin merchant, "Your crocuses are wilting. Give them more water!"

The next stall contained many different colors of tulips, which Annaleis passed by without saying a word. The merchant cried "Tulips!" as she passed.

"Yes, and quite a few other places to get tulips, too!" she retorted.

The third stall Annaleis passed was being worked by one of her favorite vendors, who had large yellow flowers with little horny monkeys sticking out of the middle. She looked carefully, fascinated. Even up close, the pistils looked like tiny monkeys. The monkey shapes even had ridiculously long phalluses distended from them. She reminded herself it was the male part of the plant, while the stamens spiraled in tiny, intricate pigtails, which Annaleis thought were adorable. A huge grin began to spread over her wrinkled face, pulling the corners of her eyes into crow's feet that threatened to pucker her ears.

"Oh, I see you've noticed my new exotic orchids!" said the stall owner. She was a nice old lady who treated Annaleis with far more kindness than the governor did.

While Annaleis was distracted, a large black man ran over and dropped an envelope in her basket. He disappeared without a trace while Annaleis was enjoying the flowers. She never even noticed him, just continued to stare at the flowers in fascination.

When Annaleis got home, she pulled the exotic flowers out of her basket. Then, she noticed the note inside the basket, wondering how she hadn't noticed it before. She pulled out the strange red envelope, wondering how it got there. Then, she noticed the address: *To the Ducels*.

Annaleis opened the envelope, puzzled as to how anyone could spell her husband's fine name incorrectly. When she read the ransom note, she was even more puzzled, and she was frightened at the same time. Distressed, she pulled out a lock of her golden hair, and the monkey orchids fell to the floor as she realized Jacob was a hostage. She screamed at the top of her lungs as she ran to find Jan. "Jan! Jan! Jan! They took Jacob!"

After a while, Annaleis could hear Jan shouting, and she rushed to his side. She immediately showed him the note, then fell to the ground and sobbed out, "They've taken our son! All is lost!" She continued to sob while Jan read the note, throwing it to the table when he was done reading.

Jan reached down to the edge of the table and gripped it with both hands. Annaleis was expecting him to throw something, but instead, he pushed the entire table over with one massive roar. The table proved too heavy for him to throw, despite his heroic attempt to lift it into the air. As maps and compasses and magnifying lenses crashed to the floor, shattering into broken glass and torn paper, Annaleis stared at her husband in terror. "What are we going to do, Jan?"

"You don't negotiate with pirates! What's she going to do? We have fourteen hundred ships! She's never going to get through us. Why would I send her a ransom when she's going to come to my city anyway?"

Annaleis felt her hands starting to shake at the suggestion, and she took a long drink to steady her nerves. "She has our son alive, Jan! She wouldn't want fifty marks if he was already dead. If she has to come all the way to Holland, you know she won't let him live. You want our son back alive, don't you?"

The governor sent his fist crashing into the nearest chair. It skidded across the carpet. Annaleis didn't even duck because she knew it wasn't aimed at her. The governor chose to take his aggression out against furniture, not people.

"I'll send the Royal Netherlands Navy after them!" he shouted. "I'll tell Admiral Flanders right away. They won't stand a chance against two hundred man-of-wars. By my father Maximillian, I vow that I'll bring my heir back alive."

Jan wrote an angry letter and sealed it before sending a servant to the docks to deliver the message. Annaleis watched that exchange, which would seal her son's fate, and she felt the blood draining from her head. She squeezed her eyelids and avoided passing out, but she retired to her room and felt ill for the rest of the day.

Chapter 24

KEELA HAD BECOME great friends with the local people who lived on La Gran Roque. Frenchmen had continued to explore the island after naming it, but they had disappeared into history long before Keela arrived. The native merchants who lived there acted like the French had never arrived at all, carrying on their usual way of life.

The natives were fishermen as well as merchants, and Keela rowed out to sea with them many times to sample the local fishing. They allowed her access to all their canoes in case the Dutch should discover them, and they provided all the fish her men could eat. In return, Keela gave the natives the protection of her strong swordsmen. And she happily paid them with treasure gathered from the slave fortress in exchange for supplies they had for sale.

Weeks later, the slave trader Keela had sent to Holland returned on a sailboat. She went down to the shore to meet him as he sailed into the cove. "What's his answer?" she immediately wanted to know.

"See for yourself," said the exhausted trader, handing Keela the letter.

She opened the letter and returned to camp at once. "Okay, everyone, listen up. He said no. So, we're going to war! No partying tonight. Get lots of rest. We sail at daybreak!"

"I'm going to stay right here," said the ex-slave trader, collapsing by the fire.

Keela saw that he would be no use. "Have it your way. Tie him up with the rest of the slave traders," she told her pirates. "He's coming with us. We're selling all of them into slavery anyway, and the gover-nor too. They're going to find out what life was like for their slaves."

Keela studied battle plans with Daniel. A detailed map of the city of Amsterdam now sat before her, having been drawn in the intervening weeks. Daniel looked worried. "But he'll send out the Dutch Navy! That's hundreds of man-of-wars," he pointed out.

"I'm counting on it," Keela replied.

"What do you mean?"

"He's getting cocky. He'll send all his ships out. That means they can't defend the city at the same time. See this river? He thinks it's his strength, but it's really his weakness." Daniel nodded enthusiastically, understanding her now. "We can get right up these rivers and canals, under the bridge, to wherever we want. We can steal some paddleboats and ships small enough to slip in under his nose. And when I get there, you'll make slaves of all the arrogant bastards of Amsterdam and sell them to make more money for our cause."

Two large ships were packed with people and weapons. Before Keela got underway, she made sure to replace the Dutch flag she had pulled down earlier. The second ship also bore a Dutch flag, so the Dutch navy would hopefully sail right past them.

As Keela sailed across the ocean, she realized how vast the sea must be. Traveling under the decks as a slave, she hadn't watched the endless ocean for hours as she did now. From sunup to sundown, all she could see was the ocean spreading in all directions. There were no islands or anything else to interrupt her voyage.

The ocean really seemed to be endless when one was sailing for weeks. Keela began to imagine things to while her time away. She fan-cied, for instance, that she would sail forever without finding Holland.

The ocean was so vast that the great Dutch Navy never crossed paths with Keela and her crew. She had expected to encounter the navy, but the ocean was so large that they never did. The pirates reached Holland unharmed. She recognized the great levees erected all around the country from the description of the walls protecting a sunken land. She found it ironic that a small country that had to defend itself with walls from the sea would conceive of throwing thousands of free people inside walls and enslaving them.

"Don't get too close to shore until after dark," Keela instructed her crew. "Let's keep scouting until we see the lights of Amsterdam." She watched the dikes slip away into darkness until the merchants' ships began to appear in the harbor. Then, she spun her ship's wheel toward a dike, and the man-of-war commanded by Daniel slipped into position behind her.

Keela watched the merchant ships come and go from all directions, and because both of her ships were man-of-wars flying Dutch flags, nobody was able to tell that the Dutch Navy was not actually at port. The four slaves she had working on the deck were all dressed like regular sailors. With the pirates' disguises firmly in place, the passing merchant ships thought of them simply as anchored sailors. They could not see the ropes Keela and the other pirates hid inside their clothing—ropes that she planned to use to bind people's hands behind their backs.

Everyone on Keela's ships looked calm and peaceful. There was no sign of any danger. Much to her surprise, the navy had left the city completely undefended. She had expected the governor to leave at least one ship behind.

Waiting for darkness to fall frustrated Keela, but she maintained her position and watched the sun sink toward the levees. Even without an armada, she had noticed swords slung around the belts of some of the Dutch sailors. Wide, black shadows churned through the water and raced toward the boat as the sun slipped behind a levee. After darkness had completely arrived, Keela gave the order to get in the boats in complete silence.

All of the pirates walked down off the ships to the abandoned docks. Keela left her lantern open so she could see the canoes, and before long, she arrived at a section of the docks where hundreds of small paddleboats rested. Their owners lay fast asleep in their beds. She waved her arms toward the paddleboats, covering her mouth with her hand to signal that she demanded silence. The crew of pirates worked with as little light as they could get away with.

As soon as Keela and Daniel were in their boats, they covered their lanterns again and joined the other people in their stolen canoes. They dropped their oars into the dark water and rowed into Amsterdam through the wide rivers, with no more sound than the trickling water dripping off the oars between strokes. It was already dark, and nobody saw them row up to the governor's mansion and into the fields beyond.

The pirates lit their torches and began to set the fields of hay and tulips ablaze with their bright flames. One pirate hesitated long enough to watch the tulips wither and shrivel in the burning heat. So, he never saw one of the field guards come up beside him and bury a knife in his neck, killing him before he could hit the ground. But Keela watched him fall and waved the other pirates forward.

The fallen man's wiser friends continued on through the fields, igniting one at a time until half of Amsterdam's prized fields and parks, tucked between the city and the markets, were full of blazing fire. The beautiful city of Amsterdam, so fair in the daylight, had become a red, glowing nightmare in the dead of night. All over the city, fires lit up the sky, and people began to scream.

Keela pulled her canoe up to the side of the river and leaped to the brick walkway, where stairs led her up to the street. All along the highway, slave traders were starting to leave their houses, ushering the slaves outside to put out the fires in the fields. While the slaves got to work, trying to cover the flowers with damp cloth, they left their masters undefended. All their masters had to protect themselves were metal swords.

Keela saw her marks and zeroed in on four slave traders in the street. She focused on the nearest one. "Hey, you!" she called to him. The trader turned in surprise, ready to strike. But Keela struck first, knocking him to the ground. He struggled, but in seconds, she had his hands tightly bound. "You're headed back to the ship. Now, you're a slave!"

Other slave traders began to run toward Keela, and as the other pirates ran toward them, blocking their progress with sword strikes, she discovered that standing in the chaos was Jonathon Omari. He continued to hold his ground even though some of the slave traders had chosen cowardice and fled. She took the advantage and pushed him up against a wall, running him backward until his head hit the bricks. He looked down at the knife blade pushed against his neck.

"You've treated me kindly before. In return, I'll give you this one chance to escape," Keela informed Jonathon.

Jonathon stared in defiance even though the blade was still pushed against his throat. "I don't want to go, Keela."

"Look, Jonathon," Keela said, releasing the pressure on his throat but refusing to withdraw the blade, "just listen to me. I'm not the same woman I used to be. If you don't leave now, I'll have no choice but to slit your throat. But if you come with me, you can be part of our mission."

Jonathon tried to shake his head but stopped as soon as the blade nicked his skin. "I can't be part of your war, Keela. What you're trying to stop is something that will never end."

Keela looked down at his belt. "You don't even have a weapon."

Jonathon smiled weakly. "I didn't come here to fight. I heard you were a pirate, and I wanted to see it for myself. Now that I've seen you, I can tell you're not going to give up your mission for anyone."

Keela shook her head, clearing her mind and growing impatient. "Fine, if I can't convince you, I'll have to walk you there myself," she said. She grabbed Jonathon by the collar and started marching him back down to where the canoes were hidden, bringing over another pirate as she walked past just by swinging her arm. The pirate followed wordlessly, and Keela was thrilled at the power she wielded. At one point, Jonathon had been able to control his servants with the same gestures, but now, Keela enjoyed the power. She was even more thrilled that, unlike the slave traders, she was able to use this power for good instead of evil.

Keela got Jonathon down to the water and pushed him into her boat. "Don't let anybody see you. Go on; get free."

"Keela," he whispered. "Come back to Santa Maria."

"You don't want me to come back. Go back to your ship. Be free. Be alive. Forget all about me, Jonathon Omari. Free your slaves. Do right by them."

Jonathon stood up in the boat, grabbing her shirt and pulling her toward him. He teetered unsteadily in the boat. "I know you remember me, Keela. I moved with you, and you moved with me. That was love that we had. I still want you back in my arms, Keela."

Keela pushed him back, and he had to sit down in the boat to keep from falling into the water. "You never loved me, Jonathon. All you did was own me." The argument had reached a fever pitch, and she had no choice but to spell it out for him. "No one is ever going to possess me again. Now, get out of here; I hear someone coming."

As Jonathon rowed away quickly and silently, a pirate burst through the bushes, making more than enough noise to cover Jonathon's escape. Keela turned around, glad to be rid of Jonathon. Now, she could continue her attack on Amsterdam. "What's the news?" Keela asked the pirate, staring him right in the face. "You might want to try sneaking next time."

"Sorry, but it's so amazing." The pirate was too excited to whisper. "When we were doing some spying, we found tunnels leading under the governor's mansion!"

"You should spy a little quieter," said Keela, growing more impatient with the bungling pirate.

"Sorry," said the pirate, lowering his voice considerably. "The tunnels were dug out sixty years ago, and the governor doesn't even know about it. They were meant to smuggle goods into Amsterdam if there was ever a siege. Some of the men in town told me about it."

Keela held up her hand and whispered back. "It's a good thing we've got friends here in Amsterdam. Can they keep this secret, or will they be gossiping to everyone?"

"The rulers will never see us coming. I paid the man who told me in coin to buy his silence. We can sneak into the basement of the governor's house right now. My friend said something about boards over the door, but I'm sure they won't pose a problem for us."

"Show me where this is," Keela insisted.

They met other pirates as they advanced, all of whom turned and followed them without a word, sensing their purpose and falling into line. Far down a rock wall, where trees grew everywhere, Keela found the pile of boulders that hid the entrance to the tunnels. The pirate pointed so that the rest of his friends could also see the disguised entrance, leading to a chorus of quiet sounds from the unwise pirates.

"Move these rocks but put them down slowly," Keela commanded. "We don't want to attract any attention." After the boulders were cleared, she entered the small tunnel first, followed by the others. Once she was inside, she started lighting torches. She gave a torch to each pirate as they passed her. Firelight was much better than moonlight, turning the tunnel a dull red.

Keela heard footsteps and voices upstairs. "Quiet," Keela whispered to her crew. As she tiptoed forward, she found the door leading to the mansion, which was sealed by several wooden beams nailed in place. "Great," she whispered under her breath. "*Now* what are we going to do? We need something to pry these beams loose."

Getting through the basement door was tricky for Keela and the pirates. The beams were sturdy and took quite a bit of work to get down. The work made noise as the boards screeched and resisted, but one by one, they fell to the floor. A round iron handle allowed the hatch to open, and Akua began twisting it, finding absolutely no resistance. His huge arms were prepared for decades of rust, but the door swung open once he pushed upward, and he wasted no time in leaping to the floor above to secure their entrance.

Finding the basement room he entered empty and unguarded, Akua let out one low wolf whistle, and all the other pirates and Keela invaded the mansion through the open door. This same door that was designed to let the previous governor receive supplies during a siege and escape if he had to now made escape impossible. Keela enjoyed the irony as she scuttled through the hatch, entering the basement in triumph.

The pirates continued assembling under the governor's mansion as Keela looked at the shelves stocked with cheeses and salamis. "We're in the pantry, right next to the kitchen," whispered Akua.

"Good," Keela said. "I have a plan." As she entered the kitchen, she raised her finger to her lips, and one of the cooks came over silently. "I'm Keela, and I'm here to free you," she whispered.

The cook who approached her bore an unattractive tattoo. She thought it was a personal choice at first. But then, the rest of the cooks and a butler came forward, eager to help her, and when she saw the same tattoos on them, she recognized it as a type of brand. The brand was just like ones she had seen on other slaves. But Jonathon had never had enough cruelty to do anything of the sort to her.

"I'm setting all of you free, too," Keela informed them. With that, the cooks were much happier and willing to help her, nodding their heads and smiling brightly. "Does anyone know where the governor stays?" she asked.

"I used to live in Amsterdam," said one of the cooks. Keela could tell the cook was younger than she was. "He can't sleep well at night, so he spends a lot of time on his balcony, at the front of the building on the third floor. You can't miss the wide staircase at the end of the inner courtyard. He makes me get him food at the strangest hours of the night."

"Perfect," Keela said quietly. "You won't have to make any deliveries tonight. Tell the rest of the slaves they are free and that our boats are waiting for you at the docks. We have room for everyone."

The kitchen was soon abandoned, save for the pirates, as the cooks left to spread the word to the other slaves. Keela continued with the pirates on into the courtyard, acknowledging the escaping servants with silent nods. Crossing the courtyard, Keela ascended the wide stairs, and the rest of the pirates followed her.

Chapter 25

THE GOVERNOR'S WIFE LEANED against the railing of her balcony and watched the stars in the sky from her tall vantage point. When the fields started to catch fire, she became alarmed and started coughing from the smoke. She watched in terror as the flames got bigger until the night was glowing from the fire and the smoke in the air. The red glow illuminated several pirates slicing people apart with their swords. When she saw the brigands, she knew they were after her and her husband, and her terror turned to panic.

Annaleis hurried into her husband's room. Jan Ducal rested in his third-floor bedroom, drinking whiskey with no ice and undressing for bed. "The whole city is in trouble!" Annaleis informed him, sitting down on the bed. "The fields are on fire, and it's your fault. The pirates are taking over the city."

"What?! Then why are you sitting down?!" Jan got out of bed and put on his heavy robe. Before he headed out to the balcony, he freshened up his drink from the tall carafe by his dresser. "Aren't you going to come and watch with me?"

"No," Annaleis said. "Absolutely not. You got yourself into this mess, Jan. I'm staying right here and bolting the door, and if they try to get me, I'll stab their eyes out." She grabbed a sharp hairpin from its place by the bed. Jan did not have to look at his wife to know she was capable of that. "They're pirates, Jan. Have you got your guns with you?"

"I left them in the office. But I've still got this." He reached under

128

the bed and withdrew his long, sharp dagger. "They won't take either one of us alive."

"Don't go to your office. They already have the mansion surrounded. They will grab you in a heartbeat. Just hold on to that dagger and hope they don't rip it out of your hands!"

"I'm not going to stay here and wait for them to capture me like a petrified animal. I'm going outside. I need to see what's going on!" Jan opened the door, moved quickly through it, and slammed it behind him.

Annaleis ran over and barred the door shut, praying that nobody could break through. She also prayed for her husband, though her heart reminded her that he was always causing these situations and needed to suffer the consequences. She huddled by the door, sniffling, praying, and clutching the hairpin so hard that the pointed gems left dents in her fingers. She hoped that her weight would help keep the door closed, but she heard dozens of footsteps on the stairs, and she realized that she was in trouble. As the pirates struggled with the handle, Annaleis heard one of the men say "It's locked" from the other side of the door.

"Break it down, then," answered a woman's voice. Annaleis realized that the bar was not going to stop the pirates from coming into the room. In fact, one kick from a boot was all it took to knock the door open, and when the door pushed inward, Annaleis rolled away from it at once. The man in front of her was gigantic, and the troupe of men behind him appeared vicious, just not as huge. A woman stood among them, brandishing a sword. Annaleis knew from descriptions she had heard that the woman must be Keela, and she realized that she was likely the pirate who wrote the ransom note.

"Get her, Akua," Keela instructed.

Annaleis brandished her hairpin, growling and trying to intimidate the huge man. Akua opened his jaw and released an earth-shattering roar that was more like a dragon than a human. Annaleis tightened her grip on the hairpin as the massive warrior rushed across the room with lightning speed. He grabbed her arms with his gigantic hands, and her shoulders vanished inside the two meaty palms that squeezed with crushing force.

Annaleis tried to fight back, stabbing Akua with the hairpin several times until it went into his arm and didn't come back out. It remained embedded in his arm, notched into the bone, but it didn't affect Akua. He was far too large to worry about a small wound. Staring into Annaleis's eyes, the monster of a man removed one hand from her arm. Without the hairpin, Annaleis stood defenseless. He pulled a sharp dagger from its scabbard.

Annaleis had time to notice that the dagger's enclosure was off-white, and she realized it was made from bone. The powerful man held the blade against her throat, with the tip of the dagger tickling her throat with dangerous pressure, making her gag with horror. While the blade was poking her throat, she could feel her hands being pulled behind her back and tied.

Akua put the dagger away, but he clapped his hand over Annaleis's mouth immediately afterward, and he turned her around to face the door. She screamed when she realized what was going to happen. But the grip on her mouth was so complete that no sound from her cries even reached her own ears.

Realizing that she had no way to warn Jan, Annaleis stopped trying to scream. She wanted so bad to fight back. She wanted to stop the feeling of being powerless. But the more she thought about it, the clearer it became to her that she had gone from being the wife of the most powerful man in Amsterdam to someone without any power at all in a matter of seconds.

As Annaleis was being marched downstairs, she saw many of her slaves walking through the courtyard and disappearing. Although she wanted to scream at them to return to work, she couldn't make a sound, and as they departed, she was aware that she had been abandoned. While the slaves ran for freedom, she saw more pirates spilling into the mansion. She understood, then, what it meant to be captive—what it meant to have every privilege taken from you, so much so that you couldn't even move your arms to fight back.

As Annaleis continued down the stairs in a forced march, her head began to spin with dizziness as terror overwhelmed her again. She felt a fainting spell coming on. And soon, she fell backward, only saved from a disastrous fall by her two captors, who kept her upright and moving even as she stumbled.

Suddenly reliant on her captors for survival, Annaleis remembered that at one point, she had relied on her servants for the same thing. They supported her by providing her with food, drinks, warm blankets, and everything else that she needed. Then, she remembered an even earlier time, when she was reliant on her mother's breast milk for survival, and she suddenly felt like an infant. She had spent her entire life working to grab hold of power whenever she could, but the pirates had reduced her to this infantile mind in a matter of moments.

Chapter 26

J AN DUCAL WALKED to the balcony, where he had a near-complete view of Amsterdam. It looked like Rome. The fields were blazing with fire, and many slaves were trying to put the fires out. Pirates roamed the streets, taking what they wanted and leaving terror in their wake.

Staring at the scene with spite and malice, Jan realized that with the navy out to sea, his entire town was defenseless. The city guards had remained when the sea forces had sailed away. But pirates were slaughtering them in hand-to-hand combat on the streets below.

The Governor grabbed a potted plant from the balcony. His biceps burned with pain, but the whiskey dulled it enough for him to get the pot onto the ledge. He stared down at the pirates fighting below him, clashing with the city guards, while he caught his breath. Even though some of the pirates carried scabbards and others carried cutlasses, they were all effective. From his vantage point, Jan could wait out the fight until the right moment. He didn't want to hit one of the city guards with the pot. The fighting was intense, and he didn't have a clear shot yet.

The anticipation tickled Jan's spine. He couldn't tell one pirate from another, but the city guards always wore their red hats, so he knew which people not to hurt. After one pirate managed to subdue several guards, he had a clear area around him. Jan knew it was time to strike, and he pushed the potted plant off the ledge.

When the potted plant hit the pirate, he fell to the ground, and Jan was elated. The other pirates stopped fighting and looked up at the balcony. Jan fought for air against the weight of the whiskey in his gut.

With his lungs filled, he shouted into the moment of silence. "Guards!" he cried. "Protect this mansion with your life!"

One of the guards responded for the rest of them. "We're doing everything we can, Governor!"

"Don't call me that!" Jan shouted.

After a few seconds, the pirates below began to roar and resume their attack. They swung at the guards with ferocious swipes. After some of the guards fell to the pirates' attacks, the surviving guards began to back away, allowing the pirates to start heading into the mansion. As Jan Ducal stared at the devastation from the balcony, he realized that his dagger was no match for an army of pirates. And his guns were still in the basement.

As Jan tried to think of a way to get into the basement undetected, he heard a woman's voice behind him. "There you are!" the voice said.

Jan thought it was his wife coming to rescue him, so he called out to her. "Annaleis?" Hearing no response, he turned around and saw Keela. She was dressed in full war regalia, with a whole flock of cutlass-wielding pirates right behind her, filling the balcony. Annaleis was not in their midst.

"What did you do with my wife?!" screamed Jan.

"Calm down, you scum!" Keela barked back. "You'll find out soon enough!"

Chapter 27

"**W**HAT DO YOU MEAN by that?" Jan asked Keela, his voice much quieter. He drew his dagger and held it before him. "You're saying that I'll find out soon enough what happened to my wife, but you're up here ready for blood?"

"Enough small talk, Governor!" shouted Keela. "Get to the point! You cowards are all the same. You always use arguments to slow things down." Keela knew that her anger would unbalance the governor, and she enjoyed messing with his mind. It caused her a great deal of entertainment as the drama started to play out, with the aging governor mincing words while he was surrounded by pirates.

"I'm trying to figure out what you're planning on doing! Are you trying to kill me, or are you going to just clap me in irons like some criminal?"

"You should have given me the money when you had the chance, you little cheapskate." Keela's voice was dangerous and low. She knew her tone already had him in her grasp. Her insults against the rich governor made her feel all the better about her escape and her rise to fame.

To Keela, the capture of Jan Ducal was even better than the capture of Annaleis. What she planned to do to them was going to be brutal, but she wasn't afraid of exacting revenge. The years had eroded during her stay in slavery, and far too much time had been wasted with her unable to move at all. In a matter of months, she had made it all the way to the seat of power in Holland, which was one of the most powerful nations in terms of the number of slaves it transferred every day to places in the

New World.

"What are you going to do?" the governor asked again.

Keela advanced with shackles. "Put these on your hands, or I'll put them on for you!"

"What are you doing?" he repeated.

"Making you a slave." Keela shook the shackles.

"No! You can't do this!"

"What did you think I was going to do?" asked Keela. "You're worth way too much money on the slave market for you to die defending your home. You're going to become a slave. That way, I still get my money. Do you understand?"

"I'll die before I become a slave!" shouted Jan. He shoved the dagger as hard as he could at Keela.

With her larger scabbard, Keela had no trouble blocking Jan's attack, using her sword as a makeshift shield. "That's funny," she said. "I used to think the same thing. But I was a slave for seven years, and you get used to it pretty fast."

Jan took a swing at another pirate who was advancing. The pirate dodged backward and swiped his scabbard expertly. Four of Jan's fingers flew clean off his hand, and with them clattered his dagger, clanging as it hit the marble floor of the balcony. Jan's screams of agony rang throughout the mansion, and a great cheer went up all the way through the residence.

Keela pointed her sword at the offending pirate. He gulped and held his silence, hoping to stave off her fury with compliance. "We're not trying to kill him, you fool!" she reminded the pirate. "He's going to make us a lot more money alive. Bandage him up so he doesn't bleed to death."

The pirate went over to Jan Ducal and wrapped a clean cloth around the stumps of his fingers. Jan screamed out loud but caught his breath once the gauze was wrapped tight. As he was dragged away by Keela's crew, he continued to kick and scream.

Some of the nearby pirates noticed the governor being hauled away. "What do we do now?" one of them asked. "We already have the ringleader."

"Take as many prisoners as possible," Keela replied. "Now that we have the governor, they will have no choice but surrender. We need lots of slaves to sell at the market."

Jan was taken downstairs, where Annaleis was already tied to a chair. Next to her was an empty chair. Jan's legs were buckled, and the pirates carried him to the chair. Annaleis was gagged and couldn't cry out loud. Keela noted her tears without any compassion.

Keela didn't need to shout orders like other leaders. Instead, she simply pointed at different parts of the room, and the pirates did her bidding. They wordlessly moved from task to task, whether it be looting the wine stash or going through fine clothing.

Jan stared down at the floor, looking defeated. His drooping neck looked broken, yet he was still alive. His hands rested in the shackles, limp and useless. He shook his head from side to side and eventually lifted it up to look at Keela. "I'm not supposed to be a slave! You and the other pirates should be the slaves. This isn't right!"

Keela wanted to keep Annaleis gagged. But Annaleis's darting eyes told Keela that she might be useful if she could speak. Keela pulled the gag out of Annaleis's mouth and stepped back.

Annaleis spoke as soon as she could. "Jan! Don't say that! They'll kill me too!"

Just as Keela was about to step into the conversation, a pirate came over and whispered in her ear. "Hold that thought," she said. "Keep an eye on those two. I'll be right back."

When Keela went down to the slave quarters with the other pirate, she found a young woman cowering in a cage in the corner. The woman's back was pushed against a wall, and her legs were pressed against the floor. Keela could tell that she'd been assaulted during her time in slavery. "Nobody's been able to get near her," said the pirate. "We keep trying to get her out of there, but she kicks us, hits us, and even bites us."

"That's because none of you men know how to deal with a woman when she's scared. You should take this as a lesson. Women are more dangerous than men. Watch this." Keela went into the cage, completely calmly and quietly. Without uttering a word, she moved to the corner where the woman huddled. Keela's arms stayed down, and her fingers stayed calm. She didn't look nervous, but it was all self-control. The woman followed Keela's progress with her eyes but didn't move a muscle as Keela walked right in front of her.

"You must be one of Annaleis's servants," Keela said, squatting down in front of her, not showing any fear. "What's your name?"

"Bridget," said the young woman.

"Both of the Ducals are tied up right now. They can't hurt you."

Fear turned to relief in Bridget, and she began to relax. She moved away from the wall and hugged her rescuer. The worst was over, but Keela wanted the young girl to have her revenge. "That woman who tortured you and terrorized you, she's right up above us, tied to a chair. You can do anything you want to her. Are you ready?"

Bridget backed away from Keela and started getting to her feet. "I'm ready," she confirmed.

Keela motioned with her arm, and Bridget followed her wordlessly. "That's how you talk to a woman," she said to the pirates as she walked past them. "Don't forget this."

Annaleis started to breathe faster the moment she saw Bridget walk up the stairs in front of Keela. "I found someone who wants to hurt you even more than I do," Keela said. She made some motions with her arms, and the pirates took Annaleis from the chair and tied her to a pole that was supporting the ceiling. Then, the pirates stripped her naked as Keela and Bridget watched.

"Make sure you don't hit her face," Keela instructed Bridget. "She'll be sold for far less money if she has face wounds. Anywhere else is fine. But make sure you don't kill her." Keela's voice cut through the room, allowing Annaleis to hear her.

Bridget walked over to Annaleis. Everyone could see the pieces of a hair clip that Bridget held out in her palm. "For this useless bauble, you had me whipped. Now, it's my turn," Bridget said with confidence.

Annaleis had her face toward the pole, but her sobs filled the room, making Bridget grin with mirth. She set the broken clip down on a table and turned around to Keela, reaching out her hand. Keela walked over and presented her with a powerful whip—one with many different strands arching out from the end. "Anywhere but her face, remember. I need to make money off her."

"No problem," Bridget agreed. "I'm going to hit her where it hurts. It's not too hard because I'm still hurting in some of those places myself right now."

Annaleis started to cry before the punishment even began. Bridget swung the whip with mighty strength. The strands of the whip arched through the air and whisked across Annaleis's buttocks and lower back, leaving her screaming in pain. The tendrils punched out holes of her skin and left red dimples on her buttocks, with blood slowly streaking to the floor. Annaleis continued to sob.

"Don't swing so hard," Keela said. "Save your energy. You don't have to stop anytime soon."

Bridget was far from done. With her second swing, the tendrils whipped so hard that several flew between Annaleis's legs in quick succession and left her so vandalized that blood now began to drip down to the floor in a steady trickle. Her screams rose higher into the night, and though they rang throughout the house, there was no one there to hear them as it had long since been abandoned.

Another swish of the whip, and Annaleis's back was bleeding too. She started to sink to the floor. But with her wrists roped to the pole, her body only sank a slight distance. With her legs shaking in pain, she made herself stand up again, forcing her battered frame to a proud and standing position.

Keela spoke from behind Bridget. "That's enough, now. She's learned her lesson. She'll never disrespect another human being again. Isn't that right?"

Annaleis could do nothing but nod before collapsing, and the proud woman now clung to the pole for dear life. Keela made another motion with her arms, and the pirates untied Annaleis's wrists, brought her down from the pole, and tied her wrists behind her back again. They made her sit in the chair beside Jan once more.

Keela started cutting Jan's expensive clothes away. He couldn't fight back because he was already shackled. Then, she threw some slaves' rags over his shoulders. His shackled hands rested inside the loose shirt. "You're not a governor anymore," Keela told him. "Now, you're a slave."

"You should just kill me now!" screamed the Governor. "I'd rather die than be a slave." He stretched his neck into the air.

"No! You want to be alive to experience this!" She could tell that his survival was pure torture because his eyes clouded over, and he started breathing faster than ever before. "Men! Take him to the ship with the other fresh slaves! Then, start getting the gold and the swords!"

"You miserable pirates!" Jan Ducal was enraged now. "I don't know what kind of sick game you're playing, but you'll never beat the Dutch Navy! They'll hunt you to the ends of the earth!"

"You'll be on a slave ship by morning, so I don't think it will be too easy for them to find you, will it now?" Keela said with a grin.

"What do you mean, I'll be on a slave ship?"

"You're a slave now, and that's where slaves go. They go on slave ships, to be slaves in other countries. That's where you're going tomorrow morning! Have I made myself clear enough?"

"Can't we just talk about this?" Jan pleaded. "I'm going to have to work in a field. I'm not strong enough for that kind of work."

Keela took a deep breath. "Sure, we have time to talk. I need to know what happened to Caitlin. What did John Deas do with her? And just in case you think I'm going anywhere, the night's still young. If you can tell me what happened to my daughter, I might just do what you want. Or I could kill you, and then you wouldn't have to be a slave."

Jan Ducal sputtered with anger. "You don't have to threaten me to find that out! John Deas is taking very good care of her, just so you know. He gave that little girl to his wife, Margaret, and she takes care of Caitlin. His castle is on the largest of the Canary Islands."

"Thank you for telling me," Keela answered. "That's a huge weight off my mind." She started walking away.

"Wait!" Jan Ducal screamed after her. "Aren't you going to kill me?"

Keela stopped in her tracks, turned around, and walked back. She didn't say anything for a minute but held her long sword up against his throat. Jan began to hyperventilate in anticipation, holding his neck against the blade greedily.

"I told you what you wanted to know. I have nothing else to offer, so please just kill me now," Jan continued pleading.

Keela leaned forward until her head was right next to his ear. As she whispered, Annaleis could hear what Keela said as well. "You know what? I lied. I'm not going to kill you. You're going to be loaded onto the boat with the rest of the captives—the slaves. And your slave wife, too."

As he saw barrel after barrel loaded with gold leave the mansion, Jan began to shiver. And as his massive armory of swords was looted as fast the pirates could slide them through their belts, he began to cry. Keela held up her hand as the pirates brought out more barrels of gold. "We don't need *all* of this gold," she said. "I understand if the freed men and women want to go back to their families rather than be pirates. If that is the case, then let them go with our blessing and a generous amount of this gold. But rather than give them *all* the gold, let those who want to fight at our side follow us and share in even more riches from future invasions. Give them the incentive to choose."

"If they want to leave, we give them gold. But if they stay with us, they can get even more gold. Simple," Akua said, confirming the arrangement.

"Thank you," said Keela. "I knew you'd understand." Jan shook his head from side to side. Keela knew he wanted to say something. "You have a question, Jan? I'd like to hear it."

"Why are they following you at all? *I'm* their master," he snarled.

His persistence irritated Keela. "Jan, why can't you understand the concept? It's not that hard to get. All you need to do is see things from your servants' point of view. Well, don't worry because you'll have plenty of years as a slave to think about it."

Keela knew this tactic had failed to change his mind as soon as he opened his mouth. "You think you're some kind of hero, don't you? You're just a pitiful excuse for a woman. Don't give away all my gold and leave me bankrupt! You really are heartless."

Keela decided to use logic instead. "If I took all your gold and put it in my ship, the boat would sink to the bottom of the sea. Your greediness is unforgivable."

Jan Ducal was hauled to his feet and taken away. When he reached the slave ship, he was chained to Annaleis. Inside the ship, Keela's new prisoners were herded into narrow shelves. Jan and Annaleis were chained in a row with the rest of the new slaves.

"Make sure these three all get to be on the same plank as Jacob," Keela said. "I promised them that they'd be able to see their son!" Annaleis began to weep. "Cheer up! You get to see your son! I promised you, didn't I? I always keep my promises." Struggling in his chains, Jan spat in Keela's face. "I'm still keeping my promise, ungrateful man! Put Jacob on the other side so they can gaze at each other for the entire voyage," Keela instructed one of her pirates.

One of the guards watching the new slaves saw Jan spit on Keela and gave him a correcting smack on the back of the head. As Jan and Annaleis were led into the ship with the rest of the new slaves, Annaleis tried to comfort her crying husband, patting his shoulder and massaging his sore head. But as all the new slaves were loaded onto their shelves, she began to whimper, finally breaking down and joining the chorus of moans and other complaints.

As the new slaves got used to their compartments, they were horrified to find that there was no way to sit up. The distance between the shelves was just enough to lie there, but if they tried to get up, they'd bump into the slats above them. The slaves adjusted to their new environment with a lot of grumbling.

Keela sailed down the coast, reaching France with a strong wind behind her sails. She was lucky enough to encounter another slave ship on her journey, and its slave traders were foolish enough to mistake the pirates for real slavers. They freely conversed with Keela and her crew.

"Where is the best place to sell slaves?" Keela asked.

The captain of the other ship spoke across the disbands. "A Coruna," he answered.

"What's a Coruna?" she asked.

"A is part of the name, woman. It's 'A Coruna' in France. You can't miss the red roofs."

Keela reached the famed city of the red roofs before sunset of that day. She anchored her ship in the harbor and waited for the next morning. She knew that slave auctions always took place in the morning, before civilized people could enter the marketplace and voice offense at the trade.

Chapter 28

WHEN KEELA GOT HER new slaves to the slave auction at A Coruna, she and Daniel surveyed the arena. The air was hot as fire, and the arena had a dirt floor, which was topped with straw to keep the dust to a minimum. Despite the straw, clouds of dust filled the air as people walked back and forth. Another slave trader was already on the auction podium, calling the prices at top volume. Six more slaves remained to be auctioned, but no one stood behind his slaves in line.

"We can go up there next," said Daniel. "We should prepare the slaves immediately."

"You know what to do," said Keela. "Get as much money as you can for the cause. Make them sound amazing."

Daniel smiled at her. "Are you kidding? I've wanted to do this for years!"

Daniel and the other pirates wasted no time getting the governor and his family and the rest of the new slaves off the ship. Keela enjoyed watching them stagger as they disembarked because she remembered feeling that same way after being pulled out of the slave ship. She also enjoyed watching them swing their arms and legs, trying to massage their hands. She knew how much their arms must be tingling.

Now that the new slaves understood what it felt like to be cooped up in a small space for days and days, they followed their captors without a word. They were respectful and did not fight back as they were led to the auction arena. And their captors never grinned at this— not even Keela. They did not want to give anything away.

Daniel stood at the auction block upon the wooden stage, looking just like a captain ready to sell his goods. The governor was up first on the auction block. He began to look nauseated. Keela finally grinned at the governor. Then, Daniel turned to the audience of bidders and began the auction.

"What do you bid for this fine specimen? He might be getting up in years, but he'll serve you well! He's very loyal. What are my bids?"

"Fifty francs!" someone shouted.

"Sixty francs!" cried another voice in the audience, from a mountain of a man.

"One hundred francs!" cried yet another voice.

"One hundred fifty," returned the big slave trader.

"Oh, come on, Homer, you know me," whimpered the slave. "I'm the Governor of Amsterdam! This is an outrage!"

"Going once!" shouted Daniel.

The smaller man bidding on the governor squinted at him and shook his head. "Sure, and I'm the King of England! Two hundred francs!"

"Going twice!" Daniel cried, keeping the gavel raised. The mountainous man shook his head.

"Think about what you're doing!" cried the governor.

"The Governor of Amsterdam would never end up on an auction block," said Homer. "You're nothing but a slave trying to give him a bad name. And now, you're *my* slave."

"Sold! Daniel finished. Please clear the way for the next person up for bids."

Homer walked forward to claim his prize, and Keela made sure that the money ended up in her hands before he walked away. Now, Jacob stood on the auction block. He stood quite a bit taller than his father and was, of course, younger.

"How much for this good, fine specimen?" asked Daniel. "This man has fine teeth, big muscles, and he's trustworthy. He will work in your fields all day long."

"One hundred!" cried the first bidder.

"Two hundred!" cried the second.

"Oh, quite a bit more, now. This one's worth a lot of francs," Daniel insisted. All Jacob could do was nod, with his eyes wide open with obedience. He opened his mouth a couple of times but said no words.

"Three hundred!" piped up yet another bidder.

"You really like this one, don't you? Look how clean his teeth are," Daniel pointed out. "Anybody like him for three hundred and fifty francs?"

"Three fifty!" cried another voice in the audience.

"Four hundred!" cried one of the earlier bidders.

"Now, let's be reasonable here," said Daniel. "He's a good specimen, but that's more than enough for him. Let's stop the bidding at four hundred."

"Five hundred!" came another bid before Daniel could drop his gavel.

"Six hundred!" The bidders continued back and forth.

"Six hundred is the top bid," Daniel asserted. "You can't just bid on him all day. So, he's all yours at six hundred. Please pay before collecting your asset." After Daniel slammed the gavel down on the auction block, he turned to face the person who now owned Jacob, who was already on his way up to the stage to collect the merchandise. "How much for this old lady here?" Daniel asked, gesturing toward Annaleis. "She might be able to help around the house. Let's start at forty, okay?" Annaleis scoffed but was completely ignored.

"Twenty francs," said the greedy bidder who already had Jacob.

"Anyone else?" Daniel asked, turning toward the crowd of bidders.

After a long pause, another bidder offered quietly, "Thirty francs?"

"Forty," responded the greedy bidder. "I need plenty of help around the house."

"Sixty," answered the quiet bidder.

"Seventy!" answered another bidder. "I'll take that chance."

"Eighty," replied the greedy bidder. "But that's it. That's all I'll pay for her."

Annaleis spat into the audience, and Daniel rewarded her with a smack on the back of her head. After a long pause, he finally dropped the gavel down. "Eighty it is. But don't you worry, folks, we have plenty of younger slaves here today, too. So, don't go anywhere! This one doesn't even look thirty," he said as a young man was led up and shown off. Daniel expected the bidding to be strong for him, but at only three hundred francs, the bidding leveled off, and he had to let the young man go for that amount.

Daniel never changed his tone as he continued auctioning off the people they had collected in Amsterdam. After he finished the auction, he returned to Keela's ship. She had on a fantastic red dress and looked every bit the lady, even though she still wore the sword at her hip.

"We made thousands of francs today," said Keela. "It was great! I have the money tucked away in the ship, and I want to distribute it after we get to sea. Are all the supplies on board?"

Daniel nodded. "Yes, we're fully stocked now. The chandlers and sutlers were plentiful here. We have ropes, tar, glue, more buckets for bilging, and plenty of food." Keela rubbed her belly. Food was the most important detail. She had seen steaks coming on board. "We are prepared for anything, and we still have plenty of gold to spare."

Keela clapped Daniel on the shoulder. He relaxed at once, and so did the people around him. "Well then, we should celebrate!" she suggested. "We'll leave in the morning, after the festivities." Keela stayed on deck while cheers began to emerge from the galley. She didn't want to dull her reflexes, so she avoided rum. When the party began to spill out onto the deck, she went into the captain's quarters, where no one would bother her.

Unfortunately, someone still wanted to bother her. She let Akua and a short messenger man into the captain's chambers. "Someone wants to bring a message to you, Keela," Akua informed her.

Keela paused to think for a second. She hadn't expected anyone to know about her stay in A Coruna. She was curious, and this eventually swayed her mind to hear the message. "What is it?" she asked.

"Just a small note, and a box, from this messenger," said Akua, handing her the folded piece of paper. He set the box down on the captain's table.

Keela looked up and saw the short messenger still standing in the room. "Your presence is no longer needed," she said. "Why are you still here?"

The messenger cleared his throat and paused. For a moment, she thought he had decided not to speak, but he eventually did. "I object, for I must know your answer before I depart."

"Fair enough," Keela agreed. The note in front of her read:

This is Captain Redbeard of the Barbarossa ("red beard") pirates. I've been impressed by your exploits and want to meet you. Come to Algiers and ask for Redbeard. You'll find me. Wear the presents if you like them.

Keela opened the red box and discovered two silver-handled blunderbusses. The hammers were plated in gold, but she knew they had to be steel or flint underneath, and the ends were wide and finely polished. She was very proud of them and slid them both into her belt, one on each side. She loved having two pistols. That way, if one were not enough, a second would be at the ready.

"I love the gifts," Keela told the messenger. "Please join us for the festivities in the tents. You are a welcome guest indeed."

The messenger nodded and left with Akua. Once she was alone again, Keela put the note in her pocket to keep it safe. Then, she headed out to the beach, where the tents were glowing, set up in the high grasses away from the other ships. Sheltered on the beach, Keela felt safe and protected.

Keela entered a tent and found it filled with lanterns, pillows, and music. She saw a great display of fresh food from the A Coruna market, and it put her in an even better mood. The young slave woman who had whipped Annaleis was also in the tent, and Keela recognized her at once. She had disappeared after Keela liberated Amsterdam.

"How did you find me?" Keela asked Bridget while also acknowledging a man and woman standing by her.

"I was born here in A Coruna," Bridget replied. "When you arrived, I couldn't help but see you again. These are my parents."

"We can't thank you enough for rescuing our daughter," said the jubilant mother, hugging Keela immediately. "How can we ever repay you?"

"Just join us for the festivities. That's all I ask of you. Sing and be merry and enjoy this life you've been given!"

As the fiddles and flutes began a new song, the merriment reached a fever pitch, and a great deal of dancing took place inside the tents. Keela joined in many of the dances and songs. When dawn came, she woke up and headed to the ship with the rest of her crew, while some of the men stayed back to tear down the tents. Once they were all aboard, they sailed off for Algiers, with Daniel at the helm.

Chapter 29

KEELA KEPT HER SHIP ALONG the coastline, following the coast of France and then Spain, knowing it would lead her to the Mediterranean and the pirate called Barbarossa. The pirate Barbarossa's reputation preceded him, and she was excited to meet him. While she traveled down the Spanish coast, she found slave traders happy to complain about how he took all their cargo and left them floating in life rafts while their ships were commandeered. And before she reached Turkey, she had heard about his exploits in Libya.

As the coast of Spain and Portugal became the Bosporus Straits, Keela was amazed at the beauty of the land. Constantinople beckoned to her from the shore, with tall minarets promising her vast supplies of gold. But she had another destination in mind.

Keela perceived the beginning of the Mediterranean Sea as a very wide river—sometimes five miles across, sometimes only two—separating rolling hills and green meadows on each side. As it widened into the great Mediterranean Sea, she understood the power hidden in this body of water. It was not just a passageway to Algeria; it was a living organism seated between two continents. It rose and fell with the tides, and the cliffs vanished into the churning water and returned, exposed and dry, hours later.

Looking at her map again, Keela reminded herself that this narrow passage was the beginning of a great ocean—a massive body of water separating two continents. But there, in the narrows, the journey could become treacherous. Portuguese sailors could attack her ship at any time. She knew that many slave traders from Portugal and France, not just Dutch traders, were still quite busy down here. Although Barbarossa had been successful in Algiers, having established an entire city for pirates, it was still over a thousand miles by sea before she reached that safe haven.

Keela struggled to imagine a more beautiful place than the coasts of the Mediterranean. But as she sailed past a slave trading post further down the coast of North Africa, she couldn't believe the number of slaves being shipped through. Ship after ship went out from the shore beneath the slave fortress. It was almost like an entire industry, with a tight schedule of deliveries, to have so many outgoing slave ships.

Algiers was breathtaking to Keela. The arches of the houses matched the scallops of the waves. Each window sat beneath a white dome, and each dome reached up to the sky. The minarets in Constantinople had been pointed, but these were smooth, rounded domes that resembled the swells on the ocean. And the beaches of Algiers had been cultivated with palm trees, growing hundreds of feet high and flourishing with ripe coconuts.

When Keela landed, she found many men wearing turbans gathered at the docks. She asked for Redbeard, and though the men in turbans laughed, they pointed the way to find him. After asking for directions several times, Keela eventually found her way to a beautiful tent on the beach, surrounded by palm trees. Young men supported by leather belts ran up the side of the trunks to grab coconuts from beneath the palm leaves. Each coconut would fall to the sand and crack on impact, so the festivities seemed never-ending, with young men and women drinking the coconut milk and dancing.

Keela heard sounds of music and laughter coming from inside the tent, and wonderful smells of exotic spices and wood smoke from a round fire wafted out. She noticed a man in a yellow turban standing outside the tent, but he disappeared into the tent as she approached. She heard someone speaking from inside the tent, and she held her tongue so she could listen.

"Master, the woman you asked for is outside. She's wearing both blunderbusses."

"What are you waiting for, then? You're keeping a woman waiting? You'll give us a bad reputation! Send her in right away."

Keela straightened her brilliant red dress and tightened her belt, determined to make a good impression. The yellow-turbaned guard poked his head and his arm out and ushered her in, with the folds of his maroon shirt rustling as he nervously whisked his arm back and forth. Inside, Keela found a man with a fantastic gold vest and bright crimson turban, who sported an equally bright red beard.

Keela spoke first. "Redbeard, I assume?"

The man drew in a deep breath and expelled a long peal of laughter. "That's *Captain* Redbeard to you, Keela the Great!"

The honorific set Keela back apace. "Excuse me? I've never heard that word attached to my name."

"Sit down. Please. You're our honored guest. You must make yourself comfortable," Redbeard insisted. Keela had noticed pillows the moment she came in, and when she sat down on one of the huge pillows, she was amazed at how soft the stuffing was and how it folded around her. "Everyone around here calls you Keela the Great," Redbeard continued. "You're famous. And those blunderbusses look great on your belt, by the way. I'm glad you like them because you're my hero. You took down Aruba! You took down Amsterdam!"

Keela had found respect with her fellow pirates, but this man had only just met her. She decided to compliment his achievements by downplaying her own. "A hero? I wouldn't say that. Actually, *you're* the hero here. You've been terrorizing Spain and Libya and fighting the slave traders at their home bases."

"That's why I wanted to bring you here," Redbeard said. "We're both fighting for the same cause, and I think we should work together."

Keela had guessed that Redbeard was looking for some kind of partnership when she had read his note. "I agree with you," said Keela. "Our forces would be strong together."

"Yes, we would be quite formidable. But instead of fighting by my side, you search for John Deas. May I ask why someone as powerful as you would have a need to stop John Deas? That little maggot isn't worth your time. He's just another slave-dealing piece of scum, like all the rest."

Keela wanted to agree with Redbeard, but her memory insisted that she reveal why John Deas was the target of her vendetta. "No, he's worse than the rest!" she insisted. "He killed my husband, he raped me, and he stole my daughter. Then, he sold me into bondage, and I didn't have a chance to escape for seven years. It's all his fault, and there's no way I'm resting until I've had my revenge."

"I have spies everywhere," answered Redbeard. "I know exactly where he's hiding. He's living on the second largest of the Canary Islands, with his wife and a little girl."

Keela was astonished she had been lied to by Jan Ducal, who claimed Deas lived on the *largest* island. "Your spies have seen my daughter? And he doesn't live on the biggest island?"

"We figured it was the daughter of an Irishwoman. How else would he get a redheaded daughter?"

Keela wanted to continue the conversation about John Deas, but she also wanted to move forward on the partnership. "Let me make you a deal. I'll join forces with you, and we'll have enough people to take down John Deas before anything else," she proposed. She expected Redbeard to mull this proposal for a while, but it was mere seconds later that he continued with his own proposal.

"I'll work with you," he agreed, "as long as you promise to help me wipe out the slave trade from here to the Bosporus. Together, we can block the top of Africa and force the slave trade through the Ivory Coast, where it's a lot easier to pick off ships. I think between your ambition and my thousands of pirates, we should have no problem getting what you're after."

"Then it's a deal," Keela confirmed. After the deal was made, Keela remained in the aromatic tent and drank strong tea and even stronger spirits, celebrating and enjoying herself until the evening became dark.

"Leave us, all of you," said Redbeard. "I need some privacy."

All of Redbeard's friends started walking out of the tent, one by one, with their curved swords flashing as they departed silently. Once they had all departed, Redbeard grabbed Keela and pulled her close by his side. She felt the heat of his body immediately. He unwrapped her turban, and her long red hair began to flow down. The hair surrounded her back and became a spectacle in the light of the fire.

"You're magnificent, Keela," Redbeard said. And then, without warning, he was inside of her. This time, it was something Keela welcomed.

The feeling of Redbeard throbbing inside of her overwhelmed Keela, and the vibrations melted through her body. Fueled by the strong drinks, every nerve in her body was engulfed in fire. His arms wrapped around her, and she cradled his hands, pulling them up to her breasts instinctively.

Keela's back kept arching forward as she shot through ecstatic waves. Redbeard pushed her hair out of the way and over her shoulder. She felt like she was being tickled from behind, and she realized it was his magnificent beard rubbing against her, which was even more thrilling.

Redbeard's thrusts grew more and more intense until he began to kiss the back of Keela's neck, and she couldn't take it anymore. They pumped harder and harder until they both exploded, and all the gears stopped working in Keela's mind. She felt like she was floating high above the clouds as she descended to the bed, completely spent and in a state of bliss.

When Redbeard finally broke the silence, Keela couldn't help but release a startled gasp. "We're going to be glorious together," he said.

Keela caught her breath before returning his vow. "Promise me one thing, dear captain. John Deas is mine to do with as I please."

"Your wish is my command," answered Redbeard.

Chapter 30

KEELA WAS EXTREMELY IMPRESSED by Redbeard's massive pirate ships with cannons poking out of the portholes. These were much bigger ships than the man-of-wars she was accustomed to. She gazed in wonder as the ships towered above the swells in the harbor. "What type of ships are these?" she called up from the dock to one of the ship's commanders.

The commander of the ship stood on deck, and after a nod from Redbeard, he spoke up. "The great Algerian warships, Keela the Great. They are led by my pride and joy, *The Radoom*. Each warship is capable of holding five hundred pirates."

"Tell your men to go after the defenders, but make sure they don't go after John Deas. He's mine and mine alone," Keela informed the commander.

The commander nodded and watched as pirates loaded armfuls of swords onto the deck to prepare for the battle ahead, as well as food, water, and medicine. Keela knew that everything would be ready soon, and it wasn't long before Redbeard asked her, "Well, are you coming aboard, or are you just going to stare at my ships all day?"

Keela walked up the gangplank to *The Radoom*, where Redbeard's pirates waited at the ready. She took his hand. "All aboard?"

A hearty chorus of "Ayes" rose up on deck, and Redbeard called out, "To the Canary Islands we go!"

Keela had plenty of time to enjoy the wonderful ship Redbeard called home most of the time. His quarters were sublime, with acres of red velvet hung against the walls and purple velvet draped across the beams of the ceiling. It did not even resemble a ship's quarters. The portholes were round, but gold from Redbeard's many plunders lined every window in stunning yellow that glistened in the sunlight bouncing off the sea.

The gold from Redbeard's plunders also graced the walls of his cabin and even the posts of his massive bed. Fine pillows and soft blankets adorned the bed with bold colors. Keela had not expected this kind of luxury from a pirate. "This is the most wonderful bed I've ever seen," she noted out loud.

"The world has been very kind to me," Redbeard answered. "I just wanted to share some of this glory with you."

"This is almost *too* much glory!" said Keela, trying to add up the weight of the treasure in her mind. What's balancing all this out?"

"My golden hoard on the other end. Don't tell anyone!"

"My lips are sealed," Keela assured him.

While Redbeard spoke with her, Keela removed her sword from her belt and placed it on the chest at the end of the bed. Beside it, she laid both blunderbusses. She knew it was a significant gesture to remove her weapons, but she had never met anyone who made her feel so safe before.

"I have acquired many great treasures in my journeys," said Redbeard, "but they are not mine because of the world's kindness. All these treasures you see here came to me because of my life as a pirate. All I've ever known is war against the Portuguese, the Spanish, and everyone else that tries to take the life of Africa away from the sacred continent. Each time I conquer one of their ships, I plunder their gold. The true kindness of the world is that no one has defeated me."

Keela sat down on the magnificent bed. She sighed and luxuriated in the soft blankets and the comfortable mattress. It felt like she was sinking into air. Even though the waves of the Mediterranean rocked the boat back and forth, inside the soft bed, she felt calm and protected. Redbeard, on the other hand, seemed excited and aroused. He appeared even more so when she started to unbutton her dress. Keela brushed her long hair back and relaxed on the bed. "Well, Redbeard, how about some love on the high seas?"

"Don't mind if I do," answered Redbeard.

Keela stood up, but before she could take off her dress, Redbeard had tugged it free from her shoulders. She had initiated the process, but he was taking control. Relaxing onto the bed again, she watched as he rose above her and stared deep into her eyes.

Hovering above her, Redbeard whispered, "I love you" into Keela's ear. Then, he lowered his head to hers, burying her in a gentle kiss that seemed to last forever. His lips were gentle, and they surrounded her mouth, bringing tingling all the way to the end of her toes. As Keela moaned in the back of her throat, Redbeard pulled his lips away slowly, only to replace them on her neck, tracing the curve of her collarbone down to the top of her smooth breast. Going lower—so much lower—he crossed her belly with his lips like he was sailing across the ocean.

All sense of direction disappeared for Keela as Redbeard lowered his head and started to make sweeping moves with his tongue, pleasing her in a way she'd never experienced. She didn't expect the kind of force that hit her when he started. She had been so built up by the tender kisses that she had reached a shimmering state of arousal. As Redbeard plowed forward, she soared higher until everything was locked inside the sensation. Even though her eyes were closed, Keela saw stars flashing all around her, and she opened her eyes to find Redbeard's head still between her legs.

Keela cried out in ecstasy until she ran out of breath and gasped for air. "It's too much!" she cried. "Just take me!" Redbeard was on top of her in an instant, entering her body with massive force. She allowed him to enter, relishing the experience as her body, long aching for the presence of a man, was filled and satisfied.

Although Keela was already satisfied, Redbeard was just getting started. As the thrusts began, one after another, she slowly began to reach another peak, pushing herself harder until she erupted with a deep shiver and surrendered herself to his body. Her voice sounded strange to her as she was so lost in the moment. A blissful paradise wrapped around her as Redbeard's embrace folded around her and filled her senses.

Keela exploded again, feeling nothing but happiness and bliss. She closed her eyes and witnessed many beautiful colors, and she only left that beautiful paradise when the thrusts reached fever strength. Then, Redbeard slowed down, satisfied, and she felt like a new life was awakening. She was catapulted out of her paradise and into the arms of her lover.

Keela rested in Redbeard's arms, silent, still, and only blinking. Redbeard remained silent and still as well. But he removed himself from Keela, moved to the side, and collapsed down on the bed beside her, folding his hand in front of him in prayer. "Thank Allah that a truly sublime woman like you has entered my life," he said. "You are the spirit of freedom." His hands remained in grateful prayer, and Keela shared in the gratitude, thankful for *his* presence as well. She rested her head on his shoulder, and the waves gently rocked her to blissful dreams that seemed to have no end.

The Radoom traveled along the African Coast, too far from shore to be noticed by enemy vessels but close enough to see the endless sands of the coastline, with glittering white cliffs on the horizon. Passing through the narrow straits unharmed, they swung around the heel of Morocco and sailed out toward the Canary Islands. In all, Keela counted eight days before the bright green Canary Islands began to rise into view above the horizon.

Chapter 31

JOHN DEAS WOKE UP TO a bright sunny morning on his island paradise. He looked out the window onto his private lawn, where his family was enjoying the tropical sunshine. Whenever he enjoyed this peaceful oasis, he would think about the chaotic slave-capturing missions he had been on. That morning, he decided not to engage in any more slave captures ever again because he would have to leave the comforts of his castle behind him.

Deas looked down at his guards at their posts, who were watching carefully for any intruding enemies. Then, he went to his restroom, where a mirror had been hung over his washbasin as a stolen prize from one of the many villages he had pillaged. He had gone through so many towns that he couldn't remember the name of the place where he'd salvaged this large round mirror.

The mirror reflected Deas's face without bias. He couldn't avoid looking at the deep scar between his eyeball and his temple, left there by a rebel from a village that had put up quite a fight. One of his men had died there during the fight, and Deas had almost perished too. If his friends hadn't slaughtered the rebel as he hovered over Deas, and had they not dragged Deas to safety, he would have been dead. The rebel had the knife right against his cheek, trying to cut him all the way to the lip. Weeks from civilization, a torn cheek would have doomed Deas.

Another long scar appeared along Deas's temple, from another encounter in which he had almost been slaughtered. He had been in the slave business his entire life, and when he was young, one of his father's slaves had broken free and tried to use John as a pawn. John's father had coldly pointed his crossbow and released an arrow without even trembling. It went right into its target, missing young John by inches and saving his life. It didn't miss his temple, though. The long streak from the arrow notch reminded John how close the arrow had come. He could still remember the drops of blood making his shoulder itch.

John Deas learned the value of cold-heartedness from his father, as well as the value of selling slaves. As he brought his father's image to mind, he could almost see his figure hovering behind him in the mirror. With a complete lack of remorse, John put his hand over his chest with pride and sent kind prayers to wherever his father rested, high above, watching over him.

Deas sighed, relaxed, and descended to his kitchen, where Margaret sat at a table. Caitlin was cooking breakfast, and he could smell the eggs frying in rich oil. The guard outside the kitchen window took surveys of the lawn but also took time to sniff the air and watch Caitlin through the window. Deas figured everything must be fine if the guard had time to watch his blossoming daughter instead of his surroundings.

Margaret had taught the young girl to be a good cook over the years, and now, Caitlin cooked for them instead of Margaret. Deas was proud of this beautiful place he had created, and he was smiling as breakfast was put on the table. He looked at the guard posted by the kitchen window as his plate was being put down in front of him. The guard was provided with his own salary and food, so Deas resolved not to let the guard have one table scrap.

Turning back to the table to bow his head and say grace, John felt nothing but gratitude during his prayers, even adding the thick-necked window guard to his prayers. When he lifted his head, he looked back at the window and noticed that the guard was gone. In that brief moment, his assumption that he was safe crumbled. A deep tingling in his kidneys prepared him to fight, and his hand reached for his hip holster.

By the time Deas's pistol was out of its holster, the castle's front door caught fire. He aimed at the front door, prepared to stop anyone who came through it. As soon as the ropes holding the door to the stones had burned through, the door fell flat against the floor, still burning. Men dressed like pirates advanced into the room.

Caitlin and Margaret backed away from the table and from each other. John stayed seated, and he fired his pistol at the first two pirates. The ball missed one of the men, but the side blow to the temple of the other pirate was enough to bring him down.

Two more pirates entered the room while Deas reloaded his pistol. He tried to pack the gunpowder as they advanced to the table. One of the pirates tripped over his fallen comrade but managed to hop until he caught his footing. As he danced across the floor, he lost his grip on his sword, and it clattered to the table.

Margaret had a dagger in her hands by the time the pirates approached, and John Deas noticed that she'd been practicing. The first dagger strike got one pirate on the inner thigh, where he bled fast enough to bring him down to his knees in seconds. The second strike was more severe, leaving the dagger jammed into the pirate's crotch. Each tug at the dagger from Margaret as she tried to extract it brought another high-pitched scream from the emasculated pirate. Each tug was followed by another one until the dagger pulled free, and by then, the pirate had perished.

One of John Deas's personal guards entered the castle through the front door, but an arrow was lodged in his back, and blood ran down his shirt. The guard managed to cut the left arm of the other pirate in the room quite badly, but the pirate turned around and punched hard enough to knock a regular man out. The guard's thick neck muscles protected him, and his massive shoulders proved to be more than a match for the smaller pirate.

The guard kept the pirate on the ground with one knee and yanked the pirate's arm clean out of its socket, along with part of a lung. The blood sprayed out, and shreds of white lung tissue came along with it, bringing a swifter death than John could have imagined. The shock in the pirate's eyes was only there for a moment, making him look unprepared for the end—naïve to the point of almost being comical.

John laughed out loud at the pirate's demise. But then, he saw the end of a sword in his peripheral vision and stopped laughing as he turned his head just in time to see a new pirate bring the sword down flat against his hands. The attack disarmed John, knocking his pistol out of his hand but sparing him the use of the hand. "You'll regret that!" he shouted.

While the other pirate's sword lay forgotten on the table, the guard had been approached by three more pirates. They were too preoccupied with the guard to notice the extra sword. The guard grabbed it from the table and brought it up against an attacker's throat, slicing it open. Then, he brought down another enemy. But soon, more had arrived, and they grabbed Caitlin and took her out the back of the castle, out of sight.

"Where do you think you're taking my daughter?!" Margaret screamed as the pirates vanished.

"Actually, that's *my* daughter!" Keela shouted from behind Margaret as she entered the kitchen. All of Margaret's bravado vanished as she whirled around to face the foe behind her.

John Deas turned in horror at the sound of Keela's voice. "You!" he shouted.

"*My* daughter. Isn't that right, John Deas? So, we meet again."

"John, what is she talking about?" Margaret asked. She was now crying. "How did her mother find us?"

As the white stucco began to peel from the flames, John struggled across the room, fighting pirates off left and right, until he got to his wife. "Margaret!" he shouted. "Get to the basement! Hurry!" As Margaret started to run downstairs, the pirates surrounded John, and soon, his sword strikes could not come fast enough to hold them back.

John Deas heard Keela yell, "Go get her already!"

The dining room was too full of pirates and guards for John to see Keela anymore. But as the pirates cleared out, running down the stairwell, he could once again see the woman he had sold into slavery. He now realized that the stories of her becoming a pirate were true!

Chapter 32

KEELA CONTINUED TO FIGHT THE guards at the front of the castle, striking down one at a time with her blade. Two fingers severed from a guard flew through the air as she unleashed her anger. Only three guards now blocked her from getting to John Deas. Her next strike removed three more fingers, but the guard tossed his sword to his other hand and kept swinging. Keela could see Deas in the room, but she couldn't confront him yet. To see her target in the room drove her mad with rage. She began swinging her sword even harder, with the long blade soaring through the air with enough force to decapitate the fingerless guard.

The last protector came to confront Keela, standing right before her. Keela dropped her sword, pulled both blunderbusses out of her belt at the same time, and pointed the barrels directly at the guard's eyes. He had no time to react to the fluid movement. Refusing to hesitate, Keela plunged the triggers of both blunderbusses, and two huge balls of lead blasted out of the guns.

The guard's eyes crossed for a split second before the huge balls shot through his head and burrowed a channel through each eye socket. White eyeball plasma squirted past the rocketing lead balls and landed wetly on the floor. The balls continued through the guard's skull unabated, and as they rocketed out the back of his skull, Keela could see through his head to the dining room behind him. She relished the look of horror on Deas's face.

No one else stood between Keela and John Deas. As Deas struggled, Keela advanced toward him. He backed up, but the hard wall of the castle was soon at his back. Keela pointed her blade at his throat, but instead of tickling it, she continued to edge the blade forward, driving the tip into the skin. A bead of red blood emerged from the cut and swelled against the blade. John's jugular vein throbbed just on the other side of the tip. The longer Keela held him against the wall, the faster his jugular throbbed.

"Remember when you killed my husband?" Keela asked at a slow pace. "Was he just another casualty to you? I *know* you remember raping me. Do you care about your wife?" Faster and faster, swelling and receding against her blade, Keela could feel the pressure of Deas's pulse pushing the sword back and forth. Relishing the feeling of his pulse in her hands, she waited there, staring into his eyes, letting an exultant smile play across her lips.

Against her will, Margaret was dragged up the stairs by the combined force of two pirates holding her arms. "Rip her clothes off!" Keela yelled to the pirates. Neither pirate disobeyed her for even a second.

Keela leaned in front of John Deas, tormenting him. The blade sunk deeper into his vein as she leaned forward and pulled back. Only the edge of the vein was nicked; the cut was not deep enough to fully penetrate his jugular. He gulped for air, holding his hand against his wounded neck.

Two of the other pirates came over to Keela, leering at John Deas. "What do you want us to do with him?" one of them asked. "Pull his guts out an inch at a time over the fire?"

Keela shook her head. "I've been waiting for this for seven years, so he's not through suffering yet. I want you to make sure he doesn't move a muscle. And get two more of your friends. I want them to hold his legs while you hold his arms. You can't trust this one for a second."

"We'll be right back," said one of her pirates. Keela was alone with John for a few moments. "It would be a good idea for you to lie down," she said. When John scooted forward and rested his head on the floor, she had confirmation that he was listening to her.

When four pirates had reassembled in the room, two of them came over and kneeled on the floor, pressing their knees into John's thighs so he was completely pinned. The other two pirates held his hands to the floor, spread-eagle, so that he couldn't use his arms either. Once John was securely pinned, Keela finally withdrew the blade from his neck, enjoying the hot rush of blood that trickled down his neck. She knew she had failed to tear his jugular vein, but the skin itself bled with plenty of vigor.

"Do you love your wife as much as I loved my husband?" Keela asked John. "As much as I love my child?" She backed away from him, but he never took his eyes off her. Keela turned to the pirates again. "You get to hurt Mrs. Deas like he hurt me!" she said to the pirates. Then, she turned to John. "And you get to watch!"

Margaret began to cry as she was quickly exposed, with the fabric of her dress ripping in sections and falling to the floor. Keela walked over to her, smiling from ear to ear. "Your husband's a murderer." She watched Margaret for any signs of acknowledgment, but Margaret refused to shudder or flinch. "You already knew that, though." Margaret's jaw began to shudder, but she said nothing. "Now, you have to pay for his crimes. Have your fun, boys!"

Keela's hostage started to cry. "John!" Margaret sobbed. "Please, no! Do something!"

Keela was not surprised by Margaret's outburst, but John appeared to be surprised by it. His eyes opened wide, and, despite his lack of negotiating position, he shouted, "Leave her alone, you sard! Don't you touch her!"

Keela told the pirates to keep going as she continued to look at John. She didn't want to look at Margaret because she felt some guilt creeping in. John had committed this horrible act against Keela, but now, she wanted to do the same thing to Margaret. She was conflicted, but she suddenly felt trapped without a choice.

In a moment of weakness, Keela felt intense compassion for the cruel man in front of her. "Do you love her?" she asked. "Yes, I can see that you do," she said, answering her own question.

Tears sprang to John's eyes, and his neck grew tighter. He struggled as hard as he could, finally finding the strength to bring his boot down on a pirate's hand. The pirate reached up to punish him, but John used the moment to kick the pirate severely. And even though John took some punches from the other pirates holding him, they had to release their grasp to throw the punches, allowing him to find enough strength to wrench his arms free.

John struggled so hard that he broke free of all four pirates and attacked Keela. She wasn't expecting that level of ferocious anger, and she wasn't expecting the pirates to be defeated. All four pirates got to their feet and began to chase John, but they all got up at different times, and he was still moving. Keela took two steps backward to give the pirates more time to catch him.

Wielding her sword, Keela aimed for John's fingers. She wanted to aim for his neck, but she also wanted him to keep suffering. So, she focused on shortening his fingers. She swung her sword as he lunged forward. Three of his fingernails went rattling to the floor, falling from his fingertips, which began to drip blood at once. He screamed in intense pain, clutching his hand.

While John was shouting, the pirates were able to catch up to him. He fought like a wild animal. And Keela caught her breath as the pirates worked at subduing him. She paced back and forth, upset that the pirates were struggling. "You've got to make him pay for that!" she shouted.

To get even with John, the pirate holding his damaged hand pressed the raw nail beds against the rough mortar holding the stones of a wall in place. John moaned in agony as his torn and tender cuticles started bleeding small tendrils of red down the mortar. "Chain him to the chair so he won't keep getting away!" Keela instructed.

Once John was chained, Keela approached, and he closed his eyes. "Look at me, you coward!" Keela shouted. John opened his eyes for a few seconds, and Keela grabbed his jaw with one hand, yanking so hard that she heard and witnessed his jawbone pop out of place. His eyes snapped shut again, and she couldn't stand the insult. "Look at me! Are you truly scared of me? That's one hell of a compliment, Mr. Deas!"

Keela let go of John's jaw, grasped his rough and tangled hair, and yanked it. John grunted in pain as his matted hair was tugged, tearing some free from his scalp. But he refused to look at Keela. She grunted in pleasure. "I'm enjoying this, aren't you, John?" John's eyelids were still squeezed shut, but his face muscles moved. "You don't want the eye-hooks, do you? That's what you did to the slaves, to make them watch, isn't it?"

John struggled, but the pirates had little trouble getting the clamps onto his eyelids. The alligator clamps yanked his eyelids open, and blood ran down the edges of his eyes. He seemed to pass out, with his head slumped forward.

"Oh, you're not done yet," Keela informed him as she threw a bucket of cold water on him. He came to his senses, sobbing. Blood still dripped from the cuts on his eyes. His wife was tied to another chair, and Keela wondered if she was unconscious. A rag had been wrapped around Margaret's mouth. Every time the pirates whipped her, she jerked from head to toe, bouncing against the rope restraints, and Keela figured she couldn't do that unless she were awake.

Keela stuck a red-hot pin under the edge of Margaret's fingernail. Margaret began to shriek in pain, and her gag did little to muffle the sound. "You let this woman take care of my child?" Keela sneered at John. "It's your turn now, John Deas. Bring in my bag," she instructed the pirates.

Keela waited while a pirate ran the errand. When John opened his eyes, Keela could see the fear in them. He had been wide awake the entire time.

When the torture bag was presented to Keela, she opened it, bringing out a small mold, along with a vial of lead. She poured a chunk of lead into the mold and hung it over the fireplace so the lead would start melting into the mold's chamber. While she waited, Keela noticed that the pirate who had handed her the bag was still gazing at her. "Where is Caitlin?" she asked. "Did something happen?"

"Nothing of the kind, Keela the Great. Your daughter is safe on our ship."

"Thank goodness," Keela answered. "I don't want her to see this part."

Keela examined the lead in the fire, but it hadn't started boiling yet.

She added more wood to the fire, making sure that the flames burned hotter so that the lead could be turned to liquid and used against John. "I've been wanting to have a conversation with you for a while now, Mr. Deas," Keela said as she waited.

Keela sat down in one of John's soft, comfortable chairs and crossed her legs, relaxing. "You know what I got really good at, John? Can you even guess what you taught me—what you put in my soul? I'm a long way from that Irish housewife you abandoned. I'm not that terrified woman anymore—that petrified woman who you raped mercilessly. And if that wasn't bad enough, you made my daughter watch!"

"Her name is still Caitlin," interrupted John, furious. "I'm not a savage!"

"Oh yes, you are," Keela replied. "And then, you gave my beautiful daughter to this tramp! Let me start with your wife first!" Keela peered into the mold on the fire. "Nope, not bubbling enough yet. Soon, I'll teach you what hot lead feels like. But first, I want you to know that the only thing that kept me going all those dark years as a slave was waiting for this day. I'm going to enjoy every minute of this. Okay, it looks hot enough now!"

Keela put the chalice of bubbling lead onto a hook at the end of a chain, and revelation sprung to John's eyes as his entire face grew animated and peeled back in sheer terror. He began struggling harder, trying to get free of his chair while also trying to yell. But he found himself muzzled with a stinking leather strap. He couldn't even cry out in protest as Keela began to spin the chalice, and precise droplets of lead hit his wife's nipples. Keela made sure that the next drop ran down Margaret's belly into her navel, leaving a streak of red behind and gaining a rising scream from Margaret as the hot lead rested in her navel.

As the droplets of lead flattened against Margaret's skin, red weals began to grow around them in small rings. Her skin sizzled and steamed from the boiling hot lead. The stench of burning flesh filled the air, and some of the pirates lost control of their stomachs, heaving in the stinking room.

As Margaret shrieked, Keela covered her own ears because it was making her eardrums vibrate. But when Margaret eventually passed out, Keela missed the sound. So, she poured a bucket of cold water against Margaret's naked body, waking her up. As Margaret looked back and forth, looking delirious, Keela laughed in a dull monotone.

"You weren't supposed to pass out that fast," Keela said, laughing out loud. "We're going to take a break before the next round. I don't want you to miss out on all the excitement." As she spoke, Keela pulled breast rippers out of the torture bag. Margaret started to wail, and then she started to cough and spit up blood. "You held my daughter in captivity, Margaret," Keela continued. "That's not ever going to be all right. You don't deserve anything less than this!"

"I thought you were going to take a break," wailed Margaret.

"Well, I can't let the lead cool off, can I?" Keela pushed the sharp tongs in past Margaret's skin until they had a good hold of the tissues, and then, she started to pull the tongs apart from each other. "It's just like carving a turkey," Keela said calmly. "The only difference is that *you're* the main dish."

As the flesh pulled away from Margaret's breasts, they became misshapen and tore apart, gushing blood as strips of tissue were peeled away. One of the pirates wrapped the fresh wounds as Margaret passed out. "Clean her up," Keela ordered. "Make sure she's not dying, and get some slave clothes on her," she said.

Margaret's unconscious body was dragged into the corner by two pirates. John Deas clung to consciousness, but spittle and blood foamed out of his mouth, and his eyelids were still peeled back by the hooks. "You're going to know every ounce of my pain," Keela told him. "This is for taking my husband from me forever and for all the years that you kept my daughter away from me. You're going to hurt *so* bad."

John screamed as balls of molten lead kept hitting him in one eyeball and then the other. Soon, all he saw was white-hot pain and then a slowly encroaching darkness. As he screamed out loud, the light continued to fade slowly away.

"You'll never see another sunset! You'll never see your wife again! You'll never see another living thing!" Keela relished John's pain as she spoke each word. As John kept screaming, he felt hot tongs rip into his tongue. Then, he could no longer scream because his tongue was missing altogether, having been ripped away with three excruciating yanks. "You'll never bark another order for as long as your miserable life continues!" Keela finished.

Unable to see or speak, John Deas was a ruined man. As he sat there in the interminable darkness, he felt white-hot pain on his member as a red-hot poker burned into it. As the layers of fat and sponge inside his penis boiled away, the blade ripped it clean away from his body. He felt another wave of agony as Keela pressed a hot blade against the wound, cauterizing it. John realized in horror that she was going to let him live, and his agony would continue.

"You'll never be able to rape another helpless woman again!" Keela shouted. She thought she would be satisfied once she had her revenge. She thought the slowly boiling rage inside of her would finally subside. But she just felt emptier than she ever had before. As she looked at the ruined man before her, she realized that she had done something important. She had rescued her daughter and avenged her husband's murder. But still, it wasn't enough.

Keela pulled both pistols from her holsters. Margaret started whimpering, so Keela knew she was awake. Keela paced slowly back and forth, thinking about her plan. Somehow, all she could imagine for these two was death. She couldn't sit with the idea of letting them live. But the dilemma she faced was knowing that John and Margaret would stop suffering if she killed them.

After loading each blunderbuss, Keela stepped behind Margaret. Leaving the barrel on Margaret's skull so there was no chance of missing, Keela pulled the trigger. After Keela's rush had started to fade, she pulled the barrel off as the congealing blood was beginning to make an adhesive mess of her pistol.

Choosing her second weapon and her left hand since her right hand was still tingling and sore from the first detonation, Keela walked in front of John Deas. He was now blind, so Keela put the barrel to his forehead so he could feel it. His last word was a deep groan. But with half of his brain torn away, the groan subsided within three seconds of Keela's blunderbuss tearing his skull open.

Keela's second rush lasted longer than the first. But when it eventually faded away, she went outside with the rest of the pirates. She immediately walked over to Redbeard.

"Well, Keela, did you enjoy it?" asked Redbeard.

"I enjoyed it immensely," she said. "Now, my daughter is safe and sound, and I feel much better. Let's go home."

"We *are* home, Keela. It's pirate law. This is all ours now," Redbeard informed her. "So, enjoy your new home!"

Keela looked around the magnificent battlements, realizing that a castle would be a logical place to have a fortress. "We should get a feast going," she suggested. "The pirates are the real heroes today. Tonight, we celebrate! In the meantime, we should do something about this mess. How many of you want to help clean it up?" To Keela's great surprise, more than a dozen of the battle-weary pirates were happy to help in that endeavor.

Chapter 33

KEELA AND REDBEARD WATCHED from the conquered castle as the bodies of their enemies were carted out to the coast and burned for everyone's pleasure. As for the fallen pirates, they would be taken back to Algiers to be given proper burials. Keela saw all the conquered men being piled up on top of a pyre, and before long, the pile of bodies burned into the sky. It was a beautiful sight to her. She wished deep in her heart that she could paint this pristine moment to trap it forever in time.

"Come, my love, there's a hot bath waiting for you," Redbeard informed Keela.

Keela turned her gaze to the proud arches of the castle and saw steam coming from some windows on the far side. She was desperate to see Caitlin, but she did not want Caitlin to see her as she was, covered in dirt and blood. "Oh, Redbeard!" Keela said. "We have a bathhouse!"

"Indeed, we do," he confirmed. "Let's go there now."

The bathhouse was magnificent. The tiles underneath the water were many colors, and the blue of the water made it all overwhelming. As Keela and Redbeard entered the warm water, she immediately became aroused. They began cleaning each other. Keela cleaned the blood from Redbeard's thick shins, and he cleaned her as well, rubbing the cleansing sponges between her breasts, then down to her thighs and between her legs.

As Keela became more aroused, she leaned back. Redbeard moved forward, taking the initiative. Not thrusting as hard as Keela expected, he ever so gently slid inside her, a fraction of an inch at a time. The new sensation was so exciting that Keela was beginning to collapse helplessly into strong shoulders before Redbeard was even all the way inside. By the time he completely entered her, she was moaning and writhing, desperate to feel every inch of him. Keela rose to ecstasy again and again, and Redbeard was relentless in touching every part of her.

After they were both satisfied, Redbeard wrapped Keela in fine robes, and himself as well. And after they were properly dressed as the new royalty of the islands, he placed a slender crown atop her head. "It's only a token position," he said. "We don't have a whole kingdom . . . yet."

"We have something more important," answered Keela, even though the idea of a kingdom sounded enticing. "We have each other."

Redbeard led her to the main room of the castle, which had once served as John Deas's personal dining room. Now, it served as a feasting-hall, loaded with steaming-hot fire-roasted boars and tables of fruit. Much of the food was gifted from the grateful native people of the Canary Islands. After years of enduring Deas's reign, they were so happy with Keela and Redbeard that they joined the festivities. By the time Keela reached the feasting-hall, many people were in the fine gardens outside it as well, enjoying the luxury previously afforded only to Deas and his closest allies.

From across the crowded hall, Keela saw Caitlin come running for her. Caitlin crossed the room too slow, it seemed. Time seemed to pause for Keela as everyone witnessed the jubilant fourteen-year-old girl race across the floor, stepping out of her way if they had to. Keela dropped to her knees, and she embraced her daughter after years apart, hugging her tightly. Tears ran down her face. To feel her daughter in her arms again brought down all the walls in her heart.

"Mommy, Mommy, I just knew you'd come back for me!" Caitlin cried out. "I knew you'd come someday."

"I would have sailed to the ends of the earth until I found you, my daughter. Nothing could have kept me from you." Keela was self-conscious about her choked sobs until she noticed tears in her daughter's eyes as well. She stood up and turned Caitlin's head from side to side. "Did they harm you in any way, my child?"

"No, Mother. They never whipped me like the other servants."

"Well, you're not a servant anymore," Keela said, her voice breaking. She quickly changed the subject, pushing a smile onto her lips to press the tears back into hiding. "Come take a look at your room."

Caitlin was led upstairs to the most beautiful view in the castle, emerging from massive bay windows that looked out over the sea and the green canyon that emptied into the ocean. Red, yellow, and green silk pillows graced a bed with a purple satin bedspread. "Only the best for my daughter," Keela said.

"Oh, Mommy, I love it so much," Caitlin gushed.

A wave of nostalgia washed over Keela as she held the green ribbon in her hand. She noticed the pain in Caitlin's eyes when she saw it. But soon, joy took hold, and Caitlin's lips peeled back into a smile that looked almost painful in size.

"Here's something of yours that was taken a long time ago," Keela said softly. She held out the ribbon, almost feeling regret that it was going back to Caitlin after so many years as the sole memento Keela held onto from her life in Ireland.

Caitlin's eyes beamed with excitement, and her hands reached instinctively for her precious ribbon. "That's my ribbon!" she cried out. "I heard that the painting in the Louvre has this ribbon, but I didn't believe it."

"What do you mean, the painting in the Louvre?" asked Keela, surprised.

"It's this fancy palace in Paris."

"I know what it is and where. I just didn't know one of my paintings was hanging there! I was even in France not too long ago." Keela tried to fathom that one of her paintings could really be hanging there.

Keela had no choice but to beam with pride as Caitlin turned around and Keela carefully wove the beautiful green ribbon, weatherbeaten but still shining, into her daughter's long hair. All her hesitation was gone as Caitlin beamed at her through the mirror, gazing at the ribbon that was once again in its proper place, woven through Caitlin's hair. "I'm going to rejoin the festivities," Keela informed her. "But you should enjoy your new room."

"After the long day I've had, the only thing I'm enjoying is the bed," said Caitlin, yawning. Then, she looked surprised, as if she'd just remembered something. "Oh, Mother, could you tuck me into bed? I've missed that so much."

Keela's heart soared in her chest as memories came rushing back to her mind, and she nodded, wordless. Caitlin crept into her new bed, exhaling deeply as she touched the satin sheet for the first time. She gently rested her head back onto the pillow. Keela carefully brought the sheets up to her daughter's neck, hands aching with sentiment as she tucked her daughter into bed for the first time in years.

A wonderful celebration was brewing in the feasting-hall by the time Keela reentered. The music was loud and raucous, composed of fiddles, drums, whistles, and any other instruments the pirates had acquired on raids. The strange harmonic tones were pleasing to Keela, and she reveled in the loud, dissonant music as the musicians played with half-tones. It sounded very different from Irish music because of the different instruments, but it provided the same vibrant mood and positive energy, and Keela enjoyed it immensely.

When Redbeard got on his knees in front of Keela, she was filled with so much joy that she couldn't even speak. "My dear, if you'll marry me, I'll be your faithful husband tomorrow. Will you accept this offer from a humble pirate?"

"Yes, of course, I accept," she answered at once. "But there's nothing humble about you."

"No, there isn't," Redbeard agreed. "We'll get married upon our return to Algiers!" he bellowed. "The celebration will last for days!" He picked Keela up in his arms and swung her around in the air, and Keela laughed with joy and dizziness before he put her down, drowning her in an extended kiss. Keela's forces—the free people and the pirates—all cheered mightily.

After the feasting had concluded, Keela went outside to look at the sunset. When Redbeard joined her, he noticed she was sad, and he ignored the marvelous sunset to speak to her. "What's wrong?" he inquired.

"I want you to know, before we're wedded, that I can't bear you any children. I know you would want them. That horrid creature I killed today, John Deas, ruined all that for me."

Redbeard held Keela close to his chest, and she relaxed into him with a sigh. "I'm a warrior and a pirate. I don't have time for things like babies. But if you'll marry me, I'll be a father to your daughter. That's all I'll ever need. I know that I'll be busy as a pirate, but I will always make time for her and you."

"Barbarossa, every day, I fall even more in love with you." Keela closed her eyes and prayed that she could hold him close until the day she died. The warm feeling in her chest told her that they would have good days together for years to come. But on the eve of 1601, trouble was brewing, and soon, a storm would come.

Chapter 34

THE DAY BEFORE Keela and Redbeard's wedding was to take place had been filled with drinking and merriment. But Keela had avoided the liquor as much as she could, hoping to avoid a hangover. She needed her sleep because the other women would wake her up before dawn.

A chorus of giggling from Keela's bridal party roused her from her slumber. It was still dark outside, and the women shrieked with laughter as they grabbed her hands and yanked to her feet. Keela hurried to her dressing area with the other women as the predawn darkness stretched a freezing hand across the desert. Shivering in her thin nightwear, she hurried, with her skin covered in ticklish gooseflesh, to the tent where she would be made ready for her wedding.

Inside the red tent, Keela's attention was immediately drawn to the spectacular dress already prepared for her. She had never seen the garment before, but the deep red swirls embroidered into the white linen with painstaking detail were brilliant to her and told her the garment was truly priceless. The red complemented her red hair perfectly, and the swirls reminded her of the ocean before her bridesmaids even told her that the swirls represented the ocean that brought her and Redbeard together.

Dressed in her wedding gown and her ceremonial turban, Keela was grabbed by the hands again and was led by laughing, dancing women. Back outside, the sun had emerged from the narrow horizon, and the hot sunlight beamed down on thousands of men and women already dancing and cheering. The marriage was a stunning affair to Keela. It wasn't the fact that she was a bride again that got to her; it was the festivities and grandeur that spoke of how well the Algerian pirates had done for themselves. She could see a lucrative, brilliant future, and she felt liberated from the troubles of her past.

Keela sat back, reclining on a wide sofa while her ladies sat beside her and giggled. She watched as everything was arranged. Women prepared baskets of flowers, and men prepared for the long procession by stretching and sword-fighting with each other, all in good humor and laughter. Keela would have been impressed by their antics had she not been fighting for years—fighting hard to free enslaved people. The thrill of the fight had worn off. She enjoyed the break from her mission, but she took the celebration in stride, conserving her strength for the battles yet to come.

The dancing stopped along with the crescendos from the pounding drums and was replaced with loud applause as Redbeard came out of his tent. His brilliant wedding attire was glistening and shining with gold in the morning sun. Keela didn't know what to do.

In Algeria, the crowds enjoyed shouting and ululating, often without any words involved. The sound was striking and soothing at the same time. The sound was striking for being unique, and it was soothing by providing something Keela remembered: it was the same shouts that many of the slaves she freed produced in celebration.

Redbeard paralyzed Keela with a single glimpse. He was a stunning Godhead in an equally striking shirt and fine pants. In her mind, he was close to divine, and she had no problem accepting the exquisite clothing he provided her. She was dressed in finery so magnificent that she had trouble looking at it. The gold shimmered with so much vigor that it made her eyes water, and she had some passing awareness of what she must look like to the crowd: a royal person, when once she was just a humble painter and fishmonger.

Keela and Redbeard looked at each other with a gaze that passed all understanding, and the crowd hushed as Redbeard approached her. He was not paralyzed like her, but he was unsteady in the knees, to her great pleasure. His sea legs were fine, but she could tell that his land legs were not quite so confident on this day.

Earlier, Redbeard had written down sacred poetry, and he now referred to his writing before he spoke. His words were deep and clear that they rang across the desert, and Keela knew that everyone could hear him because of the profound silence from the crowd. "As the ocean has brought us together," he read, "so it shall bring us good fortune in the future. These garments secure the ocean's blessing. Every spiral is a prayer that the ocean will bear us safely back home."

Keela didn't care that Redbeard needed to look at the words. The magnificent speech helped convince her that she had a good husband now. She allowed herself to be ushered into one of two beautiful chairs, both with strong arms and stable backs. She climbed into the elevated chair, and Redbeard sat down in the other chair.

"Let's get started," said Redbeard. "I want to get married!"

As all the people began to march out of the city, Keela realized that this was no small venture. Once the line was clear, the people underneath Keela and Redbeard lifted the chairs. She had never once been held aloft by others, and her hands dug into the arms of the chair. She realized she was high above the crowd, and she felt vertigo looking at the hands holding up the chairs. She left her eyes on the horizon, to enjoy the procession. Finally, her tension began to fade as she continued down the path unharmed and realized that the people beneath were strong enough to shoulder her chair for dozens of miles if they had to.

As the procession continued through the day, Keela understood it would take a while, and she realized that her assessment of the men's strength was not far off. Beyond the desert, she noticed the procession walking toward a canyon. It was so unexpected to her, facing this open desert, to find a canyon and running rivers there. But a river was, after all, their destination.

Keela enjoyed the breathtaking scenery and the handsome, well-dressed man beside her. Redbeard was dressed so royally that he almost seemed more like a king to her than a pirate in his magnificent robes. But his spectacle of color was outmatched by the vibrant flowers that grew along the river. And rapids sent mist floating through the air, watering vines that clung to the fragile rocks of the canyon walls.

The wedding venue was outdoors, in the deepest part of the canyon, by a confluence of more than ten waterfalls. Keela wanted to count them all, but she realized that each distinct river separated several times. Then, she realized that dozens of waterfalls existed here. It was so breathtaking that she couldn't concentrate on the wedding. Myriad cascades of water filled the air by the waterfalls with hundreds of rainbows. And the group of stones that made up the face of the waterfalls balanced precariously in places, creating a second spectacle among the rainbows. Keela could see the stones rocking back and forth beneath the cascades, and it appeared as though the rocks were laughing.

"This is where we get married," Keela said. The holy man who was to wed them nodded. It was a moment she'd been waiting for, but now that it was here, she didn't want it to end. The waterfalls and the rainbows shimmered before her. She felt as if the world was magical after all, and she felt inferior to the endless rainbows and the swirling mist.

"It is time," said the holy man. "Barbarossa, please give Keela your vows. And Keela, return them with promises of your own. You may begin." The priest stepped back.

Keela had not expected so much respect from a holy man. They were both pirates, after all. Caitlin stood by her side, bearing a basket of red flowers. After seven years of enslavement away from her daughter, Keela was overjoyed to have her daughter there as her maid of honor.

Redbeard stood before Keela, and two people marked down records of his words. "I, Barbarossa, promise you these things as my vows of marriage. I am not just a body for you. You have traveled further into me, with me, beyond yourself, and to me. Now, you will cross even more oceans, and I'll never leave your side. I'll be your husband until the day I die, and I'll protect you with my dying breath."

Keela could not hide a tear as it ran down her cheek. Her own vows were just as elegant. As she spoke them, she felt outshone by the powerful Redbeard, but the twinkling in his eyes told her that promises were very meaningful to her new husband. She had already written the words in her own hand, but when she spoke them, she noticed the bobbing heads and quick fingers jotting down what she said.

"Wherever I am, wherever you are, we'll now go places together.

Together, we'll break the bonds of slavery. We'll set people free and support them until they want for nothing and are completely satisfied. We will stir them with our love so they can arise and be free. And I'll fight by your side until the last moments of my life, for I want to spend my life by your side, fighting for freedom, until the slave trade is gone from Africa."

The holy man cleared his throat. "You two are now united, and let no man or woman ever tear you asunder!"

Barbarossa gave Keela a passionate kiss, signaling the end of the ceremony and the beginning of the celebration. The butchers took their cue from him and turned to the wedding cattle. The cows were innocent, and they were ignorant of their doom until the sharpened knives began to slice their throats, and they bellowed in pain and surprise. The shocked cattle boomed loud enough for Keela to hear over the waterfalls and cheers as the cattle agonized in their death-throes. She realized the wedding feast was being prepared, and she noticed the animals nearby, hanging upside down and dying. Even before the cows stopped twitching, the fresh slaughter was quickly butchered, placed onto frying surfaces above a fire, and cooked into perfect wedding food.

By the time the food was brought to the tables, the wedding attendees were already dancing by the hundreds. The drummers immediately gathered up a wild rhythm, and the music pounded through the canyon, joined with shrill flutes and the clanging and chattering of noisemakers handed around the wedding party. The cacophony surrounded the party and swept it up in a golden web of light that stretched through the canyon and made the steep walls shimmer. Everything seemed magical, and Keela wanted this moment to last forever.

Caitlin was able to spend plenty of time hanging out with the other teenagers. No longer forced to cook and clean all the time, she celebrated her freedom by spending time with the Algerian children. She played with the toys handed out at the wedding and was having a good time. For Keela, seeing Caitlin playing freely was the greatest joy of all—one which she kept close to her heart and promised to remember.

Three ambassadors—young men in fine gilded robes—approached the newly married couple. Keela wasn't surprised when she noticed

Caitlin eyeing some of the young men. As one of the men introduced himself, his soft voice spoke of a kind spirit, and Caitlin desired to meet him. She walked over to stand by Keela and held her hand. Keela smiled and did not seem to mind the intrusion. Then, she turned her attention to the young man.

"I am Prince Ilias of Morocco, and this is Princess Imane. We have brought many presents for you. My father wishes to speak to you tonight, about battle plans."

Princess Imane spoke up. "Is this the right time to talk about this?"

Redbeard said, "Why trouble our guests? We should talk about this tomorrow! This is no time or place to discuss battle plans. This is a wedding! Enjoy the celebration, and tomorrow, we shall have plenty of time to discuss these matters once we're back in Algiers."

The princess was about to lead the prince away, but Caitlin caught his attention with a smile. Prince Ilias looked at Imane questioningly, but his older sister's passing gesture gave him leave. Caitlin paused, grabbing her mother's hand in a way that made it clear Caitlin felt insecure. Keela slowly and gently uncurled Caitlin's fingers. "It's time for celebration," she said. "If you want to make new friends, that's all right. You have my blessing."

Spurred on by her mother, Caitlin squared her shoulders and marched across the grass, eager to show her best manners. "My name is Caitlin. It's nice to meet you."

"My name is Prince Ilias, and it's nice to meet you, too," the young man replied. "We have much to discuss." And with that, Caitlin and Ilias started walking off.

Keela turned back to the wedding party to find Redbeard enjoying the celebration. "Well? Aren't you going to dance with your husband on your wedding night?" he called out.

Keela laughed and eagerly ran across the grass to Redbeard, who picked her up in his arms. As the wedding dances began, the rest of the day became a blur of rainbows to Keela. When sleep overtook her, wild dreams and festivities continued in her mind until the morning sun woke her, and she realized she had to go back to Algiers.

Although Keela and Redbeard were carried back to town in the chair ritual, the procession was much slower this time because the revelers were still drunk from the night before. The ones who carried Keela seemed sober enough, and that was all that mattered to her. Long hours passed before the caravan returned to town, and by then, Keela was already deep in thought, planning her next adventures.

Chapter 35

THE NEXT DAY, Redbeard spoke with the Moroccan advisors. Poring over a map of the Caribbean, the oldest man there spoke slowly and firmly, making sure each world was clearly heard. Although the men spoke of war, their tone was reverent and thoughtful, as if they were discussing Allah instead of the freedom of thousands of slaves.

"These three islands right here are Dead Chest Island, Peter's Island, and Scrub Island," the older Moroccan man informed Redbeard. "They have all been used since the dawn of the slave trade, and all three of them are heavily defended. These slaves are starving, dying of abscesses, and suffering greatly. We must go there and get our people back. So many Moroccans have already died in these slave pens."

"We will go there as soon as we're prepared," said Redbeard.

Princess Imane stepped to the table, lending her voice to the discussion. "My father, the king, desperately needs your help, Barbarossa. Many of our people are still imprisoned on Peter's Island, but some Moroccans could also be hidden on Scrub Island. If you can free our people, you'll be greatly rewarded. We have ships, weapons, swords, and anything else you might need for this mission."

"This is going to get serious," said Redbeard. "Princess Imane, if you're faint of heart . . ." he began. But he stopped in response to a sharp look from Imane. The other advisors backed away a step.

"Never," said Imane, standing up to her full height. "I've seen far too much to turn back now."

Redbeard nodded once and turned back to the map, scowling as he studied the tiny islands dotting the blue ocean surrounding them. Working on limited data, the cartographers had only managed to sketch out the basic shapes of the islands and landmarks. "So, what's the situation?" Redbeard asked.

"Scrub Island and Dead Chest Island are the worst ones," the lead Moroccan advisor pointed out.

Captain Redbeard's first mate said, "On Scrub Island, I need five ships. There are five different points I need to dominate."

Keela spoke up. "Akua will go with you. And I'll take Peter's Island."

Daniel spoke up as well. "I'm going after Dead Chest Island. Who's with me?" Several of Redbeard's captains raised their hands.

Princess Imane put a list on the table. "These are the sixty Moroccans we know to be imprisoned there. Bring them back to Morocco so they can enjoy the rest of their lives. The rest of them, you can set free or recruit to your cause. But our people need to come home. They've been gone far too long."

"I agree with you," said Keela. "This has gone on for far too long. It's about time we started fighting back. You'll get your people back, I promise."

Redbeard cleared his throat. "I also promise your people shall be free. If anybody knows more about these islands, please tell me now."

The emotion of the moment had faded, but the discussion continued. "Scrub Island is the smallest island, but it's well-defended," the lead Moroccan advisor continued.

Keela focused on her plans. The discussion lasted well into the afternoon, but when it was finished, both parties were committed to the battle. Keela headed to her dressing room, full of nerves and excitement.

Keela prepared in her chambers, where Caitlin stayed as well. It was impossible for the two to avoid speaking, but Keela tried to be brief. "Caitlin, you should go with Princess Imane back to Morocco. She'll be able to protect you with her advisors. And I see you've become quick friends with Prince Ilias. You'll be able to spend time with him, too. But stay in Fez, where you're protected. I need you to stay safe while I'm on this rescue mission. It could take a long time for me to come home, but I need you to be patient."

"I promise, Mother," was her answer. But Keela could sense the pain Caitlin was feeling as her mother had to leave once again.

Keela went out to the docks and immediately started handing out swords to her pirates, ensuring that everybody on board her ship was armed. The armory was well stocked with swords to hand out, and the Moroccan sailors had been generous with their ships, providing ten large boats from which swords and food had already been unloaded. The boats now hung high in the water, with their decks protruding above the waves. Once the pirates had filled the ships, they would depart, ready to hide several miles from the islands to provide reinforcements.

One of the Moroccan sailors came up to Redbeard. "Our people have these amazing poison darts," the sailor informed him.

"Tell me more," said Redbeard, his eyes glinting with good humor. Keela paid attention, too. She was eager to learn more about her new arsenal.

"The blowguns are silent," the sailor continued. "You just blow into them real hard. Their target never hears a thing. It works so fast that the enemy is down on the ground in just a few dozen seconds. They don't even have time to fight back because when you can't breathe, you can't strike out. They stop breathing, and they can't even cry out."

Keela thought the plan was excellent, but Redbeard was leading the conversation. "How many do you have?"

"Only a hundred arrows poisoned so far, but they are extremely venomous. And we have many more arrows and much more poison on hand. There's also venomous frogs and spiders on the islands, which we can collect for you." Keela liked the idea of venomous insects.

"Bring these weapons on board, and as many darts as you can haul, but don't let them out of your sight. In the wrong hands, who knows what could happen to them." As he spoke, Redbeard motioned to *The Radoom*, his flagship.

Redbeard's pirates enjoyed a life of luxury in return for their hard work. They were well paid for their efforts from the steadily growing stockpile of treasure that Keela and Redbeard now shared. Keela's pirates also enjoyed good fortune, and during their first voyage to the Canary Islands with Barbarossa's pirates, they learned the finer skills of piracy from Redbeard's experienced troops.

Leaving on this dangerous mission, Keela felt confident in the strength of her pirates. Her forces met Redbeard's on the decks of *The Radoom*, and Keela could not tell their forces from each other. They were one cohesive group of sailors, all primed with excellent fighting skills and a deep passion for ending slavery that united them behind a common front.

As the boats filled with pirates, the lines of red paint used to keep the barnacles at bay began to sink down to the lapping waves. A young man with two red flags would spring to action when the red line had begun to sink into the waves. Then, he would swing his arms, and the wrench for the anchor chain would be pulled up by the engineer, the moorings would be untied from the dock, and each great ship would depart.

One by one, the great armada of ships departed the harbor in Algiers and sailed into the deep Mediterranean on their way to the other side of the world. They sailed through the Bosporus on a holy day. They knew that no slave riggers would dare to run the narrow waters on a holy day, profits or no profits. Nothing but the open Atlantic stood between them and the islands.

"Let's retire to our quarters, Keela the Great," Redbeard insisted. "I've got desires to fulfill."

"But we've only been married two days!" Keela responded.

"Too long for me!"

Keela knew that Redbeard had arranged for them to sleep together during the voyage. But she didn't realize it would be in the ship's best quarters. A great bed sat in the chamber, surrounded by books, maps, flasks of rum, and anything else Redbeard found particularly tantalizing. Redbeard smiled deviously, and it made Keela's heart race with excitement. She quickly took off her dress, and Redbeard responded by undressing as well. As she pulled him toward her, Keela was surprised when she landed on the bed, but he stayed upright. She was even more surprised when he leaned over and started kissing her toes.

Redbeard's kisses to the toes were not normal kisses. They were strong, sucking embraces with little nibbles that made shivers run all the way up Keela's leg. Then, he started to work on the other foot, and soon, both of her legs were tingling. While she began to moan with excitement, Redbeard began to inch his way up her shin with his lips, tracing the line of her shin all the way up to her knee.

Keela was starting to writhe with pleasure, but she realized Redbeard wasn't done torturing her with pleasure yet. His mouth ran up the inside of her thigh, and the sensitive skin there picked up every rustle of his beard and every tickle of his teeth until Keela felt herself going wild. But as he reached where she most desired to be kissed, he kept moving up to her belly, which she discovered was sensitive as she started gulping for air, sucking in her belly in excited reactions.

It was when Redbeard made his way to her chest that Keela really began to cry out with pleasure, enjoying the nibbling as his teeth tortured her hard nipples. Only then did Redbeard start pleasing her where she wanted, and the anticipation led to more tickling pleasure than she had experienced in her life. The experience took less time than usual, but the blast of sensation was intense enough that Keela lost track of time during those moments. She knew she was moaning at the end, but that only gave Redbeard a cue to stop what he was doing and continue teasing her. He rolled her over, and she decided not to open her eyes, wondering where his next activity would take him.

Keela was almost upset when Redbeard began to kiss her back and tease the fading whip scars with his fingers, driving her back into frustration. She had expected more direct routes, and this unknown time before he would start intercourse built a new kind of tension. Her legs, her arms . . . he found all his marks. And the strokes of his hands brought more arousal and made her more excited.

Then, Redbeard entered her without warning, and Keela realized that she had married a powerful lover as well as a sensitive one. The act had been preceded by graceful arousal, so she was more prepared for it this time. Still, its sudden impact took her breath away, and she felt a deep fullness and complete draining of her lungs. She gasped in shock as Redbeard began to pound her with more vigor than ever before, and even though she thought she would not be able to handle it, she began to feel herself lifting into bliss.

Many more times, Redbeard drove Keela to ecstasy as the night dragged on. And more than once, Redbeard and Keela both had to pause for more rum and a chance to catch their breath. Keela found Redbeard a capable lover.

When the dawn began to rise beyond the portholes, Keela noticed seagulls flying past her viewpoint. She knew it meant land was near. She didn't want to stop, but she had no choice when she saw the evidence of land. The time for pleasure had passed, and now, the time for fighting had begun.

Redbeard groaned with frustration when Keela pulled her hands away from his back. "The islands are close, my husband. Soon we have to fight."

Redbeard grabbed her naked torso and tried to pull her back into his arms. "We should make Peter's Island by late afternoon, along with the other boats. Come back for now," he argued.

"I must prepare," Keela protested.

Keela loaded her shot pouch with fresh powder and slipped it onto her belt with a leather strap. Then, she loaded her pistol with a freshly packed ball and slid it through her belt, where it hung for when she needed it most. On the other side, she slipped her long, straight sword through her belt. She liked the scalloped version of the swords the pirates used—the ones they heartily called scabbards—but she didn't care for them personally. A longsword had far more reach, and the killing power was preserved at the focal point on the tip of the sword instead of divided along the blade like the scabbards. Usually, the scabbards would leave an enemy bleeding to death. But Keela's longsword was strong enough to send an enemy to the other side in seconds, cleaving straight through necks and arms with killing power.

Keela next wrapped her embroidered bandana around her immense web of hair, tucking every strand safely inside the cloth. Although men could sometimes break through her armor, they never got to her hair. Then, Keela walked outside the cabin and made her way to the deck of the ship.

Redbeard took quite a bit longer to prepare himself. By the time he joined Keela on deck, dressed in a large red pirate jacket and armed to the teeth, Keela was already at the edge of the ship, looking over the side with deep sorrow in her eyes. She didn't even see him walk over.

Redbeard came over to Keela. "What's troubling you? You're heavy in thought, my love."

"I am thinking deeply, Barbarossa. Did I do enough to find my daughter? Did I try hard enough? What will she think of me as a warrior? I know for sure that she thinks I'm abandoning her today. How can I make her see that it's my calling to free all these slaves?"

Redbeard rubbed her shoulder. "I know that your daughter's proud of you. You tried and tried until you found her and rescued her. Your story went around the world. There are a lot fewer people than you think who would go as far as you did to bring your daughter to safety. Most people would have given up."

Keela stopped staring out to sea, unaffected by Redbeard's encouragement. "I don't think most people give up," she argued. "I just think the odds are stacked against them. They fail, but it's not their fault. All it takes is losing one battle, and you die. I've been lucky, but so many others have already fallen on Canary Island and before that. Slavery must end, and I'm going to be a part of that mission."

Redbeard smiled at her, but she didn't notice because she was still looking out to sea with a deep frown on her face. "Look," said Redbeard, "what are the odds that these evil prisons will someday be overthrown without us, much less all three on the same day? What are the odds that it happens today, even with our help? The odds have been stacked against the slaves. Without us, they would starve and suffer and die. But because of us, they'll be free tonight. You're beating the odds every day you fight this war against the slave traders. You're making your own fortune, Keela, and fate must bow to you."

Keela stood up straight and no longer leaned against the ropes. "You're right," she agreed. "It's time to beat fate at her own game. We're going to succeed, and the slave traders will have to look elsewhere to stash their human cargo."

Peter's Island came into view first, as a small tip of green poking above the horizon. Before long, Keela watched the rest of the island come into view from beyond the edge of the sea, growing by the minute until an entire peak was visible. Scrub Island was next, rising in the distance behind Peter's Island, although the peak was more off-center, rising above one side of the island. Beyond that, Dead Chest Island proved to be the smallest of them all. It was just a strip of earth poking above the ocean.

"Why is Dead Chest Island so short?" Keela asked.

"It's an atoll, dear Keela. Sometimes, we find smaller islands like this, with a big lagoon in the middle instead of a volcano. These are the easiest islands to build slave pens on because there's literally nowhere for the slaves to run. And even if they escape the dim cages, the shoreline twists around, bringing them right back to the slave pens. Dead Chest Island has been used as a trap for many years, but tonight, it's the slavers who will have nowhere to run. We're going to use their own trap against them, and they won't have any choice in the matter. Most of them are on Peter's Island. That place will be their doom."

The other pirates who were listening in laughed at the good news. Soon, their plans to overtake the islands would begin in earnest. "Horrific," said Keela in response to the information from Redbeard. The pirates were surprised by her sudden attitude and looked at her in confusion. "Nothing is sacred to these Portuguese, she continued. "They even took the Saint away from Peter's Island. Now, the island is just a blasphemy. The offense ends tonight. After we win, we'll make sure that the mapmakers return the 'Saint' to Saint Peter's Island."

Chapter 36

THE SUN BEGAN TO slip behind the horizon as the ships got into position around the islands. The slave pens were high up in the jungle to prevent escape, and it made the ships invisible to the slavers as the ships floated into position. Peter's Island had five different bays, but the traders left them unguarded, never expecting an attack from the sea.

As night fell, the invaders silently rowed into one of the harbors, slipping ashore in the growing darkness. Several deadly arrows and blowguns rested among Keela's group. As the group pushed through the jungle, one of the Moroccan soldiers put his torch by the ground, right next to a red flower. He touched the flower very carefully, and he instantly started wiping his fingers off on a bandana.

"Deadly poison!" the man hissed. "Perfect for our arrows! They will gasp their way into an early grave." He started gasping for air himself, but he grabbed a vial at once and drank the contents. "Antidote," he explained.

The soldier produced more arrows and spun them into the juicy foxglove flowers, making them all poisoned. Keela dug her sword through the foxglove flowers as well, noting the way the petals arrange themselves in large bells, protecting the poison inside. The soldier who touched the foxglove was still having trouble breathing as the group went up a hill, but he shook off the effects of the poison as he ascended further. As he went, he handed out poisoned arrows, and by the time the party reached the slave pens, everyone had extinguished their torches

191

and walked without speaking.

Knowing the plan by heart, Keela, Redbeard, and the other pirates hid in the jungle and watched the guards standing outside the massive complex of slave pens. At least thirty rows of cages sat behind long walls, with the tops of the cages poking above the walls. The rock walls keeping the slaves penned in were not tall enough to force them to remain. But many of the stones were purposely left loose in the mortar so that when the stones hit the rocks below, they would make enough sound that the guards could get to an escapee in time.

As they watched the guards, Keela counted under her breath. She counted five guards, and there were dozens of blowguns in her group's arsenal, with two different positions to shoot from. She crouched down in the bushes to get a more relaxed position because the light blowguns were fashioned from hollow reeds that moved in the slightest breeze or shaking hand. She wanted to be right on target.

Keela saw a guard look up toward the sky and walk away from the other guards by the gate to urinate. As he stood there relaxing, he continued to look up at the night sky, completely oblivious to the pirates in the bushes. In the light of the half-moon, his neck glowed.

When Keela blew as hard as she could, she saw her tiny arrow vanish into the darkness. She couldn't even see it when the arrow hit the guard's pale neck. He stopped relieving himself at once, and he opened his mouth to scream, but he was unable to do so. He leaned forward, with his face contorted in pain, but he remained standing for several seconds before finally collapsing in silence to the ground.

The other guards had not noticed the fallen guard's absence yet, but they did notice the sharp pricks as arrows began to sink into their necks. One by one, they began to grab their muskets, but the poison was working too fast. By the time they could draw their weapons, they were already starting to choke silently. One guard was dragged to the ground by the weight of his weapon as his arms and legs stopped working. He fell to the ground, with his leg kicking like he was trying to get back up.

The next guard fell at the same time as his partner, both falling backward and littering the ground with their corpses. Their hearts stopped before they even hit the ground. They had withstood the poison for a while, but in the end, it had got the best of them.

The last guard stayed up the longest, but death came fast and without grace. He stood until his heart exploded under the pressure. He collapsed without a flinch.

Keela and the other pirates quickly moved past the guards, noticing the stripes that marked several of the guards as commanders. She expected more resistance and was pleased with the results. But by the time Keela and Redbeard made it through the gate, already brandishing their swords, they met dozens of armed guards who were ready to shoot the invaders entering their prison.

One single commander chose to lead the battle, but his death was inevitable. He drew attention to himself and became the target of seven different pirates. He never stood a chance as their swords cut him into pieces. The guards holding guns kept firing their weapons, but it was futile in the close quarters. Two or three of the bullets damaged hands and legs, but even the pirates that had to limp into battle continued to give the slave traders a tough fight.

The guards were prepared to fight, but they hadn't expected to be fighting pirates in such close quarters. Without their leader, they had no formalized plan of defense. Instead, they blocked the main prison hallway with a mass of bodies as they fell.

Keela expected more of a firefight as the guards began to advance, but she quickly realized they were saving their ammunition or, more likely, had begun to run out. Realizing they expected a swordfight, she quickly raised her pistol and shot it into the oncoming crowd, blowing one guard backward. As he fell, he knocked over the two men behind him as well. The other guards surrounded the fallen men to protect them, but the edges of the hallway were starting to narrow.

The natural hallway between the rows of cages served to the guards' disadvantage. As the guards were focused on the people at the front of the battle, other pirates had begun sneaking around other corridors, opening cage after cage and releasing the slaves within. One by one, the slaves retreated to the far end of the compound.

Inside the heart of the battle, more soldiers had arrived on the other side. They surrounded the pirates, but the slave traders were still unprepared. Two of the pirates looked at each other, advanced toward the press of slavers at the same time, and went down the line, fighting back the slavers' sword blows and dealing lethal cuts to their thighs. They dealt tricky blows that the slavers didn't see coming.

As tendons were torn and people began falling, the spirit of the remaining slavers greatly diminished, but not everyone had given up. Keela, Redbeard, and some of the other pirates ended up trimmed off from the rest of the group, and though a tense struggle was happening beside Keela, the pirates couldn't break through to help her. She fought slavers off two at a time, using two swords to build a wall of defense around her. Anyone who came close was fended off, and one of Keela's comrades would finish them off.

The slaver now opposing Keela raised his sword in front of her, and she wouldn't take that. As his sword was raised, she sliced her long, straight sword across his belly. The men on each side of her didn't back down, though. They drew closer to her, antagonized by their fallen comrade. Keela noticed they were defending their bellies, and she saw a good advantage.

"You're all just picaroons!" shouted one of the slavers.

"Yeah, just rotten bilge rats! Crawl back to your ship!" another chimed in.

Keela was disgusted by their insults and stupidity. Instead of trying to kill her, they were trying to degrade her. "Who do you think you are?" asked Keela, not blinking.

"Huh?" asked the slaver, confused.

Keela's eyes lit up brightly with humor just before her sword began to swing mercilessly through the air. She couldn't believe they were going to insult her when she had a deadly weapon in her hand.

"Wait!" cried one of the men as he fell from her swing.

"Too late for you," Keela said, not even turning around as his head flopped to the ground. Blood leaked out of his mouth as he tried to breathe through the stream of blood coming from his gut.

Watching their gutted friend, the men challenging Keela expected a gutting as well. Not wanting that slow death, they drew their swords back and forth through the middle, defending their guts. Keela swung her sword by their midsections with low strokes that drew their blades lower. She could tell their attention had been diverted because they now kept blocking their torsos.

Since the men were focusing on their lower bodies, they left their throats undefended. Without smiling, Keela struck twice at a high angle, and both soldiers fell at once, with their necks spurting blood and their eyes wide in shock and surprise at their sudden demise. Only after they stopped spurting blood did Keela allow herself to smile. Even as they lay on the ground twitching, their arms kept flapping through the air, trying even in extremis to claim more casualties.

"Kill the scallywags!" screamed one of the slavers, driving the fervor and keeping the slavers fighting a hopeless battle.

Keela continued to hew her way through soldiers until nearly half of them were gone. Then, she began to smile. She sliced an opponent through his gut, but as he fell, she struck his neck as well, sparing him a slow death. As she began to turn her head from the man dying in front of her, Keela saw Redbeard fighting at her side. But she also saw a hooked Portuguese blade quickly come up behind him.

Before Keela could pull her own sword out of the slaver's neck, the hooked, cruel Portuguese sword sliced through Redbeard, slipping through his armor like butter and ripping through her beloved's body in a heartbeat. Keela was shocked at how fast it all happened, although it seemed like time was grinding to a halt and she was the one experiencing death and not Redbeard. The terrible moment seemed to take forever, but she knew that, in reality, less than a second had passed.

As Keela's sword rose in reaction, she wondered why Redbeard had not fallen yet. But as she drew her blade to the killer's throat, she realized that the Portuguese sword was still sticking through Redbeard and leaving him suspended in the air. As she sliced through the neck of her opponent, not sparing a single ounce of energy against her husband's killer, the soldier's entire head lifted clean off his shoulders, flying helmet and all through the air. Keela had not realized she possessed enough fury to decapitate another person or even the strength in her arms to drive the sword that deep. But witnessing her husband's death gave her the strength she required.

Time began to resume its inexorable march. Keela wanted to fall to her knees in grief, but the guards surrounding her gave her no time to grieve. She continued to hew through bodies until nobody was standing in her way. She had no idea what to do when the bodies stopped falling and she realized they were all dead. She swung her sword once more, eyes glazed and blurred, and through the haze of battle, she heard the cheers and dropped her sword. The fight was over now, but if it had taken just a few minutes less, Redbeard would still be alive.

Keela stood there, gasping for breath as a suddenly passive witness to the scene. The slaves had been freed, and their captors were dead. But deep in Keela's heart, she felt cold, empty, and hollow, like a wind was blowing through her chest and alienating her from the warm embraces of her successful companions.

Keela looked down at her feet. Among the pile of bodies was Redbeard's corpse. The other warriors standing beside her were motionless, waiting for her cue. "Get him back to the ship!" she cried. "And the rest of you, start cutting all these cages open. Don't waste your time on the locks!"

As the men started to walk among the slave pens, slicing the ropes holding the cage doors in place, Keela pulled the records from her pocket and called out names. "Horace Kimbi!"

"Here!" cried one of the freed men, stepping forward without fear.

"Get to the ship with the red sails," Keela instructed him. "You're headed back to Morocco! Victory Mnguni!"

"Here!" cried another voice.

"You're free now! Go to the ship with the red sails. You're headed back to Morocco!"

As Keela rallied the people from Morocco, one of them pleaded, "There's so many of us here! They kept us in different parts of the pens to keep us less inclined to escape. You have to find us all."

"I'll find every one of you. I promise," Keela reassured the man as she sliced through the ropes. A door swung open in a haphazard fashion, dangling from the padlock. Victory stepped through the open doorway and began to scream in the moonlight before he raced out past the slave pens and out the open prison gate to freedom.

Keela continued searching for Moroccans, setting each survivor free as she found them. Before long, she found an open pit where corpses had not been buried yet. The smell led her to the corpses, but she had no idea who they were.

In the open pit, Keela found four bodies that her new friends could identify as people from the list. The others were not from Morocco, but they were dead just the same. Staring at the bodies, Keela felt a deep sense of sorrow at their passing and forced her eyes to turn away. As she walked away, she felt like her heart was being pulled from her chest. It was like a strange, cold, sucking vacuum that haunted her and teased at her heart muscles, making the veins in her neck flutter with fear. She wondered if the ghosts could sense her fear, and then she wondered if the living could.

As Keela tried to honor the dead in her mind, the face of Redbeard appeared before her. She chewed on that ragged place inside of her, stroking the pain to find the courage to walk and speak and breathe. She walked among the empty slave pens, staring into their dim depths, piercing the darkness with her torch. Inside every cage, she smelled the stench of death, reeking filth, and rotting and decaying food the slaves were forced to consume or face starvation. The buzzing sound of large jungle insects feeding on the decay and despair of the slave pens could be heard everywhere.

Inside her heart, Keela felt sickened by the horror around her. She walked out of the slave pens after ensuring that not a single living soul was left trapped inside their horrible depths. As she walked out of the great doors guarding the now-useless slave pens, Keela felt a great weight lift off her shoulders at her victory over the slave traders. But at the same time, another weight settled down inside her soul as she pondered the fact that Redbeard couldn't share the victory with her.

Leaving the jungle and returning to her ship, Keela found Redbeard's body already inside his coffin. "It was such a horrific sight, my lady," one of the pirates said. "We didn't want people to have to see him that way."

Keela smiled at her men, though tears were in her eyes. "Clean him up, then. He deserves a proper send-off." Although she retained control while looking at the men, when she turned her back and exited to the deck, she couldn't hold back her sobs.

Chapter 37

D ANIEL APPROACHED DEAD CHEST ISLAND, looking at the slave pits with scorn. The tiny atoll was almost swallowed by the sea, even at low tide. At times like this, when the tide was high, the waters flowed into the deep lagoon in the middle of the island.

Daniel and his forces landed on the opposite side of the lagoon from the slave pens and quietly slipped onto the shore, trying to steer clear of the noisy tide pools as they sneaked around the narrow strip of sand. Some went in each direction so they could corner the slave traders inside their nest.

When all the forces had surrounded the pens, Daniel lifted a conch shell from the beach and blew as loud as he could. The haunting tone of the conch shell echoed between the walls surrounding the pens, and the traders began to run outside to defend their precious cargo. Even before Daniel's pirates could use their arrows, Daniel heard screams from behind the slave pens as his forces attacked the traders from the far side. This distracted the traders ahead of him, and they turned around to look.

As the traders were distracted, Daniel noticed a group of slaves tending the small fields. Daniel pointed at the traders with his sword, and the slaves looked up and understood at once. Within seconds, the hoes and shovels became weapons that were quite effective. As the sharp hoes sliced through the necks and arms of the guards surrounding the slaves, the guards began to bleed to death. Daniel knew that the guards' chances of survival were absolutely none with the dung-fertilized dirt covering the hoes and shovels. If the hoes and shovels themselves did not kill the guards, the disease pushed through the guards' blood would eventually claim their unfortunate souls.

As Daniel continued to watch, he saw a guard fall instantly as his solar plexus was ripped open from side to side. He jerked as he fell, and he did not move again once he hit the ground. Daniel didn't mind the sight of these traders dying. In fact, he relished every second of their suffering and hoped that their deaths took as long as possible.

Daniel's feeling of revenge against this vile slavery overwhelmed him, and he realized he needed to release his anger or be consumed by it. Rage boiling in his eyes, he screamed a warning of "Fire!" as the guards began to fire their muskets from long range. The guards' shots went wide, missing his people and only serving to encourage their wrath. Many pirate eyes flashed with sharp rage as arrow hands pulled away and released deadly feathered arrows, which had far more accurate range than the Spanish muskets.

Some of the guards' muskets backfired, exploding in their hands and sending plumes of smoke into their faces. One man cried out and tore at his eyes in anguish, damaging his eyes even further in the process and causing him to drop his weapon from his charred hands. As the arrows were loosed, they swept across the beach and found their targets. They missed the man with the ruined eyes, and Daniel relished more than anything the sight of his squirming, flailing body crawling around on the beach like a sea-crab as he pummeled the sand with his useless feet and waited for death to take him.

As the guards began to fall to the sand, Daniel led the charge across the beach. One of his warriors grabbed the keys from a dead slaver. He threw the keys to Daniel, and Daniel grabbed the chain out of the air, adding it to his arsenal. The weight of the swinging keys produced brutal injuries to the traders foolish enough to get in his way. Trapped in from both sides, the slave traders fell and were defeated. Daniel relished the irony that their own keys were their downfall.

The man on the beach was still trying to die, unwilling to face a life without his eyes or his hands. But try as he might, his time would not come. He banged his blinded head against the rocks in frustration, and

Daniel knew the man was almost beyond his senses by the time he walked up behind him and slid his sword between the bones in the man's neck, separating them and severing his spinal cord. Even with the sword wedged between the man's vertebrae, long moments of survival persisted. His head continued to shake up and down until Daniel pulled the sword free, and the man finally stopped moving. For the first time, Daniel felt that a merciful death was a good thing.

Breaking through the wide wooden doors surrounding the slave pens, the rescuers entered the prison. They discovered row after row of cages arranged across the beach without any covering from rain or the beating sun. "Get these people out of these cages!" one of the pirates yelled. "They're human beings, not cargo!"

As the cages were quickly unlocked, Daniel noticed that each key on the ring he held had a symbol and that each row of cages had a symbol too. Unlocking all the cages was quite easy with their labeling system, but what made it more difficult was the terrible smell coming from the cages. Some of the slaves had perished before they could be rescued, adding the stench of death to the smell of human waste and decaying food that permeated the slave pens. Daniel stared in horror at the dead bodies and moved on to free the slaves who were still breathing.

One of the slaves Daniel rescued was just a young girl. She was barely breathing, so instead of setting her free, he opened the door and raced in to help her. The young girl's parched lips had cracked in the hot sun, and drops of blood had hardened on her half-open lips. "Water! I need water in here!" cried Daniel.

The young girl stared at him, unable to speak from the dryness in her throat. Her eyes said it all, with the deep horror and helplessness that comes from being locked in a cage and starved. Her eyes and her withdrawn arms spoke of mistrust and terror, and Daniel could do nothing but smooth her tangled and sand-covered hair, repeating, "It's going to be all right. You're safe now."

A woman arrived with some water in a canteen, and Daniel put the canteen's small mouth to the girl's bleeding lips as soon as possible. She gulped with greed, consuming the water as fast as it could be released from the canteen. She belched and looked around in wonder as her senses returned.

"Take her to my ship and take good care of her," Daniel ordered the woman. "No more of these slaves are dying on my watch. Today, they are all free, and I'm not losing one on their day of freedom."

The woman lifted the young girl into her arms. She lifted her with ease because the girl was emaciated and lighter than a bird after weeks trapped in the horrible slave pens.

Chapter 38

A KUA STOOD ON THE yellow beaches of Scrub Island and waited for his companions to join him there. If it hadn't been a place where slaves were held, he could have imagined taking this island for his own once the battle was done.

Once all the boats had scraped ashore, the men advanced into the jungle and headed for the prison. The dense jungle revealed itself to be teeming with snakes, frogs, and other dangerous creatures. The men were not fooled by the bright, beautiful colors. They knew these jungle denizens were toxic. Some of them were so toxic that the men delicately twirled their arrows through the slime on the backs of the frogs, being careful not to touch the slime with their fingers.

When the slave pens were in view, the advancing men hunkered down in the bushes while also protected by jungle trees. They blew their blowguns as hard as they could. At the same time, they fired muskets, but many of the musket balls missed their mark and hit trees instead. Even though the muskets were good at short range, they were terrible at long range. Hundreds of arrows sailed through the air as well as the pirates continued their attack.

One of the warriors noticed a guard sneaking toward them in the grass. The guard was trying to hide in the darkness, but the moonlight flashed on the metal of his musket, and one of Akua's warriors buried a poison dart into his neck. Already on the ground, the man gasped for breath but found enough strength to lift his weapon. The small warrior that had shot him saw the musket flare and ducked in time, but the shot whizzed past him and dug into the ribs of the pirate behind him, who fell to the ground, gasping for air.

As more pirates advanced across the meadow, the pirate shot by the musket started to gurgle as blood filled his airway. Nevertheless, he ran as best he could across a field, half in terror and half in rage. He raised his sword and used it to tear apart the enemy forces. The other pirates joined him in hot pursuit, happy to join the carnage, screaming and whooping as their swords sliced through their foes.

As the pirates reached the slave pens, the jailors were the fiercest fighters. Two of them worked together and managed to bring one of the freed slaves to the ground, screaming as he was slain. One of the jailors buried a pike through the man's heart, shattering the ribs with a fatal series of cracks. They bent over his body, continuing to slice him as he shook, dying.

The two jailors were unprepared for the sword blows that brought them their fate. They never saw Akua behind them before they died, falling on top of the slain slave. The rest of the jailors fought back, but before long, they had fallen too.

The last trader lost all motivation, realizing he was the last one alive. He threw his keys to the pirates, surrendering himself, but he was surrounded and slaughtered as well. The pirates didn't make it simple for him. First, they removed his legs, and then, when he still drew breath, they took off his arms. The loss of blood was too great, and he stopped breathing, staring up at the sky in impotent defiance.

Chapter 39

KEELA SAILED BACK TO Morocco with the freed people and a few of her trusted sailors. When she arrived at Morocco's coastline, she landed and brought the survivors across the desert to the capital, Fez. She had never been in Fez before, but she had heard stories about its red walls stretching higher than the palace itself. The red walls topped with blue designs high above were striking and intimidating to her, and she welcomed the bright smile on King Ahmad's face. His people sent up a cheer when they saw her.

In a rush, the freed people returned home to their city, cheering and hugging relatives and loved ones. Despite the celebration, Keela's face remained grim. Now seeing the same frown on Ahmad's face, the people of Morocco began to quiet. Keela spoke into the silence, bearing the words everyone dreaded to hear. "I brought your people back to you, but I couldn't return Redbeard. He died a hero, trying to save your people. I'll fight for his honor for the rest of my days."

Keela's nerves were on fire, threatening to break her stance. While she struggled to maintain her composure, King Ahmad lowered his head. "I am so sorry for your loss. Redbeard was a great hero."

The people of Morocco did not suffer from Irish emotional fortitude. They cried at the loss of a beloved friend. The tears of pain rolled down their faces and dropped to the red dust. As Keela stood before them, they noticed she was not crying, but she was far from peaceful. Both her hands shook, but she held her tongue. For her, Redbeard had been her husband, but she understood that to the people of Morocco, he was a hero.

"We have a place off in the jungle where the bodies of our heroes remain undisturbed," King Ahmad informed Keela. "It would be a fitting place for a hero like Barbarossa of Algeria. It would be a great honor to have his body here."

Keela nodded, shedding tears. "He would love it here. He would be honored to rest in this beautiful land of yours."

King Ahmad nodded sagely, smiling in gratitude, though his eyes were still sad. "You and all your pirates are more than welcome to attend his burial, as well as anyone else who wishes to be there. Barbarossa had many friends in his life. Spread the word far and wide that the new leader of the pirates is now Keela!"

Five of Keela's pirates brought Redbeard's body forward, bringing the coffin slowly to the front of the crowd and pausing. Ahmad raised his voice, waving his hands toward himself. "Bring him to the walls and keep watch over him. Our laws prohibit us from keeping the dead inside the city. I will send guards to make sure his body is not disturbed. You are free to join them."

"Thank you," said Keela, "we will."

Keela waited outside the city, flanked by her supporters and the city guards, and as evening fell, concerned comrades tried to convince her to go to bed. Her knees were becoming weak from the effort of standing so long. At first, she was reluctant to leave Redbeard's side. But they kept cajoling her, and after another hour without seeing any roving bandits, the weight of weariness fell over Keela. She agreed to follow her people inside the city walls to a quiet hut where they convinced her to lay down in a soft bed.

Keela fell asleep that night after convincing her friends that she was all right and bidding them goodnight. As she curled up in the bed, she thought about how Redbeard would never sleep with her again, and she felt cold inside. In this deep web of despair, she entered a dreamless sleep.

Just before waking, Keela dreamed of Redbeard. He was still alive in her dream, warm and naked. And she could feel his pulse throbbing wherever she touched his body. But suddenly, the deep, earth-shuddering pounding of Moroccan funeral drums outside the city walls woke her, and she went outside to look. She already knew, before looking outside, that it meant Redbeard was leaving.

It was impossible for Keela to miss the funeral procession. She rose to her feet, dressed, and was able to reach the procession before the Moroccans had started to advance into the hills. She followed the coffin and the funeral procession as everyone walked in silence into the hills, which were surrounded by jungle trees, thick ferns, and bright flowers.

As Keela ascended past large flowers and tall coconut trees, she realized that this was indeed a fitting place for a pirate to be laid to rest. The cemetery was remote and isolated, high up on the hills, far from the city below. Where Redbeard rested in a meadow, dozens of tall head-stones bore the names of ancient pirates—proud men and women laid to rest long before Redbeard. Keela knew she was not the first woman to be a pirate, but she was still surprised to find Queen Teuta and Chang-Shi in the graveyard of pirates.

Keela stood with the rest of the mourners, but she was given special privilege and was allowed to stand beside the open grave, even as Redbeard was being lowered in. Out of respect for her, nothing was said during the procession until his body was lowered. Even then, the people held their tongues, looking at Keela until she realized it was her place to break the silence. She tried to capture Redbeard's life in her words.

"Today, we remember the great pirate, Barbarossa. He was known to his friends as Redbeard, known to me as my husband, and known to the world as the greatest pirate that ever sailed the Seven Seas. Because of him, your fellow countrymen have been freed from bondage, and the yoke of slavery has forced the traders to their knees. Now, we have a chance to fight back. Because of Redbeard's sacrifice, we have a chance to survive!"

All the people gathered at the cemetery cheered loudly, and Keela felt a spirit of life entering the quiet resting place. Every person was filled with liveliness. And now, Keela realized she could turn Redbeard's eulogy into a true battle cry.

"Now, we need to keep that momentum going," continued Keela, with a slight nod from the holy men, spurring her on. "We need to strike back where it hurts until the entire Mediterranean coast is cut off from the slave traders. We'll take down one city at a time until the slave traders go back to hell where they came from! Are you ready to make Redbeard proud?" Another great cheer arose from everyone. "Then once we bury this man, you must all promise me that he didn't die in vain. Promise me you'll fight in his honor until you've reclaimed everything you've lost from these evil slavers!"

Another cheer erupted, longer and louder this time, and Keela did nothing to quiet it. Instead, she reveled in the power she felt as the crowd thundered around her. She felt energized and proud. Somehow, the great swelling of power within her was enough to let her lift the first spade full of sod and drop it upon Barbarossa's coffin. Then, she walked to the side and let the other mourners finish what she had started.

Although Keela had come to the funeral with many people following her, she left the funeral alone and returned to the city alone and unguarded. She commandeered a horse and returned to Algiers, where she began a ten-year campaign of violence and piracy. She fought up and down the coast. From Algiers to Tetouan, she went back and forth along the coast, sacking city after city. Her pirate ships bulged with white flame as cannons shot into the slave fortresses, destroying their doors and freeing the slaves. Chests full of gold poured in from Keela's efforts as the slave traders' vaults were drained. All the spoils went to her treasury in Algiers.

Every time Keela returned home to Algiers, she shared the gold with everyone she'd freed, presenting lavish gifts and not asking for anything in return. But the freed men and women returned her kindness anyway, by sharing treasures of their own. She blessed them all and sent them on their way with pockets and purses full of gold, telling them to buy clothing, blankets, and food for their families.

Keela's home had a fantastic ballroom, and all her celebrations were open and free to everyone, no matter who they were. Powerful dignitaries would attend her parties as well as the freed people and the pirates. With the interaction between freed people and dignitaries, some of the ambassadors began to realize that Keela's mission wasn't such a threat after all, and they even began to convince their countries to end the slave trade. After years of communication, Keela's concepts managed to convince the Spanish armada to stop its slave gathering expeditions in Africa.

Five years after Redbeard had been murdered, the pirates owned the coastline from Algiers all the way down to Tetouan, forcing the slave traders to bring their merchandise through the Ivory Coast. There, raids from Morocco attacked the slavers and set the slaves free. The morale of the slave traders began to dwindle.

In 1611, which marked ten years since Redbeard's death, Keela threw a special ball, where she made an announcement. She wore a lavish dress and held her drink high in the air, speaking loudly and clearly. "For ten long years, we've been fighting to stop the slave trade on the Mediterranean, and now, there's one last stronghold we need to destroy before we're done. We need to take out Istanbul, and then the slave trade will be effectively crushed."

Keela found no shortage of supporters for her mission because all her guests shared her vision. Her legions of pirates sailed out to the last slave fortress, outside of Istanbul. Portuguese galleons determined to stop her met her ships in the narrow bay, but when they realized they were outgunned, they had nowhere to run. When the cannons stopped blazing, the ships attempting to detain Keela's were gone. Hundreds of pirates suffered injuries during the cannon fight, but less than ten lost their lives. On the other side, not one Portuguese defender was left alive.

The last slave traders on the Mediterranean lifted their hands in surrender as they stood on the shore, not even daring to flee as Keela's pirates closed in and took them prisoner. They knew, without Keela telling them, what their fate would be. They would be sold as slaves to American slave owners, who had never given up on the slave trade. It was the best way to deter them from committing the same acts again.

Keela's reputation had grown along with her success. After fighting for ten long years, Keela returned to her home base in Algiers and fortified the city with stronger walls. She wanted her stronghold to last for hundreds of years so that the specter of slavery would never rise in

Africa again. Even with her enemies defeated, she knew that more would arise, and she wanted to be prepared.

Chapter 40

WHEN KEELA RETURNED TO Algiers and commanded the pirates to begin fortifying the city's high walls, she asked to have the architects brought to her. When they arrived, Keela outlined a daring plan. "We need to build a school for the children and a medical center for the people. And we will need to build many more houses. I need people who can build and someone to organize them."

"I can arrange that," said one of the architects. "Everyone knows me well."

"Good. Get started on it. For now, the priority is tents for the wounded until the clinic is ready. And the rest of the people you round up should start on the houses."

The builder went down to the taverns and the other hangouts where he could find many willing people—some freshly arrived, others living there for years. When they found out they would be well rewarded for their efforts, they immediately rushed to his side and signed up to begin working the next morning. Keela established that one of the biggest tents would be used for negotiations and other sensitive affairs. The new workers worked through the next night—to avoid the heat of the day—to prepare the tent with the best cushions and rugs and the finest tea. It was much richer than the other tents.

When Keela had command of the new tent the next morning, she opened the tent to traders of all kinds. She amassed a wealth of clothing, blankets, pillows, and rugs until nobody wanted for anything. Countless negotiations took place in the tent, as well as thousands of trades and arguments as well. Keela felt that the tent was a place of creation—a holy place where good things were created.

Many romantic trysts took place in the tent, and Keela swelled with pride as baby after baby was conceived there. As the children grew and ran around the city and the fields, Keela felt convinced that her life was truly blessed and destined to continue getting better for the rest of her life. When her own daughter turned twenty-four, Caitlin traveled to Fez to meet with a Moroccan prince, and Keela had advanced warning that she would be departing.

1612 was a year with much significance to Keela when she learned that her daughter was returning. Caitlin arrived hand in hand with the prince, with them both happy and smiling as their boat sailed into the harbor and anchored at the now-peaceful docks. Keela admired the bright red sails and noticed that the Moroccan colors had never altered.

Keela stood by the docks, watching the ocean while stealing glances at her newly-fortified marketplace. The market was wonderful. She had spent many weeks rebuilding the market with new buttresses. These defenses would keep the overhanging ceilings supported in case of an attack. Explosives were becoming popular, and she didn't want merchants to die without purpose. Despite the peace, Keela was still preparing for battle.

The maroon sails bearing her daughter safely home filled Keela with joy, and although she searched the ship from stem to stern as it sailed into the harbor, she could find no defects at all. It was a perfectly sound vessel. She felt much better once she knew her daughter was safe and sound.

Keela followed the ship's progress along the dock, and she walked over to ensure that she would have a first-hand glimpse of her daughter the moment she left the gangplank. As the ship's anchor disappeared into the blue depths of the harbor, the white ropes came spinning out over the railings. The ropes were caught in graceful swirls by the dock-hands, who helped rope the ship to the tall moorings. They tugged on each rope before they waved an all-clear to the waiting Moroccans.

The gangplank fell down against the dock with a crash, and footsteps began to rumble down it. It was no surprise to Keela when a beautiful young woman was the first to run down to the docks and enter her arms without a word. "Welcome home, Caitlin," said Keela.

"I'm so happy to see you again," answered Caitlin, hugging her mother tight.

Prince Ilias and several Moroccan advisors disembarked as well. "Prince Ilias, what brings you here?" asked Keela.

"More than friendship. My father, the king, wants me to give you a message and bring back your reply."

Keela opened the precious envelope she was handed. The note inside read:

Please let me have the honor of marrying the beautiful pirate leader who freed many slaves. You shall thereafter be known as the Pirate Queen. I anxiously await your reply.

Keela considered the offer for a minute. Then, she responded with, "Tell your king he has to come here and ask for my hand himself. Then, we shall be married. I will not leave my city for any man! Remember, our gates are always open to Morocco."

"I will deliver your message, Keela the Pirate Queen," answered Prince Ilias.

Keela covered her surprise at already being called the Pirate Queen. "I shall await the King's arrival," she said.

Chapter 41

KING AHMAD'S ADVISORS and Prince Ilias sailed back to Morocco to bring Keela's reply to the king, who waited for it back in Fez. When they arrived, the advisors were weary from their long voyage and eager to be done with their mission. The buildings of Fez stretched for miles, carved out of the rock of the hills or built above their slopes out of dark red bricks. Guarding the whole city was a great wall, rising hundreds of feet high and covered in blue and red designs sacred to Morocco.

A massive gate welcomed the men back to the city. It was covered in splendid artwork and was always a wonder to behold. The advisors walked down Fez's wide streets to the great palace, which was designed to be the endpoint of every major road in the city. It was a sprawling red-brick fortress deep in the heart of the capital.

The advisors slowed themselves inside the palace so they wouldn't bump into the passing servants and guards. But they continued to walk as brisk as possible until they reached King Ahmad Al-Wattassi in the throne room. His handsome face commanded everyone's attention. Proving this point, the other people in the throne room paid the advancing men no mind. As for Ahmad, he stared at them with his piercing blue eyes, ignoring his subjects.

"My most trusted advisors, at last, you return. What is the Pirate Queen's answer?" Ahmad asked.

"Your Majesty, may we please speak privately?" asked Prince Ilias.

"Let us go at once," the king agreed.

The king led the advisors and the prince through a curtain to where they could speak in private. It was far from a secret place, but it provided enough room for them to be free from the prying ears of the court subjects. "What does the pirate lady say?" Ahmad was eager to know. He frowned as he waited for a response.

"Keela says she will not leave her city for any man. She accepts the offer of your hand, but only if you can provide it in person. She wishes to keep defending her city."

King Ahmad pondered the matter, still frowning. "Well, this pirate, Keela, sounds like a powerful leader indeed. I want her as my queen now more than ever. She has released thousands of my people from bondage over the years. I plan to marry her and build her a palace as great as this one, for although she is a mere female, she is a hero in my eyes and has fought harder than any man I have ever met. Let's go there at once. There is a trail that will take us over the mountains, and we shall cross the land to reach her."

Ahmad's word was law, and the advisors nodded, understanding that they had to follow the king's directions. Even so, the advisors shuddered because no king had ever asked to leave the capital of Fez before. One of the advisors could not help protesting. "But, Your Majesty, this is unheard of! No king has ever left Fez, not even to be married. It's unbefitting of your position to leave your capital and go elsewhere for marriage. Besides, the mountain passes are difficult and covered in snow this time of year. The men will be uncomfortable in the cold."

Ahmad shook his head, and the advisor knew at once that his argument had not been accepted. "Then they'll have to be uncomfortable, won't they? Since when did being a Moroccan mean having comfort? We've been in a state of war with the Spanish for centuries, and it's about time someone else started fighting back. Keela's strength is making Morocco look weak, but if we are united, Morocco becomes even stronger. I want this woman by my side. Let's go! I don't want to wait another minute!"

"But, Your Majesty, we still have to assemble the men for the journey," the advisor continued.

"Well, go assemble them, then."

"Father, you can't be serious!" cried Prince Ilias.

"Oh, I am serious, son," answered Ahmad. "Why do you question me now, when she has already accepted my proposal?"

"She's done nothing but fight for ten years," answered Ilias. "She's a disgrace! How can you even think of marrying that monster?"

Ahmad looked at his son with scorn. "No, son, you don't understand. She has changed the future of our country for the better. If she wants me to visit her there, I'll go to her side. Things can change, son."

Ahmad tried to maintain his composure, but Ilias grew angrier with each rebuttal. "No, they can't! Things never have to change. Violence just brings more violence. She's a rule-spurning pirate. She's a reckless rebel, and I can't stand her! A rebellious pirate becomes a high and mighty queen? I won't stand for it!"

Ahmad was becoming tired of the prince's insubordination and slammed the base of his scepter across the floor, making sure that his point was heard. "You *will* stand for it, and you *will* do as I say! I am the king. I can make new rules. Don't go against my authority! How dare you question me!"

"You're not even thinking clearly, Father. You're dishonoring yourself!"

Prince Ilias clenched his fist and looked ready to attack. This offended Ahmad, and he roared loudly to silence his son. "No! it is an honor to me! It is an honor to marry her!" Ahmad stood up, intimidating and tall.

Ilias would not be silenced. Instead, he continued to belabor the point. "Father, she's killed hundreds of innocent soldiers, not just slave traders. How does that make her a hero?"

"Because she's saved thousands of our people from slavery! Don't tell me you support these slave traders, son! In every war, some innocent people always die. It can't be stopped. You've been a warrior long enough to know that."

Ahmad was beginning to clench his fists in rising anger, but Ilias continued to argue. "You know what really makes me angry? You let her pirate husband be buried here, among our honored ancestors, our fallen heroes. And he wasn't even a Moroccan!"

"I won't hear another word about this, Ilias. I think you are the one who has dishonored the ancestors! Now I must appease them!" Ahmad grabbed a bowl of tea from the table and hurled it into the ever-burning fire. The king was screaming as he continued. "She *will* become the Pirate Queen, and there's nothing you can say about it! This conversation is over!"

Ilias fell silent, staring at his father and not daring to breathe a word. The fire crackled and hissed when the tea was poured across it, and a huge ball of steam floated up from the fire. After the quiet that ensued, Ahmad spoke with venom in his words. "Guards! Escort Prince Ilias from the palace immediately!"

The guards took the wordless prince by the arms and escorted him from the throne room, though they let him go before he was out of the castle, fearing him too much to follow through on the king's commands. Prince Ilias returned to his chamber, but he had no intention of following his father's wishes. Meanwhile, back in the throne room, Ahmad turned his attention to the advisors, who he noticed were still in the room. The advisors looked at him silently, not daring to breathe a word.

"Assemble the party now!" Ahmad bellowed. The advisors left immediately.

The king arranged to have the castle guarded in his absence. Then, he walked outside, where his nobles were already gathering. Beyond the nobles, thousands of soldiers had begun to converge on the palace. Ahmad looked at all his people and then at his advisors, and finally, he smiled.

As the soldiers got gathered and organized, the advisors looked at Ahmad with curiosity in their eyes. "We are beginning a dangerous journey. What have you got to smile about?" one of them asked.

"At the end of the journey, I get to marry the amazing Keela, who has freed countless Moroccans and other slaves from bondage. That's what."

Thousands of shields shone in the sunlight as the great mass of people made its way through the hills. As the hills gave way to stone-covered mountains, the progress was slower, with the men reduced to single file as they went along the narrow path leading through the mountains. The soldiers began to grumble and grimace as the snow whipped around them, torn away from the slopes by the driving wind.

The winds alone were treacherous, making men lose their footing on the sharp path. As one of the men traversed the passage, the wind shifted, and he lost his balance on the ice-covered rocks. He grabbed the edge of the rocks to stop his fall, and the other men tried to drag him back up. But his hands were too slippery, as ice had begun to form on his fingers. Soon, the rescuers felt the man's fingers slip free.

Screaming, the man crashed thousands of feet down the mountain slopes, bouncing off the rocks, before the others couldn't see him anymore. Ahmad's men traveled onward, inching past the broken rocks and the smear of blood on the edge of the gap where the man's frozen hands had sought to grab the sharp edge. Long before he disappeared, his screams were lost to them, torn away by the whipping wind and making his descent a silent one. They presumed he was dead and continued forward after pausing to pray for his merciful passing.

Although the summit was in view, the going was still treacherous. Even when they made it to the top and looked down the other side, some of the men got vertigo from the great height. Some had to sit down for a minute, and one even tumbled down the other side—down to Algeria, far below. He spun down the slope, and as he began to tumble, his head smashed into a rock, sparing the rest of the men his pitiful screams. The rock smashed his skull apart, driving him to the other side at once, with his life ending before they even had a chance to pray for him.

Ahmad would not stop the procession even then. He insisted, "You must keep walking. The longer we stay up here, the longer we are in danger. Let's move." They started walking again, and as they descended, they prayed more often that they would not meet the same fate as their fallen comrades.

As the men reached the end of the area of snowfall and welcomed the arrival of trees, they were ecstatic to leave the snow behind them. Ahmad stood on a tall saddle and looked down at the majestic view in front of him. The rock-built mountains gave way to jungle-covered hills and valleys. Beyond the green valleys, the rocky lands reached all the way to the sea, with the ocean shining like a white band on the horizon, gleaming in the sunlight. Deep in the valley shone the white bricks of the walls of Algiers, and Ahmad knew he had reached his destination. To Ahmad, Algiers was a shining jewel by the coast, where his beloved waited.

The rest of the journey took little time, as the soldiers and nobles fared much better in the jungle. It was familiar to them, reminding them of the jungles of Morocco. Smiles were beginning to break out on the men's faces.

As the procession reached the gate of Algiers, which had been well fortified by Keela over the years, Ahmad could see all the work she had done. Huge doors blocked their path. The doors rose hundreds of feet into the air—much higher than the gates of Fez. Huge bolts and metal beams reinforced the great doors, and as the men marveled at them, the chains pulled away, dragged off by mechanisms underground.

The gates swung open, and Keela's pirates emerged from the city with Keela in the lead, far ahead. Too far ahead to be defended by the pirates, Keela stood before the great King of Morocco and his army, his noblemen, and his advisors. Ahmad's advisors produced a fine silk cloth and placed it at Ahmad's feet. King Ahmad knelt before Keela, with both of his knees on the cloth.

"You are the most beautiful and brave warrior I have ever seen," Ahmad began. "You have the body of a soldier and the heart of a lioness. You freed my people from slavery—something far braver than I have accomplished in many years of war with the slave traders. Will you do me the honor of being my queen?"

Ahmad's advisors produced a large cone-shaped metal case and placed it in front of the kneeling Ahmad. Its lid was decorated with wings and flowers. Removing the large conical lid, Ahmad presented Keela with wedding gifts. Among them, bolts of fabric from faraway lands greeted her.

"The cloth is to keep your people warm on cold nights," Ahmad informed Keela. Underneath the fabric, Keela found a large container of brown cane sugar. "For a happy life," Ahmad said. She looked further and found necklaces with strange gems and wooden carvings she had never before beheld. Ahmad said, "Those necklaces are to keep you and your warriors safe in the heat of battle on the seas."

Keela beamed a white smile in the king's direction, but she knew Moroccan customs. Before they were married, the only thing she could do was kiss him on the forehead. She stood on tiptoe because he was taller than her, even when kneeling, and she planted one kiss on his forehead. Then, she took a step back.

"These gifts are fantastic!" Keela declared. "I accept your offering, and I am happy to be your queen. But I wish to remain here and defend my city."

"And you shall," agreed Ahmad, to the shock of his advisors. "You shall have a palace of your own, right here in Algiers. I shall rule with you here."

Chapter 42

BY KEELA AND AHMAD'S FIFTH wedding anniversary, in 1617, Keela had further fortified the city and become a powerful ruler. The anniversary celebrations were grand, and she was having the time of their life, feasting on wild boar and other African delicacies.

When Prince Ilias arrived at the feast, Keela noticed that the look on his face was somber, in contrast with the festive surroundings. "What news do you bring?" asked Ahmad, smiling at the prince, though Keela was no longer smiling.

"Your daughter, my king. She has passed away. They are having the funeral this week. You must come at once."

Ahmad rose to his feet. "This is a celebration of the queen's fifth anniversary in marriage to me. I'm not leaving her side for anything. I never have, and I never will. And you certainly can't ask me to abandon her on our anniversary!"

Prince Ilias disagreed, shaking his head and raising his voice. "Your Majesty, please listen to me! Your presence is requested, as is customary to our people. When a child dies, the parents must attend the burial, or the spirit of the departed will surely hunt them down! This is the truth I understand."

Ahmad stepped closer, but his son refused to back up. "Not even a funeral will distract me from Keela, my son. I have made a solemn vow to her."

"Father, please listen to me! You need to come to this funeral! It's very important. Why do you have to be like this, Father? You didn't listen to me last time either. Now, you spend more time with Keela than you do in Fez. You're abandoning all of us!"

Keela wanted to get involved, but it was clear who was and wasn't involved in the conflict, and she leaned back against the soft back of her chair.

"You will respect the queen!" roared Ahmad. "Bow down before her and apologize!"

"I will not! You're nothing but a coward, Father!" Ilias retorted.

Ahmad slapped his son across the face. Keela took note of this, but she still didn't step in. "How dare you insult me like that, Ilias!" Ahmad reprimanded him. "I could have your head for that! I promised Queen Keela I would never leave her side. I don't take promises lightly. I even built her a palace. My people have held promises in the highest regard for thousands of years. I am not about to break a promise now."

Caitlin spoke up as well, to try and defuse the situation. Now twenty-nine, Caitlin was impossible to intimidate. Instead, Keela had noticed her demanding that people be civilized and expecting nothing less of them. And Keela could not disagree with her daughter's attitude because she wanted people to be more civilized as well.

"It's all right, everyone," said Caitlin. "Let's calm down before someone gets hurt. I'm sure the prince will make amends in time. You may go to the funeral if you wish, King Ahmad. We don't mind."

Keela spoke up as well. "My daughter has given her blessing. Now, I give mine as well. You may go to the funeral if you wish. I won't be offended."

"No, Keela," answered the king, staring back at her defiantly, though tears of thanks twinkled in his eyes. "When my people make a promise, it's a promise to the death. Strike up the music! This is supposed to be a celebration!"

As Caitlin exhaled, Keela sat back in her chair again and tried to keep a relaxed look on her face. But she knew that things were once again changing. Caitlin stood up, and Keela knew where she was going before she took her first step. The prince walked out of the hall, and Caitlin followed behind him. Keela watched her go but didn't try to stop her. She knew that Caitlin was in love with Prince Ilias, and she knew better, after her lifetime of heartbreak, than to be the one to stand in the way of love.

Turning to her husband, Keela spoke softly. "Why don't you take a hot bath, Ahmad? You know that always relaxes you."

"I believe I will," he answered.

The bath was already drawn and hot, with a low fire below keeping the water hot and steaming. To add to the healing, Keela poured some special Egyptian salts in, which soothed the king's tense muscles. Ahmad disrobed and entered the bath slowly, letting the hot water wash over his tired muscles. He had been king for a long time, and age was beginning to wear on his body. Although his face was still handsome, Keela could see the pain in his body from the tension drawn across his shoulders.

Keela sank into the bath after Ahmad, smiling. She floated in the water, then winked and went across to a bench in the bath. The bench was just right for sitting in the hot water, and Ahmad crossed over to her, sitting beside her. The hot water had already begun to soften his tense muscles, but rubbing his shoulders, Keela still found knots.

"I can make all that tension go away, my love," Keela soothed. She straddled Ahmad and slowly brought herself down on his erect penis, feeling shock as he entered her with his large member. Hot water infused with healing salts also entered her, adding to the sensations she felt.

The soft aroma of the salts perfumed the air as Ahmad filled Keela's senses with ecstasy. As she rode above him, his hands ran up and down her back, driving her into ever-increasing shudders of pleasure. She moaned louder and louder, but when it was all over, his cries overwhelmed hers. Waves of tension left his body with each pump. Keela's whole body tingled with each thrust, as though her body were absorbing the stress and sending it elsewhere.

The deep peace in Ahmad's eyes told Keela everything as she separated from him, thrilling again at the new rush of hot water that entered her. She sat down on the bench beside him, feeling thrilled all over. She quietly held him as they sat in the water.

Ahmad breathed in the sweet smell of orchids and lotuses from

Keela's hair, admiring the way she smelled. With every moment in the water, he found more peace and relaxation with her. He felt so content in the bath that he never wanted to leave, and it was only hours later that the two of them finally curled up in bed together after another bout of lovemaking.

"Happy anniversary, my queen," Ahmad whispered before they went to sleep.

Chapter 43

OUTSIDE THE FEASTING HALL, Caitlin ran through the darkness, crying out to Prince Ilias. "Let me sail away with you! I feel the same way you do!" Prince Ilias glowered at her for a moment. "Come on, don't glare at me like that," Caitlin pleaded. "You have known me since I was a child. Your sister was so kind to me as well. You know I should be at Imane's funeral with you. I'll take my mother's place, and it will appease the nobles."

Prince Ilias held out his hand. "Come along, then." And with that, Ilias's boat sailed away, carrying them back to Morocco.

The funeral procession led up into the hills. Caitlin and Ilias walked briskly, but their companions were slower afoot, delayed by their mourning rituals. When they reached the large meadow where the dead rested, Caitlin and Ilias waited among the stones for the rest of the procession to arrive. The funeral itself was rather short, but the prince found time to vent his rage during the burial, interrupting the holy men before the time for speaking had arrived and earning their disdain.

"King Ahmad decided not to come here today. Now, Imane's spirit shall haunt him!" Ilias announced. Recognizing his speaking before the burial as a sin, the other people in the crowd lowered their heads without a word. "Is this the king you want?!" Ilias cried out.

One of the holy men blinked several times. "Watch your words. It is not time to speak yet. You're at a funeral!"

"I know exactly where I am! That's *my* sister! And where is the king? Why isn't he here at his daughter's funeral? It's because he made a promise to his queen that he wouldn't leave her side!"

The holy people officiating the burial began to raise their hands in protest, and the prince finally ceased his ranting. One of the holy men seized the opportunity to speak. "Peace be upon you. If your sister's spirit is troubled, it's you she's troubled by. Let her rest in peace."

The prince hung his head, bowing to the superior wisdom of the priests. But those beside him could see his glowering eyes that never blinked. He stared at the ground without closing his eyes. Even in submission, Ilias refused to give in to wiser minds, insisting instead on merely retaining his anger. "Lay her in the ground, then!" His bitterness was clear through his acidic voice. Even his respect for the holy men could not hide his bitterness.

As Prince Ilias left the grave, Caitlin supported his back with a gentle hand. As they walked away from the cemetery via a different route than they had come in by, the prince began to sob. Caitlin stopped and led him to the side of the path, where he could cry in peace on her shoulder. "There, there," she soothed him. "I know you loved her, and so did I. But don't let the anger get in the way of mourning her."

Ilias retired to a tent where he waited for the air of death to leave him. The next evening, he and the rest of the mourners would be allowed back to their houses, after the lingering traces of death had left them behind. Inside the tent, fresh changes of clothes had been provided for the next day. Caitlin rubbed Ilias's shoulders as they sat on the bed. "It's going to be okay," she continued to soothe him.

"No, it's not!" Ilias cried, still looking at the carpet.

Caitlin began to brush his back with soft, lingering kisses, letting her lips rest on his back for a while before lifting her head. She wearied of his tears and wanted love from him instead. His halting breath slowed at her touch and began to regulate. He turned around to look at Caitlin, and as he did, she took the words away from him, drawing his mouth into an intoxicating kiss and tearing him away from his woes and heartache.

Ilias felt himself melting as the power of Caitlin's romance overcame him. As he looked at her hair flowing all around him like a red velvet waterfall, he realized that he was on his back. By the time he could realize this, she began to kiss him again. By now, she had his full attention. As she moved down his chest, slowly kissing him lower and lower, her red hair dragged across his face, and he breathed in the deep smell of her hair.

Unable to think of anything else, Ilias closed his eyes and opened himself to the raw feeling of being surrounded by Caitlin. She enveloped him in love, crushing his boundaries and setting his heart ablaze with arousal. She lifted her face away from him, eyes full of desire, and in the interceding seconds as she rose above him, his mind raced with doubts, wondering what she would do. But she sat firmly astride him and began to give him the best lovemaking he'd ever experienced.

Caitlin went full speed as she rode Ilias to a powerful climax. When he entered the peak of the moment, he could see her face, and she seemed to be deep in the throes of passion, with her eyes closed, head thrown back, and mouth wide and gasping. As he looked at the beautiful woman above him, he realized he would do anything she asked of him.

Later, as Caitlin and Ilias held each other in their arms, she began to whisper in his ear. "I know how to overthrow the king and my mother. I could make *you* king."

"But my father would have to die." Ilias's face was neutral, but his voice was dark.

Caitlin continued to press him. "She's got this friend from Ireland, Millie, and she trusts Millie completely. She only lets Millie serve the drinks, and it would be easy for me to distract her because I'm family."

"That actually sounds like a good idea," Ilias said. "Keep talking."

"All you have to do is get the poison in the red wine. The king loves red wine. My mother only drinks white."

"How would the killers sneak in?" asked Ilias.

Caitlin knew he was starting to accept the idea, and she continued. "She has a few guards you need to take out, but just dress the killers up as pirates, and she'll let them in without a question."

It seemed like a grand solution to Caitlin, but Ilias raised one issue. "What about your mother? Won't she know what's going on? She never seems to get hurt."

"Don't worry; I'll take care of my mother because I know her weaknesses better than anyone. It's not going to be easy because my mother will never back down from a swordfight, and she's a fearless fighter. But with your people, we will be able to outnumber her forces. With your men, I can talk her into surrendering. I'll send her off to some dungeon, and then nobody can stop you from being king. Don't you want to rule forever, with just you and me—nobody else interrupting us?"

Caitlin kissed Ilias, nibbling his earlobe and pulling on it sensually. Her lust for him and for power, and her lingering feelings of abandonment from Keela putting her mission to end slavery before their relationship, had finally turned Caitlin against her mother.

* * *

The next night, after Caitlin and Ilias had been allowed to reenter the city of Fez, she seduced him again in his bedroom at the royal palace. She gave him passionate kisses and even more passionate lovemaking than before, noticing how much he desired the pleasures of the flesh. She wondered how little experience he had with women. It made him so much easier to manipulate when he was satisfied in his body.

After Ilias seemed happy, Caitlin began to whisper. "I know you can get your people on your side. They told me they will do anything for you."

"Why are you helping me so much?" Ilias asked.

"Because nobody understands you like I do—not even your friends," she answered.

The overwhelming truth of that statement made Ilias quiet for a few moments. But then, he asked, "There's more, isn't there?"

"I never told you this before, but after Redbeard was buried, I visited you here in the capital, and your father treated me like an outsider. In fact, he was downright cruel. I'm on your side, Ilias, and there's no love lost between me and the Pirate Queen. My mother left me on an island ruled by the worst slave-dealing scum ever while she went on and freed everyone else first. Then, she freed more people, keeping at her mission but leaving me alone again and again. Why did she keep abandoning me? What does she care about promises? She's a hypocrite, and your father is no better."

Several nights later, Caitlin finally convinced Ilias. She told him about an upcoming harvest festival where lots of drinking would take place. She knew that she had him convinced when he began acting like he had come up with the plan himself. In the heat of conversation, he blurted out, "This plan will work! In two weeks, I will be at the harvest festival, pretending to pursue peace. Then, I will overthrow my father and become king."

Prince Ilias called for a private meeting of his war counselors. Caitlin knew he was preparing for battle. Despite having hatched the plan herself, she let him meet with the counselors alone while she stayed behind in his royal quarters, hoping that everything would go according to plan.

Chapter 44

THE HARVEST FESTIVAL WAS a splendid occasion. By the time Caitlin arrived, people were already dancing to energetic music. Vegetables and fruits were everywhere. A great tent had been erected for all the revelers, while the castle had smoke coming from the turrets. Caitlin could tell the cooking was taking place at the castle, so she went there at a rambling pace, ignoring the traitors dressed as pirates who were trying to look inconspicuous as they approached the tent.

As Caitlin approached the castle, the traitors began to sit down at tables with other guests. Six other tables stood between them and the tent's entrance, and even more tables between them and the king. They spaced themselves apart to keep close to each of Keela's guards.

The king and queen sat at one of the tables, just like the common people because, at the harvest festival, everyone was equal. They all shared equally in the bounty of the harvest and the bounty of Keela's rewards. Many ambassadors and guards sat near the king and queen, and their presence at the tables was the only thing that set the king and queen apart from the other revelers.

Caitlin entered the castle and found the kitchen without drawing any attention to herself. She quickly grabbed a pan from the wall and backed away into the hallway without anyone noticing. Then, she threw the pan as far as she could across the floor. It bounced across the floor, clattering and banging as it went and banging hard when it hit the far wall. It created the diversion she wanted.

The maids ran over to pick up the pan, and that's when Caitlin walked into the kitchen and slipped the curare into the red wine. When Millie and another maid finished retrieving the pan, they returned to the wine tray. Millie went back to arranging the glasses for the wine, never noticing Caitlin disappearing out of sight down the hallway.

Caitlin made it back to the tent, still unnoticed, and when she sat down at a table, she almost felt safe. She had disposed of the curare vial on the walk to the tent. Then, she saw Keela looking in her direction, and her piercing gaze froze Caitlin for a second. Caitlin pulled a smile onto her face as fast as she could, and Keela didn't seem to sense the hesitation. The queen's attention was diverted by the arrival of Prince Ilias anyway. Silence fell over the room as he entered.

"What brings you to the harvest festival?" asked Ahmad, already sounding suspicious.

"Peace," answered Prince Ilias.

"What do you mean, peace?" Ahmad asked, sounding confused by his son's answer but not weak in mind.

"I have thought about it, and I have seen the error of my ways. Many of you have borne witness to our feuds in the past," Ilias said, addressing the rest of the people seated at the king's tables. The men at the tables mumbled quietly in response. "You're a noble man, Father, for holding true to your promises. This festival is glorious. Can you forgive a foolish son?"

"Yes, absolutely, I can. Let us toast to your good health."

Millie came walking out. Hearing the King's call for a toast, she brought the wine tray. Caitlin became nervous, and she tried to look the other way. Keela grabbed a glass of white wine. Millie kept walking, and the king grabbed a glass of red wine. Caitlin sighed in relief as she saw the trap was set.

"A toast to forgiveness!" cried the king.

Caitlin watched Keela raise the glass of white wine to her lips, drinking the contents. As Keela drank, she locked eyes with Caitlin, and the look in Keela's eyes suddenly shifted. She picked up the king's glass of red wine and sniffed it carefully, never taking her eyes off Caitlin, and then she seemed to become furious.

"Monkshood!" screamed Keela. It was the name of the plant that produced curare, and a name that everyone would recognize. She threw the glass of red wine to the floor, where it shattered and left a red stain on the sand. But the king had eager lips for wine as well as lovemaking, and by the time Keela's arm reached the glass, he had already drunk heartily from it. Caitlin knew she'd accomplished her goal.

Chapter 45

KEELA KNEW THE KING WAS poisoned when he started touching his face. Then, his hands started shaking. Before he collapsed, he fought for breath and started to grab at his throat. "Ahmad! No!" Keela cried out. She could still see his eyes locking onto her, but the light in his eyes was fading fast, and she could tell he was dying. "Don't leave me!" she cried out, sobbing as he died.

Keela stood over Ahmad's body, protective of him even in death. Then, she stared into the crowd. Although Caitlin and Ilias were still standing before their table, they both began to back out of the tent before Keela could breathe a word. Luckily for them, the betrayal had taken the wind out of her lungs . . . for a moment.

As soon as Keela could draw breath, she pointed at Caitlin and Ilias and screamed, "Don't let them get away!" The soldiers were ready to fight Ilias, but before they could act, people dressed in regular pirate clothing began to pull swords from their belts and attack Keela's guards. Her guards were kept busy with sword combat, leaving her with no protection.

Keela realized that she'd been overtaken, and she knew that her time was up. Three guards had already fallen, but the rest of them continued to fight to protect her life. Then, two more guards fell, and then another. Soon, there were only two protectors left. Keela knew she was outnumbered, and she threw her hands up in surrender.

"Enough!" Keela screamed loud enough for everyone to hear. The clanging of swords stopped, although many swords remained raised in the air. Even Keela's surviving guards waited, unsure of the resolution because she had never surrendered before. "I won't have any more bloodshed," she continued. "So many have already been butchered here. Let the rest escape with their lives."

Prince Ilias raised his right hand, still wielding his sword in his left. "I promise the bloodshed will stop. I am now King of Morocco and have replaced my father. As for you, Keela the Pirate Queen, you are done. Your rebellious days are over." He marched across the floor toward Keela, sword raised and ready to strike her down.

Caitlin raced up behind Ilias, grabbing his arm and diverting the fatal blow. "No, let me do it!" she insisted. "That's *my* mother! If anybody's got the right, it's me!"

Keela was still numb from the shock of her first surrender and her daughter's betrayal. She could feel nothing as Ilias handed the sword to Caitlin with a huff and moved to the side, ushering her forward. Without another look at Ilias or even a word, Caitlin marched toward Keela, grabbing her by the arm and leading her to a staircase. "You're coming with me," Caitlin said.

Keela knew the staircase led to the dungeons, but she had no choice but to go with Caitlin. In her mind, she reasoned that at least Caitlin wasn't taking her to the killing fields to be slaughtered. As they kept walking down the spiral stairs, they passed the doorway that led to the dungeons. Going deeper, Keela became confused, and her shock started to wear off. "Caitlin, this doesn't make any sense!" she cried out. "The only place down here past the dungeon is the ocean!"

Caitlin didn't even turn around as she answered. "Exactly, Mother! Don't you get it yet?!"

As they rounded the staircase to the sea, Keela saw the wide, stony beach with high cliffs arching on both sides of it. Deep inside this hidden cove, a place Keela thought would never be found, a ship with red sails, small and unobtrusive, floated in the deep water. Keela didn't even see the boat at first, nor the dinghy by the shore.

"Mother," said Caitlin, finally looking at her with tears in her eyes, "I don't know where they're planning to take you in this boat, but you've got to leave and never come back. Do you hear me? Don't you ever come back, Mother, because if you do, I'll kill you myself!"

The oarsmen in the boat looked less patient than Keela's daughter, so Keela sat down in the small dinghy, and the oarsmen pushed off into the waves that looked small but still rocked the dinghy side to side. The oarsmen rowed her across the cove to a waiting ship. Caitlin watched her like a hawk until she boarded the ship, but Keela never once turned around to look at her daughter. Instead, she held her head high and turned her back on Caitlin. As she entered the ship, she felt a baby kick inside her belly, and she touched her womb with great tenderness, knowing that the fallen King Ahmad had left one final treasure for her.

After Keela was deposed, the slave trade began again in earnest, as if the slavers were making up for lost time. Fortress after fortress of pirates was overthrown as the slavers fought back until the pirates had lost all the ground they had gained. Ilias never once tried to stop the spread of slavery. Slavery was once again a way of life for many people, and Caitlin's reign was marked by sadness.

Years later, after Caitlin had children of her own, she found a need to clear out some of the rooms in her palace. As she was going through chests with her children, her son got her attention. "Mommy, what's this?" he asked, holding up a green ribbon.

"It's a ribbon your grandmother used to have," she said. "Is there anything else, little one?"

"Yes, I see some diaries in here," he answered.

Caitlin looked through her mother's writings and discovered that Keela had thought about her every day. It was not just when Keela escaped from slavery or when she rescued Caitlin, but she had kept her daughter in her thoughts and prayers every single day, right up until the day she was overthrown, which was when the entries stopped. It was only then that Caitlin realized she was wrong to depose the Pirate Queen.

Chapter 46

AN OLD LADY WITH dazzling white hair sat in her rocking chair in her small house. She got up unsteadily, using her cane for support, and she hobbled slowly to the door of the house for her daily ritual. Once outside the house, Keela hobbled to the back yard and across grass that she was too old to tend anymore. She knelt before a rock in the Irish ground. As she cleared the grass, the name Joseph became clear before her upon the stone.

The old lady spoke to Joseph with a crackling, ancient voice. "I'm afraid this is the last journey I'm going to make here. I'll see you in heaven soon." Then, brushing some dried grass away from the edge of the stone, she got up and returned to her rocking chair. Knowing the exhaustion was not just sleepiness, she lay down and rested in her bed.

As Keela lay in her bed, her grandchildren came over, and they looked at her with concern. They could see how frail she was getting. As she looked over their shoulders, she saw Joseph standing there too. "How nice to see you again, Joseph," she whispered with faltering breath.

As the grandchildren wiped Keela's eyes, her grandson said, "You'll always be a hero to us, Grandmother—the fearless Pirate Queen who sailed the seven seas."

Caitlin came to Keela's bedside as well, staring deeply into her eyes, all spite and hatred long gone. She held out the ribbon that she'd treasured all her life, and the old lady recognized it as an offering of peace. She nodded, unable to speak anymore but fully aware of the meaning of the ribbon. With her arms too tired to raise, she watched as Caitlin carefully tied the ribbon into her snow-white hair.

After leaving Keela's beribboned hair where her mother could see it, Caitlin dropped her head and sobbed. "I'm so sorry for everything I've done. I know now that I was wrong. I found your diaries, and I had no idea that you thought about me so often. Can you forgive me?"

Forcing herself to speak, Keela said her last words. "My daughter, I already forgave you many years ago, and I will always love you." She knew from the pain in her chest that she could breathe no more. She met Joseph's gaze, and as she locked eyes with him, she felt something break inside of her. Then, she felt nothing.

Keela's grandchildren buried her outside the house, beside Joseph. After her snow-white hair with the green ribbon disappeared beneath the lid of her casket, those who knew her best saw Keela lowered into the ground. Keela passed from the world in the same way that she entered: anonymous and unknown. But the legend of her life lives on to this very day, and the world shall never forget the legend of the Pirate Queen.

From the Publisher

Thank You from the Publisher

Van Rye Publishing, LLC ("VRP") sincerely thanks you for your interest in and purchase of this book.

VRP hopes you will please consider taking a moment to help other readers like you by leaving a rating or review of this book at your favorite online book retailer. You can do so by visiting the book's product page and locating the button for leaving a rating or review.

Thank you!

Resources from the Publisher

Van Rye Publishing, LLC ("VRP") offers the following resources to readers and to writers.

For *readers* who enjoyed this book or found it useful, please consider receiving updates from VRP about new and discounted books like this one. You can do so by following VRP on Facebook (at www.facebook .com/vanryepub), Twitter (at www.twitter.com/vanryepub), or Instagram (at www.instagram.com/vanryepub).

For *writers* who enjoyed this book or found it useful, please consider having VRP edit, format, or fully publish your book manuscript. You can find out more and submit your manuscript at VRP's website (at www.vanryepublishing.com).

Thank you again!

Acknowledgments

I WOULD LIKE TO THANK the many people that have supported me through the long journey as a writer. The acknowledgments for this book are deeper, though. I acknowledge Sayyida al Hurra, the original pirate queen, and many other pirate women throughout history. I also want to acknowledge the women who still fight today. Your battles have not been forgotten!

—Melissa Saari

About the Author

M ELISSA SAARI grew up in Butte, Montana, which is Evel Knievel's hometown, and Montana is the setting of her romance novel *Mystic Lake*. She graduated from Southern New Hampshire University with a Master of Arts and Literature, with a concentration in screenwriting. Melissa loves animals and has taken care of many cats and dogs, including her two current dogs, Marla and Leo. She loves dogs because of their loyalty and protectiveness, which are traits of the characters in Melissa's young adult novels *Curse of the Lion People* and *Curse of the Black Dragon*, as well as her horror novels *The Red Satin Shoes* and *Blue Satin Diary*. Melissa currently lives in Central Washington, where the wild and mighty currents of the Columbia River flow past her door with an air of power and mysticism that further informs her writing.